THE CIRCLE OF EIGHT

A James Acton Thriller

By
J. Robert Kennedy

James Acton Thrillers
The Protocol
Brass Monkey
Broken Dove
The Templar's Relic
Flags of Sin
The Arab Fall
The Circle of Eight

Detective Shakespeare Mysteries
Depraved Difference
Tick Tock
The Redeemer

Special Agent Dylan Kane Thrillers
Rogue Operator
Containment Failure

Zander Varga, Vampire Detective
The Turned

THE CIRCLE OF EIGHT

A James Acton Thriller

J. ROBERT KENNEDY

ISBN-10: 1492333034

ISBN-13: 978-1492333036

First Edition

10 9 8 7 6 5 4 3 2 1

For the bravest girl I know, my daughter.
You have no idea how proud I am.

THE CIRCLE OF EIGHT

A James Acton Thriller

PREFACE

In June 1979 an unknown person or group using the alias R.C. Christian, hired a granite company to build a monument to exacting specifications in Elbert County, Georgia.

It has become known as the Georgia Guidestones, and nicknamed the "American Stonehenge".

The structure is inscribed in eight modern and four ancient languages including Babylonian, Classical Greek, Sanskrit and Egyptian hieroglyphs.

To this date nobody knows who built the monument, or why. However what is clear, is whoever they were had a message to deliver to us, for carved on these Guidestones are ten guidelines, or commandments, they wish us to follow:

1. Maintain humanity under 500,000,000 in perpetual balance with nature.
2. Guide reproduction wisely — improving fitness and diversity.
3. Unite humanity with a living new language.
4. Rule passion — faith — tradition — and all things with tempered reason.
5. Protect people and nations with fair laws and just courts.
6. Let all nations rule internally resolving external disputes in a world court.
7. Avoid petty laws and useless officials.
8. Balance personal rights with social duties.
9. Prize truth — beauty — love — seeking harmony with the infinite.
10. Be not a cancer on the earth — Leave room for nature — Leave room for nature.

Though it is disturbing to not know who would have the gall and power to build a monument then abandon it for the State to maintain, what is more disturbing is how they intend to deliver on their guidelines. For if they were to succeed in implementing them, over 90% of the human population would need to be wiped out.

Unknown Location

"Professor Acton, I will count to ten, and if you do not tell me what I want to know, she dies."

The hood over his head was suddenly torn away, the light glaring at him blinding. Professor James Acton tried to raise his hands to block it but they were bound behind him by what felt like zip ties rather than handcuffs, the hard plastic biting into his wrists.

"One."

"Wait!" he yelled, leaning forward in the unforgiving chair he was bound to, peering into the darkness behind the light, trying to find the source of the voice. "I don't even know what you're talking about! What do you want to know?"

"Two," said the voice. "We want to know where it is."

His heart was already slamming into his chest from their ordeal. Police had burst into their room, arrested them, thrown them in the back of a police vehicle, and then drugged them. He had been awakened only moments before with a slap to his hooded face.

"Where is what?" he cried as his eyes finally adjusted. He still couldn't see who was asking the questions, they were hidden in the darkness, behind the light, but he could see Laura, sitting in a chair of her own, facing him, tears running down her cheeks, her mouth gagged so she could say nothing, all he could hear were her sobs. He turned to the darkness. "If you hurt her!" But he didn't finish his sentence.

"Three," echoed the voice. "We will not *hurt* her, Professor Acton. We will *kill* her. I promise she won't feel a thing."

"I don't know what you're looking for!" he yelled, then sucked in a breath, trying to calm himself down, fearful he might anger them and speed up the count. His stomach was in turmoil, like butterflies had filled it and were now desperate to get out. He was pumped full of so much adrenaline his hands were shaking and he was sweating profusely, his chest soaked, his forehead dripping. "Please, tell me more. I'll tell you anything you want, just don't hurt her. I just need to know more about what you're looking for."

Professor Laura Palmer, his fiancée, the love of his life, the first woman he had ever truly loved, who excited him in every way a woman should despite their relationship approaching three years, fixed hers on him. He looked into her eyes, trying to convey that love to her, and he could tell she knew how he felt, and how sorry he was.

"Four." His ears roared with the sound of his blood pumping. "We want the Catalyst, Professor."

"The Catalyst? I've never heard of it. What is it?"

"Five." He felt himself becoming lightheaded. He widened his stance for balance, the zip ties holding his ankles to the chair legs giving him little play. Taking in several deep, slow breaths, he tried to steady his racing heart. "It is something that we once possessed, and was lost to us centuries ago."

His heart was still slamming in his chest, but he was beginning to regain control. He had to be careful. It seemed apparent that every time he spoke, and they responded, their captor would increase the count. He had at most five more questions before his beloved would be dead.

"What makes you think I have it?"

"Six." Acton strained as hard as he could against his bonds, but nothing. "You were seen holding it in a photograph."

Acton's mind began flicking through every photograph he could ever remember having been taken of him, but there were thousands if not more, and he quickly found himself only seeing photographs of Laura, smiling, laughing, kissing him in self-shots.

"If you show me the photograph, then I'll know what you're talking about."

He heard footsteps echo through the room, the sounds giving him the impression it was large, mostly empty, little to absorb the sounds bouncing off its walls. Suddenly a robed figure entered the light, the long flowing dark brown cloth silhouetted against the light, the face nothing more than a black emptiness.

"Seven."

The voice still came from the background, not from the man in front of him. A photograph was shoved in front of his face, and it took a moment for his eyes to refocus. It was him with several of his students, each holding a different object. He remembered it instantly. "That's from the south of France, just outside St. Tropez," he blurted, elated he was finally able to answer a question and perhaps save Laura. "I was asked to inventory a private collection; some billionaire had died. There were hundreds of pieces. Over a thousand, actually. Are you saying that one of these items is your Catalyst?"

"Eight."

"Please! Which one? Which artifact?"

A finger pointed to a cube being held by one of his students.

"That? That's the Catalyst? We didn't know what it was so we just catalogued it."

"Nine." The man in the robe retreated into the darkness. "Where is it?"

"But that was over ten years ago! I don't know where it is," he cried, tears welling in his eyes as he knew he had no way to give them what they wanted." All he could think to do was to keep talking, not give the man a chance to end his count. "All we did was catalog the collection, then it was

5

sold at auction, I think. We didn't keep any of the pieces. I'm sure if you check the auction they'll tell you who bought it!"

"So then *you* can't tell us where it is."

"No, but I can find out. I'll do whatever it takes. Please! I'm begging you! Please don't hurt her! Kill me instead. Shoot me! She has nothing to do with this! I didn't even know her back then."

"Ten."

"Oh God, Laura! I'm so sorry! I love you! I love you!" He struggled against his bonds, shifting in the chair, pulling with all his might, blood flowing down his wrists as the plastic sliced through the skin. He pushed forward hard, trying to get as close to her as he could, but it was all to no avail. She was sobbing freely now, her face red, her eyes pleading, crying through the gag, he could tell she was shouting that she loved him too.

Footsteps echoed, then the dark robed figure stepped between him and Laura, a gun held in the man's right hand.

"No, please! I'll do anything!"

The man raised his right foot and pushed Laura's chair over. It collapsed backward and Acton lost sight of her as she fell behind the light that had illuminated her. The man stepped into the darkness and Acton heard the most precious thing in his life scream.

Then the crack of a gunshot broke his heart for the last time.

Security Office, Le Grand Hotel, Geneva, Switzerland
One week earlier

First Sergeant Phil "Stucco" Reeves shivered, grabbing his arms in a hug, rubbing his hands up and down as he stood up.

"Cold?" asked Command Sergeant Major Burt "Big Dog" Dawson as he sipped a coffee that was still piping hot. "Coffee's fresh and a hell of a lot better than back at The Unit." Dawson was in command of Delta Team Bravo, a unit of the elite Delta Force, arguably the best counter-terrorism unit in the world, but not necessarily baristas when it came to making coffee. At Le Grand Hotel in Geneva however, they had access to some of the best.

Especially when the night manager was sweet on one of your men.

Stucco, the man in question, shook his head as he continued to hug himself, walking about the tight security room, the screens flashing images of the entire hotel. They were on a babysitting mission, the Secretary of State meeting with various representatives from the Middle East and other "concerned" states. There had been a specific threat against him from reliable sources so security was beefed up beyond the normal Secret Service guards.

"Nah, just got a shiver. Like someone walked on my grave."

"I didn't know you were superstitious," said Sergeant First Class Will "Spock" Lightman. "Explains a few things."

"Yeah, like how he tosses shells over his shoulder when he drops a clip," offered Master Sergeant Leon "Atlas" James, his impossibly deep voice echoing through the tiny room.

"Or when he breaks a mirror it's bad luck unless he cancels it out by saving a black cat."

Stucco looked at Spock, mimicking his signature trademark by cocking an eyebrow.

"You guys really need new jokes."

"Bah, you just want us to find a new target," said Spock with a knowing glance at Atlas.

Stucco turned to the screen to watch the night manager hurry down the hallway.

"Do you guys even understand what a figure of speech is?"

"Umm, the stripper the announcer's talking about at Sharky's?"

Dawson snorted his coffee, trying to remain slightly professional as he kept his eyes on the screens. At this hour however there was little going on. He had a two man team on the Ambassador's door full time, Atlas and Spock were manning the security room, while he and Stucco were roamers. At the moment they were taking five.

There was a knock at the door.

"That'll be Maria," said Stucco, jumping up to get the door. Spock and Atlas exchanged grins, jumping to the wrong conclusion. Stucco had already told Dawson about how much Maria Esposito reminded him of his little sister back home, almost "a spitting image" with many of the same mannerisms. Stucco now seemed to have taken on the big brother role of being her protector, though she didn't know it, her responses to his attentiveness one of what any young girl might have to a good looking, slightly older man with a gun.

Gaga crush.

But Stucco, stuck in little sister mode, didn't notice, and instead kept leading her on unintentionally by paying her too much attention.

"Maria!" he demonstrated as he opened the door. "And how are you tonight?"

Maria beamed a smile at Stucco then nodded to the rest of the room.

"Tired, but hoping one day to move up to day manager."

"That's life!" said Stucco, motioning to his chair. "You have to put in your dues before you get the big seat."

Maria's head bounced in agreement.

"Sometimes I wonder if I chose the right career. I should have gone into brain surgery or something."

The room was silent.

She burst out laughing.

"You guys are too polite. You remind me of Canadians! I'm just joking. Do you think if I had the grades for medical school I would be here?"

Stucco laughed as did the others, when Dawson saw something on the screen. He leaned forward and pointed.

"We've got activity on the Ambassador's floor."

Maria leaned in and looked.

"Oh Christ," she muttered. "That's that asshole Martin Lacroix. Big wig at the World Bank. Completely full of himself. He's constantly criticizing our staff, complains at all hours, makes demands, insists we make things off menu." She shook her head. "He's a pig."

"And apparently popular with the ladies," said Atlas as they watched him groping a girl one third his age against the wall next to his room. "I'd say 'get a room' but that would be redundant."

"Does this guy not have any shame?" asked Spock.

"I don't know about shame, but he should know that all this stuff is on camera," said Dawson.

Suddenly the girl pushed Lacroix away, slapped him, and stormed toward the elevator.

"Spock, Niner here. We're hearing some shouting from our position. Do you have anything on camera, over?"

Spock activated his mike.

"Just a lovers' quarrel. Nothing to worry about."

"Roger that."

The girl left on the elevator and Lacroix entered his room, the excitement over. Maria looked at the coffee service.

"Can I get anything for you gentlemen? More coffee, something from the kitchen?"

"Don't worry about it," replied Stucco. "If we need anything, we'll call them ourselves. You've got more important things to do than wait on us."

"More important maybe, but not more entertaining," she replied, casting a glance at Stucco and blushing.

Stucco smiled, still not getting it, and pointed at Spock and Atlas.

"Now don't you two give her a hard time when I'm gone."

"Wouldn't dream of it," replied Spock.

"I'm renowned for being a perfect gentleman," boomed Atlas.

Dawson rose from his chair.

"Time we got back on our rounds."

Stucco nodded and was about to say something when Maria's phone beeped on her hip. She grabbed it and read the message then hit the speed dial.

"What is it this time?" she asked, sounding exasperated. She listened, shaking her head more and more as the person on the other end of the line explained something. "And when did we last clean his room?"—"And that was after he left it this morning?"—"And he hasn't been back until now?"—"And you're sure we cleaned it?"—"He said what?"—"Fine. I'll go tell him personally."

She ended the call, looking around the room.

"Sorry about that. It's our favorite guest. He's demanding we send a maid to clean his room, which was already cleaned, and that she better be sexy."

Stucco's eyebrows raced up his forehead as his head dipped toward his chest.

"Excuse me?"

"Exactly. What a pig!" She put her hand on the door knob. "I need to go tell our honored guest that there is no maid service at this time of night." She opened the door. "Let me know if you need anything."

The door closed and Dawson watched as one of the cameras showed her heading for the elevators.

"Man, she reminds me so much of my little sis," sighed Stucco.

"Eww!" exclaimed Spock. "That's just wrong!"

"Huh?"

Dawson laughed, opening the door and stepping into the hallway.

"I'll explain it to you on the way," he said, holding the door.

Stucco, still puzzled, joined him in the hall and they made their rounds mostly in silence. As they rode up the elevator to the Secretary of State's floor, Stucco turned to Dawson.

"They actually thought I was attracted to her?"

Dawson nodded, battling to suppress the smile desperate to break out.

"That's so wrong!" exploded Stucco. "That's my little sister! Well, you know what I mean."

"I hear yah."

"Aw, man!" muttered Stucco as the doors opened. "My *sister!*"

Dawson looked left, and all was clear. The Secretary of State's room was to the left, but their job was to check the floor for anything unusual then switch off with Sergeants Carl "Niner" Sung and Gerry "Jimmy Olson" Hudson.

"Oh my God!" exclaimed Stucco. Dawson's head jerked right to see Stucco racing toward Maria as she stumbled out of the pig Lacroix's room, falling into Stucco's arms as the door shut behind her. When Dawson arrived Stucco already had her lying on the floor, her bloodied face almost unrecognizable, her shirt torn off, hanging from her wrist, her bra missing, her skirt hiked all the way revealing her panties had been removed.

"What happened?" cried Stucco.

"Help me!" she whispered, her voice barely audible.

"Did he do this to you?" demanded Stucco, pointing at the door.

"H-he raped me!" she cried.

Dawson stood up, standing back from the scene as he activated his mike.

"Spock, we've got a problem. Contact local authorities. There's been a rape. We're going to need police and an ambulance, over."

"Spock here, Atlas is contacting them now. I've got you on camera. Please tell me"—there was a pause, and the voice that continued was subdued—"tell me that it isn't Maria."

"Sorry, but it is. Better contact the day manager."

Another pause, then all business.

"Roger that. Let us know if you need anything."

"Better wake the others, we're going to be busy here so we'll need them to cover our rounds."

"Done."

There was a roar from behind him and Dawson spun to see Stucco kick open the door to the World Bank honcho's room. Before Dawson could get there Stucco was already inside, yelling for blood. Dawson rushed into the room and found Stucco with the naked man by the throat shoving him toward the ground. The man's head slammed into the carpet, and Stucco rained blow upon blow on the man's face while screaming obscenities at him, each syllable emphasized with a punch.

Dawson grabbed Stucco and hauled him off the now crying man, the coward begging for Stucco to stop. As soon as he was freed of his attacker he scrambled to the other side of the room, cowering in the corner, covering himself with a pillow taken from a couch.

Stucco struggled to free himself from Dawson's iron grip as Dawson tried to calm him.

"Take it easy, you got him. The police are on their way," said Dawson.

"Let me at him, BD. That bastard has to pay for what he's done!"

"And he will. In a court of law. Now how about you go watch Maria until help arrives?"

This seemed to work, Stucco relaxing slightly.

"I'm okay," he muttered and Dawson let him go. Stucco left the room and Dawson turned to the naked man.

"Now you just stay put until the police get here, or what he did to you will seem like a light spanking."

The man stood up, still pressed into the corner, showing no shame in his nudity, though a forbidden locker room glance showed Dawson the man should be. The man grabbed a robe from the back of a chair and put it on, tying the belt with a snap, the cowardly SOB beginning to transform into the arrogant pig that Maria had described.

Dawson looked about the suite, larger even than the Secretary of State's, but then this was the World Bank, unanswerable to anyone on how they spent our money, its financing in the form of taxes paid by Western governments to the organization based on treaties signed long ago by people no longer in power, without the knowledge or understanding of most voters in the contributing countries.

To his left there was a large table filled with stacks of files, color coded maps, and paperwork spread across it. He walked over to it, something catching his eye, several black folders with what appeared to be a large rose with a Christian cross in the center, embossed on the covers, the design intriguing.

"Don't look at those!" yelled the man.

Which made Dawson all the more curious, but as a trained soldier, he understood his job. And this wasn't it. But it also wasn't to obey the orders of rapists.

Dawson looked at the man who had puffed himself out to look far more important than he had moments ago.

"I must insist you leave my room at once."

"Why? So you can have a shower and try to wash away the evidence?"

"Evidence of what?"

Dawson's eyebrows shot up.

"Evidence of what?" he repeated. "Are you kidding me? You just raped a woman."

"I did no such thing," said the man, lighting a cigarette in the non-smoking room, the small plastic signs displayed in several places, not the least of which was the very table he was standing beside. Dawson had met people like this on many occasions, almost always government of some type, who thought the rules didn't apply to them because of a title bestowed upon them that indicated *I'm better than you.*

"The woman lying in the hallway beaten to a pulp and stripped nearly naked will most likely disagree."

The man took a long drag on his cigarette then smiled.

"She was a willing participant."

Dawson wanted to tear the man's throat out. It would be worth ending his career killing a man like this.

"We'll let the police decide."

"If the police set one foot in this room, you and anyone you care about are dead."

Dawson took several steps toward the man, raising a finger and pointing at him.

"I *highly* suggest you learn to shut that mouth of yours. You'll find that threats usually result in broken bones around me. Understand?"

The man's bravado broke for a split second as he took a step back, his hand shaking as he took another pull on his cigarette. The broken door was pushed aside and several policemen entered. Dawson stepped aside, the four men spreading out, quickly searching the suite to see if anyone else was present. A fifth man in plainclothes entered, his suit and ankle length jacket suggesting he was a detective.

"I am Inspector Pierre Laviolette of the Geneva Police. What is the problem here?" asked the man in French.

Lacroix immediately began to spout off when Dawson interrupted, pulling out his fake Secret Service ID.

"I'm Special Agent White, assigned to the United States Secretary of State's security detail. Perhaps I can be of assistance."

Inspector Laviolette raised a hand, cutting off Lacroix.

"You are American?" he asked in accented, but excellent English.

"Yes, sir." Dawson showed him his ID.

"And the man outside?"

"Part of our detail."

"This man"—Laviolette cocked his head at Lacroix—"claims that the other man assaulted him for no reason."

"Untrue. M. Lacroix physically assaulted and most likely raped the young woman outside."

"He claims she was a willing participant in rough sex."

Dawson kept control of his anger, but just barely.

"I know this woman, and was there when she was called to this room. She's the hotel's night manager, and was coming here to tell M. Lacroix that his request for a sexy maid to clean his room would not be fulfilled. M. Lacroix returned to this hotel from an unknown location less than an hour ago, had an altercation with a woman he was with in the hallway, which resulted in her leaving, and M. Lacroix then entered his room and moments later requested a 'sexy' maid to clean his already cleaned room. I think his intent was clear."

"Indeed."

"Listen, do you have any idea who I am?" yelled Lacroix from the corner. "I'm—"

"I know very well who you are, monsieur, and I strongly advise you to not say anything." He motioned to the other officers. "Arrest him. Suspicion of assault and rape."

Two officers grabbed the man, handcuffing him as he cursed in various foreign languages, finally settling on English, glaring at Dawson.

"Forget what you saw here today, or you and your friend will pay dearly."

Dawson didn't respond, instead glancing at the table of documents, then back at Lacroix.

"You were warned," growled the man as he was led outside. As he disappeared through the door, he proved he wasn't finished. "Slut!" yelled Lacroix, to which a flurry of curses burst from Stucco's mouth, out of sight of Dawson as the door closed.

Alone, the inspector looked at Dawson, his face grave.

"This will probably end my career. Both of our careers. But this man has to be stopped."

"What do you mean?"

"You really don't know who this man is?"

"Not really. He wasn't my concern, vetted by another team since he was staying on the same floor. My understanding is he's a high ranking member of the World Bank, clean record, respected in his profession, a patron of the arts, and disliked by this hotel's staff."

"He is all that, and he is also suspected in over a dozen rapes across the world, all of which have been covered up with what you Americans I think call 'hush money', or worse. He is rich, very powerful, and in his world, our laws don't apply."

Dawson frowned. "In my world he'd be assassinated."

Laviolette smiled slightly, looking at Dawson.

"I've dealt with Secret Service many times. You are *not* Secret Service."

Dawson ignored the statement.

"What can we expect next?"

"It depends on how far she wants to take it. Normally they're offered more money than they can ever hope to make in the next decade or two, and they take it. That will be the end of it. If she chooses to pursue it to court, then the witnesses might get bribed, or worse."

"Worse?"

"It wouldn't be the first time that somebody has died at the hands of this man's security force."

Köln, Germany
1472 AD

Dietrich kissed Heike for the last time with a passion he didn't know he had in him. It was enough for him to question his decision, and as she moaned in his arms, their forbidden love swelled in his chest and at that moment his decision was made.

"I love you," he whispered as their lips broke.

"And I you, my darling," replied Heike, staring into his eyes, lost in their little world. He a doctor, she the daughter of a local cobbler. They were in different stations, her father fairly well off, expecting her to marry a business man whose family would complement their own. A doctor was not in her father's plans. Certainly he made a reasonable living, and since he had been invited to join The Order five years ago, his lot had improved greatly, but doctors were still not considered an honorable profession unless you needed one, then they were as holy as priests.

He grabbed her, pulling her in tightly, and his heart and head united in their decision. Despite the warnings, despite everything he had to lose, they would be together, forever.

And he would have to tell his master that his future apprentice could be his no longer, for his heart belonged to another.

The thought of that encounter caused both his heart and mind to falter. Not in doubt that he loved Heike, of that there was no doubt. But in fear. For the master was terrifying. Insanely intelligent, impossibly prescient. He could read people so well, it was as if he knew what they were thinking, and he never corrected anyone who might think he could indeed read their mind.

It had been a moment like that just this morning that had sent his heart racing in terror.

"If you are to be my apprentice tomorrow, you must give up any notion of love, of being with a woman in any way other than carnally. Marriage is forbidden to us, bachelorhood our sworn commitment."

"I understand, my master."

"Are you certain?"

His question had made Dietrich pause as he debated on what to say. He decided to err on the side of caution.

"I will end it with her tonight, my master."

"I am pleased you admitted to it, my son. Should you not have, you would not have become my apprentice tomorrow."

Dietrich had bowed deeply, then left the master's chambers, immediately seeking Heike out. They had spent the evening together as he tried to figure some way to tell her it was over, but every moment together was agony, his love growing with each touch, each glance, each shared laugh and smile.

But what will the master do?

It was a terrifying thought. He had never heard of an apprentice rejecting his master before. He had of course heard of apprentice's dying during training, and he wondered if they had indeed died from it, or had been executed for betraying their masters.

He shivered.

"Are you cold, my darling?"

"How could I be cold when you warm my heart so?" he asked, enveloping her in his arms. Suddenly he pushed her back, holding her by both shoulders. "If we are to do this, we must do it tonight."

"What, my darling? What do you mean?"

"We must tell your father of us, and if he does not bless our union, then we will leave this place and start a new life elsewhere, far away, where no one knows us, where no one can judge us."

She threw herself into his arms, clawing at his back as she wept.

"Yes oh yes, my darling! I only want to be with you, forever!"

Dietrich took her hand and they quickly made their way toward her home at the top of the cobblestoned street as a gentle mist began to fall. He heard a foot scrape down an alley and he turned to see who might be there, but he saw nothing, including the robed figure ensconced in the darkness.

Martin Lacroix Residence, Republic of San Marino
Present Day

"This meeting of the Circle of Eight is called to order."

The voice was deep, hollow, serious. In the entire time Doctor Martin Lacroix had heard it, he had never once sensed any emotion, any compassion, any passion. It was as cold a voice as any he had encountered, the bottom end rolling like distant thunder through his earphones, the images on the screen cloaked in the traditional brown robes, faces hidden in the shadows of their hoods.

He had met Number One on many occasions, but to describe him would be impossible. He was of average height, his build hidden by the robes, but the boney hands suggested he was thin, and the lack of liver spots or severe wrinkling suggested he wasn't as aged as some in The Circle. But with the knowledge and money available to The Circle, the state-of-the-art research they had access to, one's age was no longer as easy to guess as it once was.

Anti-aging treatments were one of the most compelling reasons to join The Order. What once was science fiction had become science fact. The ability to extend useful human life well past the century mark existed—it was simply expensive and not well known, as it created a two tiered society. Those with the money who could afford to extend their lives, and those without, doomed to die in their seventies or eighties, with the last ten or twenty years of their lives a growing set of chronic and painful problems that turned living into existing.

But not within The Order.

Medical experimentation was encouraged, hailed if successful, studied further if not. Members were welcome to volunteer for radical treatments that hadn't yet even been approved for human testing, and it would be funded and performed by The Order. In fact, most cutting edge research had some sort of funding component from The Order's various fronts, giving them access to all the research and materials necessary to conduct their own procedures.

It was fascinating, and each time Lacroix read of a new breakthrough that had been successfully tested on one of their own, his heart raced in excitement. Treatments abandoned by the mainstream scientific community because of their adverse effects on a small percentage, were embraced, The Order's thinking that those who it didn't help were simply inferior genetically. Why should those who weren't be denied this knowledge?

And that was the fundamental driving force behind The Order. To gather knowledge, all knowledge—medical, scientific, historical—it didn't matter. The Order particularly prided itself on collecting forgotten knowledge, forbidden knowledge. Forgotten knowledge had been their mainstay hundreds of years ago when they were founded, but over the past fifty years so much knowledge and wondrous advances had been made and forgotten due to politics and poor funding priorities, they had taken it upon themselves to preserve and expand upon it.

Sometimes these scientists were brought within the fold, usually unwittingly, and if they showed the correct attitude toward The Order's philosophies, sometimes invited inside. And sometimes, like with himself, you made it into the ultimate inner circle, the Circle of Eight, the ruling council of The Order. Unknown to the membership except as shadowy figures who were to remain anonymous, their directives absolute, to be followed to the letter, without question.

He himself had been a member of The Circle for almost ten years, chosen by his master as his replacement almost thirty years ago. He had trained, learned the history, learned the forgotten sciences, and sworn allegiance to an organization over six hundred years old, and more powerful and anonymous than any he knew to be in existence. They were a secret, an absolute secret. Those in The Circle were sworn to remain bachelors with no connections that they may betray their secrets to. They were responsible for choosing their own replacements before they died, the identities held secret until the day of their deaths when a secret messenger would deliver the identity, and the person, to the swearing in ceremony that occurred exactly seven days after death.

And today, this impromptu meeting over secure channels was because of him. Because of his error, his screw-up, his inability to control his sexual urges.

They'll have you killed one day.

"Gentlemen. We have a problem. Or should I say, we *once again* have a problem, with Number Eight," said Number One.

"Again?" asked another, his voice filled with the exasperation Lacroix was certain they all felt for him. Even he felt it about himself. If he remained sober, he was usually fine, but as soon as that first glass of wine or scotch graced his lips, he was drinking for the night, then determined to have female companionship, whether she willingly participated or not.

But in Geneva he had crossed a line.

And got caught.

"This is getting ridiculous," said another.

"Agreed," rumbled Number One. "How do you propose to solve this problem, Number Eight?"

Lacroix looked over his shoulder at the door that had remained closed since his apprentice had left.

Where is he?

He took a drink of water to moisten his suddenly dry mouth, then leaned toward the microphone sitting on his desk.

"I have an operative identifying all of the witnesses involved, and should have a report shortly."

"And what do you intend to do?"

"They will be paid off, or otherwise encouraged to remain silent."

"But there is something unique about this encounter, is there not?" rumbled Number One's voice.

"Y-yes," said Lacroix, his voice cracking at having to admit it to The Circle. "I had several of our files in plain sight, and they were seen."

Cursing and other sounds filled his headset as The Circle erupted in anger. At that moment the door behind him opened and he turned to see his apprentice enter, a grave expression on his face. Lacroix motioned for him to hurry up.

His apprentice rushed over, handing him a file.

"We have a problem," he whispered.

"What is it?"

He flipped through the folder and stopped on a page showing the Secret Service agent who had beaten him. His apprentice pointed lower on the page.

Oh shit!

"The usual payoffs will not be enough," said one of The Circle. "They must be silenced."

Lacroix cleared his voice, leaning in again.

"Gentlemen, we may have a bigger problem than I thought."

"Explain," said Number One.

"The men we thought were Secret Service aren't."

"Then what are they?"

"Delta Force."

Stucco's Residence, Maas Drive, Fort Bragg, North Carolina

Stucco stood on the doorstep of his military issue residence, it a small, old, humble and perfectly adequate home that they could call their own while he was stationed in Fort Bragg. Most of the married guys in The Unit lived within a five minute walk of each other, the single guys either in barracks or off base in their own apartments.

But all close, all within shouting distance if anyone needed help with something, or just wanted to hang out and shoot the shit. Or shoot something. It was a family. A big family that extended far past The Unit, and far past the base. The military was a family. When one died, everyone hurt. When one did something heroic, they all felt the pride.

It was something that had been missing from his life, his own dad having abandoned him and his mother when he was three, only showing up a few times in his life, mostly to argue with his mother. But he hadn't shown up when his mother had died, killed by a drunk driver. He had been ten. The rest of his life was spent bouncing from foster home to foster home, the system never able to find him parents willing to adopt a kid so old that was a "problem child".

He had to admit it now that he was older and a father himself that he had been acting out. *I was a holy terror!* The hell he put those foster parents through wasn't fair, and it wasn't until he was sixteen when he was at yet another home, pulling the same shit, that the family's eldest son had returned home from Afghanistan, all spiffy in his crisp Marine uniform, that he stood up and paid attention. The young marine sergeant had taken him under his wing for the four weeks he was visiting, then returned to Afghanistan.

And died.

Stucco had signed up the day he turned eighteen, opting for the Army, and eventually working his way up to Sergeant and a position in the Delta Force. It had been the proudest day of his life, and though he had no parents to share his success with, he had found the woman of his dreams, Sheila, and they had married between tours in Iraq, and about a year later, little Christa was born. She was six now, tall enough to answer the doorbell he had rung, but there was no answer.

Odd.

It was a ritual. He'd come back from an op and surprise them on the doorstep. Christa had always delighted in the surprise, and Sheila too. It had started with a forgotten key, and the joy on their faces had made it something he wanted to see every time he came home, so now he never unlocked the door himself.

He always waited for them to answer.

But it was never this long.

He rang again, checking the driveway for the umpteenth time.

The car's still there!

He put his ear to the door, but heard nothing.

He shrugged his shoulders. It wouldn't be the first time they hadn't been home when he got back. With the wives a close knit family when their husbands were off on ops, it wouldn't surprise him if they were off with one of the other families in the park.

He fished his key from his pocket and unlocked the door, pushing it open. He stepped inside and could smell something amazing wafting its way from the kitchen.

"Hi hon, it's me! You home?"

He heard a sound in the kitchen and dropped his duffel bag in the entrance, kicking off his shoes as he made his way down the hall toward the tiny seventies style kitchen, Sheila's one complaint about their home.

He turned the corner and cried out at what he saw.

Colonel Thomas Clancy's Office, 1st Special Forces Operational Detachment-Delta HQ, Fort Bragg, North Carolina
A.k.a. "The Unit"

"You realize the shit storm you've created for me, Sergeant Major?"

Command Sergeant Major Burt Dawson nodded as he stood at attention, his boss, Colonel Thomas Clancy sitting behind his desk, barking at him while he had a pencil tightly clamped between his teeth as he continued to battle his addiction to cigars. It flicked up and down with each syllable, a constant distraction that if it weren't for the verbal tirade the pencil seemed to be conducting, it might be comical.

"Yes, sir!" he replied, realizing full well what was going on, the State Department representative standing to the right of Clancy almost smiling in glee.

"What the hell were you two thinking getting involved in a civilian situation like that?" Clancy held up his hand. "Don't answer that! I know damned well what you were thinking! Nothing! You weren't thinking a damned thing! You were acting on instinct, just like we trained you! To protect innocent lives, wherever they may be! I understand that! Don't you think I understand that? But that wasn't your job! Your job was to protect the Secretary of State! Not a hotel maid"—Dawson decided not to correct him—"then assault one of the most powerful men in the world!" Clancy sucked in a lungful of air then ripped the pencil from his mouth, tossing it aside. "You and your team are suspended from duty until this mess is straightened out. Understood?"

"Yes, sir!"

"Now get out of my office!"

"Yes, sir!"

Dawson snapped a salute for show, then spun on his heel and exited the room, closing the door behind him. He winked at the smiling Maggie, Colonel Clancy's longtime secretary, who knew exactly what was going on.

A show for the State Department.

Clancy would never actually punish men in his unit for saving a woman from a rapist. Dawson was already scheduled for a second meeting once the State Department rep had left. He made his way to the cafeteria and grabbed a bottle of water. Chugging half of it down, his phone buzzed.

Stucco?

He would have figured the young husband would be well into some post-op nookie by now, not calling his "boss".

"Hey, Stucco, what's up?"

"BD! You gotta help me!"

Dawson tossed his bottle in the sink, rushing for the door, the panic in his friend's voice obvious.

"What is it?"

"I don't know what to do! My wife, my kid, oh my God, BD! I think it's him. It has to be. It has to be that bastard Lacroix!"

"What is it? What's wrong?"

"You gotta help me, BD!"

There was a scream in the background that sounded like a woman's.

"Oh no!"

The line went dead.

Dawson raced toward the parking lot, speed dialing Red, his trusted friend and second in command.

Red's groggy voice answered. "Hey, BD, can't a man sleep after an op?"

"Something's wrong at Stucco's. Just got a weird call from him and heard Sheila scream. Get a team together, meet me there, and let the Colonel know what's going on. I'm on my way now."

"Consider it done," came the alert reply.

Dawson jumped in his 1964½ poppy red Mustang convertible and started it up, gunning it toward the married quarters and his friend.

Köln, Germany
1472 AD

Dietrich held Heike's hand, their fingers intertwined as they pushed their way up the steep road to her father's house, perched on the hillside with a spectacular view of the Rhine river below. It was dark now, a little light provided by the mostly blocked out stars and a half moon, as well as the candle and firelight from inside the homes spilling out the cracks in the shuttered windows, lending a sheen to the quickly dampening cobblestones.

Another sound behind them and Dietrich turned. His heart raced up his throat as he saw a dark robed figure following them.

He urged Heike forward.

"What's wrong?" she asked.

"Nothing. Let's just get you inside before it starts to rain."

She thankfully picked up her pace without further question, and he could tell by the tightening of her grip on his hand that she too was now frightened. More footsteps behind them and he broke out into a run without looking. As they passed each alleyway he would look down it and see another robed figure stepping out, and looking ahead he could see between each house a figure coming into view. Before they could reach the top of the hill a line of darkly robed figures blocked their way on all sides except their left, where a waist high wall protected pedestrians from the roaring river fifty feet below.

As they closed in upon them, Dietrich pulled the only weapon he had, a dagger, and moved toward the only wall without members of The Order blocking their way. He looked over the side at the river below, and knew it was too treacherous to attempt a jump. The rocks below, mostly hidden, the rushing water breaking upon their concealed stubbornness, seemed to glow a warning of their presence in the faint light.

The robed figures closed in on them as he held Heike behind him, his dagger held out in a useless threat, his arm trembling so much the blade threatened to clatter to the ground.

None of the approaching figures had any weapons displayed, but he knew they would be armed. They always were when robed. For they were The Order, of that he had no doubt.

He did the only thing he could think of.

"Master, if you are here, please listen. I told her it was over. We had one last kiss and I was bringing her home. Please, let her go, she has done nothing wrong."

The Order were shoulder to shoulder now, forming a semi-circle of impenetrable human flesh, there now being nowhere to go but over the wall at their backs.

The figures parted and a lone figure stepped through, the ranks closing behind him as he stepped forward, stopping only inches from Dietrich's outstretched dagger.

A hand reached forward, and he recognized it as his master's immediately, a deep scar on the top from years ago revealed as the sleeve of the robe slipped up.

Dietrich relinquished the blade without protest, Heike gasping behind him.

"Master, please. I beg of you, let her go. She is but an innocent in this and knows nothing of us."

His master put a hand on his shoulder, applying gentle but firm pressure, his intent clear. Dietrich stepped aside, leaving his master to face Heike as he still clasped her hand. She looked up at his master, tears of fear rolling down her flushed cheeks. He wished it were daylight so his master could see her brilliantly blue eyes, her golden hair, her impossibly pure skin. Surely then he couldn't harm a hair on her childlike self.

But it was dark.

It was damp.

And all that could be seen were the shadows, all that could be heard were her sniffles and the roar below. His master caressed her cheek with his left hand, approaching her so they were mere inches apart. She looked up at him, her neck bent back far, his height imposing even to Dietrich. A glint of moonlight revealed a frightened attempt at a smile from her, and nothing from his master.

Please God, help her!

Suddenly his master stepped forward, shoving her with both hands over the barrier. She screamed, as did Dietrich, spinning to try and brace himself on the wall, his left hand still holding hers, her gloved fingers slipping. He tried to reach around with his other hand but felt an iron grip on his forearm. He struggled, but all he could do was watch the terror in his darling Heike's eyes as she hung on, looking up at him as they both eyed the silk slowly flowing from his fingers.

Then there was none.

She fell, a final blood curdling scream cut off as her body was dashed on the rocks below. He spun around and rushed through the already parting members of The Order, racing down the hill to where he could see the river again and arrived just in time to watch her body slip along the water before it rounded a bend in the river and disappeared forever out of sight.

Footsteps behind him caused him to jump and spin in rage, his fist raised. He felt the dagger at his stomach, and he didn't care. All he wanted right now was to die so that he might be with her at her side as they entered Heaven and the afterlife.

"Now you can focus on your studies."

The dagger was tossed over the side and into the river below as his master walked away, leaving him to cling to the wall, sobbing at his loss, and how he alone was to blame.

Inside Stucco's Residence, Maas Drive, Fort Bragg, North Carolina

"Okay, just stay calm, honey, and I'll figure a way out of this."

Stucco's wife didn't seem convinced. And he didn't blame her. She was duct taped to a chair by her ankles, wrists and upper chest. And his precious baby, only six years old a few weeks ago, was taped to a second chair in the same manner, both back to back, the chairs taped together as one.

With enough C4 taped to his wife's chest to take out the entire house and then some.

The bomb had just beeped a moment ago while he was on the phone with Dawson, eliciting a scream from his wife and wails from his daughter.

You have to calm yourself down. Treat it like a mission.

He sucked in several deep breaths, closing his eyes, regaining control of himself as he tried to push away the thoughts of losing his family.

This is no different than any other op, so treat it that way.

He opened his eyes.

"Okay, everything is going to be fine," he said in a perfectly monotone voice. "I need you both to remain calm and quiet as I take a look at things." He looked at Christa. "Can you do that for daddy?"

She nodded, her wailing stopping as she tried to stifle her sobs.

"Good. Now you need to be brave for mommy, and I'm going to take a look, okay?"

She nodded.

He dropped to his knees to get a better look at the device. There was a pressure cord around the two of them that if broken or stretched too far, would most likely detonate the weapon. Both of their chests were heaving, stretching on the cord, and Stucco put a hand on his wife's shoulder.

"Now listen to me very carefully. I need you to control your breathing, okay? It's very easy. Just close your eyes, take a deep breath in through your nose, all the way into your stomach while counting to four, then hold it for four seconds, then slowly let it out through your mouth, counting to four." She sucked in a breath, and he counted off with her. "Good. Now just keep doing that for me until you feel your heart rate start to slow down. I'll keep working."

He listened to the rhythmic breathing, and smiled as he heard little Christa trying to do the same thing, and soon heaving chests were calmer and sobbing had stopped.

Screeching tires outside were ignored as he examined the device. It was advanced. *Very* advanced. It was out of his league, and the fact there was an antennae sticking out the top of it made him think there might be a remote detonator involved.

There was noise at the front door as it was pulled open.

And a beep from the device.

"Stucco, you in here?"

"Kitchen!"

Boots hammered on the parquet flooring then came to a halt.

"Jesus!"

Stucco looked over his shoulder and saw Dawson standing there in shock.

And another beep from the device.

"Sit rep."

Stucco pointed at the device.

"Enough C4 to take out the block, pressure trigger joining the two of them, mercury switches if they move too much, and probably more. Plus there's this." He pointed at the antennae sticking out the top.

"Looks cellular," said Dawson.

37

"Agreed."

"Okay, I'm going outside to get a landline, I don't want to risk using my cell here or your phone again. I'm going to get the bomb disposal equipment, evacuate the area, jam any cellphone signals and solve this problem."

"Okay, thanks BD. And BD?"

"Yeah?"

"You know damned well who's behind this."

Dawson nodded.

"It wouldn't surprise me one bit. I'll get word out to Inspector Laviolette to warn the other witnesses."

"Make sure Maria is safe."

"Worry about your family, let me worry about the rest."

Dawson left and Stucco heard the front door open then close.

And the device beep each time.

Outside Stucco's Residence, Maas Drive, Fort Bragg, North Carolina

Dawson strode across the street as Red and several of the others arrived, most running on foot from their homes or nearby barracks. What he had seen was disturbing. Innocent people, innocent children, terrified. His friends, terrified. It was wrong, and if that bastard Lacroix was behind it, he would pay.

Dearly.

Dawson pointed at Danny "Casey" Martin. "Call the MP's. No cellphones. Have them cordon this entire area off and begin evacuations. Tell them we've got a large amount of C4."

Casey nodded and ran up the steps of the nearest house, hammering on the door to use their phone.

"Atlas, call the Colonel, tell him Stucco's wife and daughter have been bound to two chairs, back to back, with a bomb strapped to his wife's chest. The trigger looks professional. Very well done."

"Jesus Christ," muttered Atlas. "Is this because of what happened in Geneva?"

"We'll worry about that later," said Dawson. "Just contact the Colonel, but let him know that we think it might be connected, and that the other witnesses should be contacted immediately so they can be taken into protective custody."

Atlas ran to the next house as the residents of the house Casey was borrowing the phone from exited, jumping in their car and pulling out of their driveway. The man driving who Dawson recognized but couldn't remember the name of, rolled down his window.

"You need anything, you take it. Once I get my family out of here, I'll come back and give you guys a hand with whatever you need."

"Thanks," said Dawson, turning to Niner.

"Niner, contact the bomb squad, give them the rundown and tell them to get their asses out here ASAP. We need cellphone jammers, the works."

Niner sprinted to the next house without the usual wisecracks, concern for his friend and his family the only thing apparently on his mind. In the distance the sound of sirens could be heard as the base scrambled, police, fire and ambulance services being deployed. Within minutes the place would be crawling with people.

And if Dawson were a bomber, that would be exactly when he would trigger the device.

Inside Stucco's Residence, Maas Drive, Fort Bragg, North Carolina

"What's this all about, honey? Who's this Maria girl?"

Stucco was lying on his back, looking at the bottom of the chair to see if there were any triggers there, but it seemed clear. As he was about to push himself out from the chair, he paused, noticing a strip of tape, white, the same color as the legs of the kitchen chairs, running from the seat to the floor. He flipped over on his stomach and examined the bottom of the leg but couldn't see a pressure trigger.

"Talk to me!"

The device beeped, and Stucco paused.

"You have to calm down, babe, or this thing might go off."

"Who's Maria?"

Is she jealous?

Stucco didn't discuss his missions with his wife, and despite what had happened in Geneva, hadn't planned to now. But she did deserve a little tidbit since Maria's name had been mentioned.

"I can't talk about the mission—"

"Don't give me that, mister! I'm strapped to a bomb here!"

Another beep.

It had to mean something. It had beeped when Dawson had left. Twice. Was it hooked into the front door somehow? It beeped when Sheila got excited, suggesting a pressure trigger or a mercury switch being activated by her movements.

But if things were being triggered, why wasn't the device going off?

Maybe they're warnings?

That was possible, but to what purpose?

Stucco thought about it. Most bombs he dealt with were basic. They were meant to be triggered and once triggered, detonated. That was the entire purpose of a bomb. To go off. Why delay it then?

More victims.

The amount of explosives here would certainly wipe out the house, and the shrapnel it would create could injure or kill those gathered outside. He could hear the sirens in the distance and knew the homes would be evacuated, but he also knew his team.

They'll stay until the end.

"Are you going to tell me who Maria is?"

Another beep.

Christ, she is jealous.

"She was the night manager at a hotel we were at. She got raped and we helped her. I beat up the guy who did it, and now it's going to court."

He eyed the floor. The linoleum had a cut in it. He followed it all the way to the hallway where the flooring turned into parquet.

"Oh."

Her voice was subdued, almost embarrassed.

Yup, she was jealous.

"Is she okay?"

"Pretty beat up, but she'll live."

Bingo!

There was a wire running all the way to the front door, neatly tacked along the baseboard. Something he wouldn't notice in his rush from the door to the kitchen.

It's wired to the door.

He stood up and went to the back door at the rear of the kitchen. He immediately noticed the wire coming up from under the linoleum and the pressure switch it was wired to.

The front door opened and the device beeped.

"Wait!" he yelled, but it was too late, footsteps already stomping down the hall. He rushed toward the hallway as the device beeped again with the closing of the front door. He nearly ran headlong into two men in full bomb squad gear. He noticed another man heading up the steps and Stucco yelled, running for the front door. "Stop! It's wired to the doors!"

The man outside heard him and froze, backing up several steps. Stucco turned back to the two new arrivals and realized it was Dawson and Casey.

"It's wired to both doors. I'm not sure what else. Each time a door opens or closes, the device beeps."

"Sounds like an event countdown trigger," said Casey.

Stucco's stomach flipped.

If it were true, it most likely meant there were a built in number of warnings, then the explosive would be detonated.

"How many warnings have you heard?"

Stucco shook his head.

"I-I don't know."

"Take a breath, and think," said Dawson calmly.

Stucco closed his eyes and began to tally everything in his head.

"I came in, then you did, BD. Then you left, then you guys came in. So that has to be eight right there. I heard it go off three of four times when my wife was talking, so maybe eleven or twelve."

"It went off once before you got here," said Sheila. "I tried moving and it beeped, so we froze."

"Twelve, maybe thirteen."

"If I were a gambling man..." began Casey.

"Which you are..." continued Dawson.

"I'd be betting on thirteen," finished Stucco.

Dawson and Casey nodded in agreement.

"Okay, we can't risk triggering any more warnings. We'll have to wait until the evacuation is complete, then we'll start looking at this a little closer."

"But what if it's on a timer?"

Casey shook his head.

"I doubt it. They had no way of knowing when you'd be home."

Dawson disagreed.

"No, he's right. The first time the door opened it might have started a timer. I don't think we can assume there isn't one."

Casey sighed.

"You're right." He shook his head. "This thing is deadly sick. Whoever designed it is twisted. They want you to be here, they want the first responders to be outside, but they also want the civilians in the area out. This is targeted at *you*. They want *you* to be here, *you* to go through a delayed trauma, then for *you* and your family to be killed when we try to deactivate it."

Stucco's daughter whimpered.

"But don't you worry, little girl, we'll get you out of this," said Casey, patting her head.

The two men began taking pictures and video of the device.

"I'll transmit these to HQ and get some other eyes on it."

"Is it safe to transmit? I mean, there's an antennae on that thing," said Stucco, pointing.

"There's so much cellphone traffic in this area, if it were one of the event triggers, this would have gone off long ago. More likely this is a decoy," replied Casey.

Stucco sighed in relief. At least as long as they did nothing, and there was no timer, they would be safe, but the question was whether or not there *was* a timer.

"Jesus!" muttered Casey.

"What?" asked Stucco, looking over to see his friend had flipped what appeared to be some sort of night vision gear down.

"I can see through the tape. There's two LED displays on the front of the unit. The first, on the left, has the number 'two' displayed."

"That's probably the event countdown. We were close on the thirteen guess, or we counted wrong in the first place."

"Yeah, but the other one is a timer. Counting down."

The room became silent, even Sheila and Christa holding their breaths.

"How much time do we have left?" asked Dawson.

Casey looked up at him and shook his head.

"Not enough."

Palais de Justice, Geneva, Switzerland

Public Prosecutor Yves Benoit shook Maria Esposito's hand, clasping it tightly in both of his as they stood on the steps leading into the Palais de Justice where the trial would be held.

"Thank you very much for being so brave," said Benoit. "We have been trying to put M. Lacroix behind bars for years, to no avail. Your testimony, your courage, will finally let us put this man where he belongs so he can no longer hurt anyone else."

Maria smiled slightly, embarrassed at the man's words. If truth be told, she was terrified. Her courage, her bravery, were fronts. If she had been raised differently she would have quit her job and disappeared into the mass of humanity that was the European Union.

But instead she had decided to stand up for what was right. To fight back against this man, regardless of who he was. The prosecutor had assured her she would be safe, and so had Inspector Laviolette. She would have a detail assigned to her at all times once the charges were filed later today. At the moment she had been assured that Lacroix had no way of knowing what was coming. And it was that surprise they were counting on. Once the charges were filed, the press would have a field day with it, and the media firestorm would be her protection.

"He won't dare touch you once it's in the press."

She hoped his words were prophetic.

"I hope so," she murmured as he let go of her hand. "I have to get to work."

"Have a good day, Mademoiselle."

She turned and took the stairs two at a time as she eyed her watch.

You're going to be late.

She knew she wouldn't get in trouble. The hotel was backing her on this, they had no choice. Once the United States government became involved and insisted the tapes be turned over, they became very cooperative. It wasn't every day that officials that high up called the hotel.

She was pretty certain it was those Secret Service agents that were helping move things along. They had seemed like nice guys. Stucco had seemed really nice. And cute. She wondered what might have happened if the rape hadn't occurred. Would they have perhaps gone out on a date? He had seemed interested, but in a strange way. Almost as if he was oblivious to the fact he was showing her more interest than any man had in months, and that she was returning the interest.

Maybe he's the shy type? And what kind of name is Stucco?

She smiled then winced, her bruising still fresh, her broken nose still aching. She ignored the looks of those around her, it difficult for most to hide their shock at seeing a young woman in her condition. She had offered to work behind the scenes at the hotel, and they had gratefully accepted her offer, even moving her to the day shift to make life easier for her.

The most difficult thing had been talking to her mom and dad on Skype the day after it happened. They immediately caught a flight to be with her, and were still staying with her in her tiny apartment. And she wouldn't have it any other way. Her mother had cried, her dad had kept the proverbial stiff upper lip, but his glassy eyes had revealed everything she knew he was feeling deep inside. She needed them now more than she had ever before. She was certain there was no way she'd be able to sleep alone in her apartment, not with knowing that man was still out there, and that the people that worked for him were still on the streets, perhaps looking for her.

She reached the curb and heard a horn honk. She looked and saw her father and mother in her car on the other side of the street, her father in the driver's seat, her mom standing beside the car, waving. Waving back, she briskly made her way to the crosswalk and waited for the light to change.

A city bus picked up its passengers in front of the court house then accelerated toward the light. She could hear the engine strain as the driver tried to make the green. She glanced to the right and saw it turn orange. The engine didn't ease up, instead it whined louder. She waited for the bus as it rushed toward the intersection, then suddenly felt someone shove her from behind.

She stumbled out into the road, spinning toward the bus as it rushed at her. She screamed and she saw the bus driver's eyes shoot wide open. The sound of brakes being applied was cut off as she felt the large windshield slam into her entire body, the glass splintering with the impact, the front of her body roaring in agony as every nerve caught fire, her pain receptors sending an inferno of signals to her brain.

She didn't register anything beyond the pain until she felt the bus come to a halt, her own body continuing with the transferred momentum into the center of the intersection, her head slamming into the ground.

Her head lolled to the right and she saw a large pool of blood rushing out onto the asphalt, then in the distance, her mother rushing toward her, screaming in horror as her father struggled to get out of the car.

Then nothing. Nothing but the ever growing darkness, and the flashes of bright lights that came with it, as her life slowly, completely, drained from her.

A witness for the prosecution no more.

Inside Stucco's Residence, Maas Drive, Fort Bragg, North Carolina

Stucco looked at Dawson then Casey.

"How much time?"

Casey shook his head, not saying anything. Stucco grabbed him by the shoulder.

"How much!"

Casey had been his friend since he arrived at The Unit with him, almost straight out of Delta training. They were both experienced soldiers, you had to be to get into Delta, both Sergeants—another requirement—and had bonded well with the long established Bravo Team over the past couple of years. They were part of the family, but Casey and Stucco would always share a slightly closer bond as the outsiders who had joined a tightknit group, earning their way into the circle that was The Unit.

And the look in his trusted friend's eyes was horrifying.

"Less than five minutes."

His wife gasped a cry, his daughter thankfully oblivious as to what that meant.

"Is the block cleared?" asked Stucco, his mind racing as to what they could do.

Dawson nodded.

"Yes, it's all clear."

"Then get out of here."

"What?" Casey stood, shaking his head. "We've got five minutes, give me time to figure it out."

Stucco stood, putting a hand on his friend's shoulder, the other on Dawson's.

"Let me say goodbye to my family."

Dawson nodded.

"On condition you come out in time."

"Deal. Now get out of here."

Casey grabbed Stucco's hand, still on his shoulder, and squeezed.

"I'll see you outside in three minutes." Casey looked at Sheila, saying nothing, his eyes conveying the pain he was feeling. He turned and walked down the hall, the door opening and a beep from the device startling them all. Dawson said nothing, just squeezed his hand, looked at Stucco's wife and daughter grimly, then left, the door not eliciting a beep.

Stucco leaned out into the hallway and saw someone had propped the door open with a chair.

He dropped to his knees, taking the two most precious things in his life into his hands, turning their faces toward him.

"I'm so sorry this is happening," he said, his eyes filling with tears, unable to control the pain he felt inside, his chest tightening, his stomach muscles contracting as he fought the bile that was rushing into his mouth.

His daughter looked at him, her eyes flowing tears down her cheeks as she saw her daddy cry, something she probably hadn't seen since the day she was born. It had been the happiest day of his life, and now he would be here to see her die, something no parent should see, especially in this way.

He tousled her hair, then squeezed her cheek.

"Daddy loves you, always remember that. And I'll see you in Heaven, okay?"

"Okay."

Her voice, so innocent, seemed to accept his words at face value with no fear. He turned to his wife, her face red with tears, but her sobs controlled in an effort to not scare her daughter. He looked into her eyes, the eyes of the only woman he had ever loved, the woman who had helped rescue him

50

from a life almost wasted, a life almost spent alone, who had given herself to him completely, given him the most beautiful daughter in the world, and had loved him despite all his faults and this life of danger he thrived on.

"I love you," she said, her voice cracking.

"I love you too," he said, kissing her for the last time. "I'm so sorry," he gasped, his sobs taking over. "I shouldn't have got involved."

She shushed him.

"You wouldn't be the man I loved if you hadn't helped that girl. You did what was right, and that's why I married you. You have a good heart. Never forget that."

"Thirty seconds!" yelled Casey's voice from outside.

"Now go, go before it's too late," she urged, staring into his eyes.

Stucco kissed her, placed a kiss on his little girl's head, then walked down the hallway to the front door. Across the road he could see his entire team waiting for him, everyone else gone, urging him to hurry.

He stopped in the doorway, looked back, hearing the gentle sobs of his wife, then his daughter's tiny voice.

"Where's Daddy going, Mommy?"

Stucco looked at his friends, then raised his hand, and waved. He kicked the chair holding the door open, then as it slowly closed, the pneumatic door closer doing its job, he sprinted down the hallway as he heard shouts from outside. He turned into the kitchen and fell on his knees, his arms opened wide as he slid across the linoleum and into the only family he had ever known.

And as his arms enveloped them, the device beeped one last time, and tore a family apart.

Outside Stucco's Residence, Maas Drive, Fort Bragg, North Carolina

The world was dark, hot, loud and reeked. Dawson's body ached all over as he pushed himself up on his elbows. Fortunately he still had his EOD gear on, the only part he had removed was his helmet and visor. He looked around, shaking his head. The house was gone. Completely. It was if it had been originally made from matchsticks, everything now wood splinters and drywall dust, only the slab the house had been built on remained.

On either side the neighboring houses were heavily damaged, one in flames already, the other starting to smolder. Dawson could barely hear through the roaring in his ears, but he thought he heard sirens in the distance. He turned his head to look down the street and saw several fire trucks rushing to the scene, already holding out of range of any possible explosion.

Casey!

Casey had been the closest, having run for the door when he saw what Stucco intended. Dawson looked for him, but didn't see him. He had chased Casey, but was too slow to stop him, the damned EOD gear bulky, and Casey having a good twenty foot head start.

A hand grabbed his shoulder as Red came into view.

"BD! You okay?" he yelled, his own face and clothes covered in dirt and debris.

Dawson nodded.

"Casey?"

Red looked behind him and nodded.

"He's fine. Good thing he was wearing the gear."

"Get me up," said Dawson.

Red pulled Dawson to his feet and helped him strip out of the EOD gear, it no longer needed. Freed, he walked over to Casey who was now sitting up.

"How bad a hit did you take?" he asked.

Casey shrugged and winced.

"Mighta cracked a rib. Hurts to breathe a little."

"EMT just pulled up," said Atlas as the team broke to give the professionals room to work.

"Why'd he do it, BD? Why?"

Casey's voice broke, but he maintained enough control to prevent any tears threatening to spill over from doing so.

Dawson put a hand on the man's shoulder.

"You've got a wife and kid, don't you?"

Casey nodded.

"Wouldn't you?"

Casey closed his eyes, a single tear escaping, cleaning a path down his soiled cheek.

"Yes I would," he whispered.

Casey was lifted onto a stretcher and hurried away by the EMTs within minutes, leaving the rest of them to mull around and watch the fire department do its job.

"What the hell is this?" asked Niner.

Dawson turned to see what had caught the attention of their Korean-American team member. Niner was walking over to a telephone pole where a single sheet of paper was tacked to it. It was conspicuous since posting labels on military property was strictly forbidden.

Niner reached forward to pull it down when Dawson finally made out the drawing on the paper.

"Wait!" he yelled, running over to the pole.

Niner stood with his hand out but frozen.

"What?"

"Don't touch it. It's evidence."

"Evidence?"

The others gathered around as Dawson carefully looked at the paper and how it was attached to the pole.

"It's rigged."

Niner stepped back, as did the rest of the team.

"Looks like they dug a small hollow out in the post. There's probably a pressure trigger in there. Pull that pin holding this thing in place, release the trigger, say goodbye to your head."

Dawson gently held the bottom corners of the page down.

"Get some pictures of this, then get the bomb squad over here. They can deal with this."

Atlas stepped forward with his phone and quickly began taking pictures of the page as Niner went to find the EOD team that had been instructed to stand down by Dawson, he and Casey instead commandeering their equipment, every bit as qualified as the men that had shown up to deal with the bomb.

"Okay, everyone back," said Dawson as the EOD team arrived, having been holding only a few hundred feet away. Dawson explained what he thought was going on, and the team went to work. "Try to save the paper, it's evidence."

Dawson stepped over to the team who were all looking at the photos Atlas had taken.

"What is it?" asked Spock, his trademark eyebrow far up his forehead.

"Some sort of symbol. Looks like a rose with a cross in it. Why is that familiar?" asked Atlas.

"I don't know where you might have seen it before," said Dawson as he took the phone and looked at the drawing. "But I've seen it once before."

"Where?"

"Geneva."

Chênes-Bougeries, Geneva, Switzerland

Inspector Pierre Laviolette pressed the fob, his "Rosso Red" Fiat 500 Turbo chirping pleasantly as it flashed its lights at the end of a long day.

A very long day.

His witness was dead. A freak accident. She had stepped out in front of a bus and died instantly. There were dozens of witnesses, including the girl's own parents. There was no indication of foul play, no indication she had been murdered, no indication that slippery Lacroix was behind it at all.

She had just stepped out in front of the bus.

His heart told him it was an accident. As a devout Catholic, suicide was a sin, but he wouldn't blame the poor girl for having given in, given in to the pressures of the case, and for having decided to end it once and for all with a simple step forward, into traffic.

And his brain told him it must have been an accident, a terrible coincidence that was life. It wouldn't be the first time a witness had died on him from perfectly natural causes, or at least causes unrelated to the case.

He was certain it wasn't suicide.

Not in front of her parents. Nobody would do that!

He had met the distraught Espositos. When the mention of suicide came up, it was angrily shouted down. But they had no explanation, except that perhaps she wasn't paying attention. They had pulled surveillance tapes from the area and all they showed was a cluster of people, too thick to see many details, other than to see her surge forward into the crosswalk with the bus racing the amber light.

There was no evidence anyone had pushed her.

None.

He wished there were.

At least then he could pursue the case and try to pin a murder on the beast that was Lacroix.

But instead he had received a phone call from Lacroix's lawyer, he was sure one of dozens, within hours of her death, asking for the charges, which hadn't even formally been filed yet, to be withdrawn, to avoid any "embarrassment" to either side.

He had told him to "Piss off, the body isn't even cold yet!", or words to that affect, and slammed the phone down on its receiver. But a call from the Public Prosecutor moments later suggested he got the same phone call, and was handling it a little more delicately.

"I have no choice but to not proceed. Without her as a witness, I don't have a case."

"But what about the witnesses. The photographic evidence. The DNA!"

"The witnesses didn't see the attack. Lacroix will claim it was consensual and that she was a willing participant. It will become a 'he said, she said nothing' trial. There's nothing more I can do. I'm sorry."

Laviolette had slammed the phone down on him as well.

His phone rang in his pocket as his keys hit the door. He fished it out and took the call from the office as he turned the key in his lock.

"Oui?"

"Sir! I'm so glad I reached you. There's been a development in the case."

"What?" asked Laviolette as he pushed open his door and stepped inside. "I'm home!" he called to his family.

"We just received a phone call from the United States. Their State Department."

Laviolette kicked off his shoes, his aching feet sighing in relief.

"Yes, what is it?"

57

"Your witness, the Agent Green I think his name was, the one who attacked M. Lacroix"—Laviolette froze, his heart beginning to pound in his chest—"is dead. His wife and child, along with Agent Green, were blown up. A bomb in their house!"

But Laviolette wasn't listening.

His usual arrival at home would solicit pounding feet from the far reaches as little legs carried little bodies to him from wherever they were, and a return call from his wife, who would usually be in the kitchen preparing dinner.

But none of that had happened.

In fact, there was no evidence of any dinner being cooked. No sounds from the kitchen, no delicious aromas wafting through the air.

There was nothing but silence.

"Monsieur? Are you there?"

The phone was still pressed to his ear, but forgotten.

He stepped deeper into the house, toward the kitchen, the floorboards creaking slightly as he made his way, a sound he was so used to it didn't annoy him anymore. But the day they had rented the place, needing something bigger, it had bothered him to no end. But with their fourth child on the way, they had needed more space, especially with the fourth being a boy. A boy couldn't be holed up with his three sisters in one room, not as he got older.

He entered the kitchen and found nothing. No evidence of a dinner being prepared, no evidence of a dinner even begun.

"Sir! Can you hear me? Are you alright?"

He left the kitchen, and entered the living room and cried out, dropping to his knees, the phone clattering to the floor. All the furniture had been pushed to the edges, leaving the center of the room empty, and in the middle lay his family.

Dead.

His wife was in the middle, her arms stretched out to the sides, her legs tightly together, like Jesus on a cross. And his four gorgeous children encircled her, his two youngest, only three and five, at the top, their feet touching his wife's hands, their hands her head, their bodies stretched out as if to complete the arcs of a circle. Their eldest, seven and eight years old, completed the bottom of the circle surrounding his wife.

And in the middle, surrounding his wife, was a pool of blood so large, so complete, it gave the entire scene an almost artistic look, the shimmering red pool appearing as if it had been meticulously painted, rather than running from the arterial cuts that had been strategically made so the blood drained into the center, rather than outside, spoiling the image.

Laviolette stared, not sure of what to do. It was unlike anything he had ever seen. All he could do was sob at the sight before him, at the loss of his loved ones, and in a moment of final weakness, he decided he had to be with them

He pulled his service weapon, and placed it against his head.

Then pulled the trigger, begging God to forgive him for this ultimate of sins.

Outside Stucco's Residence, Maas Drive, Fort Bragg, North Carolina

"You saw this in Geneva?" asked Red, his shaved head scratched and bleeding. "Where?"

"On some file folders in that Lacroix guy's room."

"So then this *is* payback."

"Almost definitely." Dawson lowered his voice. "Split into teams. Family men with single guys. Get to your homes, collect your families, and get them to The Unit. Don't pack anything, just get them safe, then we'll go back and clear the houses and pick up anything you may need."

"Do you think he's going to target all of us?" asked Niner. "I don't have family on base, but my folks are in California. This has me worried."

"Call them. Call whoever you think this guy might target and get them to safety. I'll have the Colonel contact the locals and try to get security details assigned for the time being. I'm guessing though only Stucco and I have anything to worry about. *Had,* I guess." Dawson paused as they all bowed their heads for a moment. "I'm guessing we're the targets, since we're the witnesses," resumed Dawson. "But I'd rather be safe than sorry, so protect your loved ones. I'm going to meet with the Colonel."

The team split off into groups as Dawson strode toward his Mustang parked safely down the road. To say he was angry would be putting it mildly. He was furious. Enraged. If Lacroix were in front of him now, he'd tear his throat out and watch him bleed to death while pissing in the hole he had made.

They needed closure on this, and the only closure he could see would be against the books.

Revenge.

He pulled his cellphone from his pocket as he climbed in the car and dialed his sister's place. It rang several times then her old style answering machine picked up.

"Sis, it's me, Burt. You there? Pick up if you are, it's important"—he paused for a few moments—"okay, well, as soon as you get this message, I want you to take George and Jenny to the nearest police station, okay? Don't stop to pack, just go. Once you're there, call me and let me know where. This is urgent, Sis, it's important. Please don't ignore it. Love you."

He hung up and prayed not only that she'd get the message and act on it, but that there was no reason to, this insanity over.

Köln, Germany
1472 AD

Dietrich stood in the shadows in front of Heike's house, the rain now hard and heavy. And cold. He shivered as he watched the door open occasionally, the concerned look on her mother's face obvious from the lantern that hung outside, left to light her way home.

He desperately wanted to step forward, into the light, and tell them what had happened to his beloved Heike, to their precious daughter, but he couldn't. He feared any contact with them would put them at risk. Instead, he remained hidden, and when the door closed once more, he plodded down the hill, the cobblestone slippery, causing him to lose his footing several times before he finally reached the bottom, his heart aching as he passed the wall where she had met her fate, again when he passed where he had caught his last glimpse of her, and one final time as he walked past his childhood home, his parents long dead from a return of the plague ten years ago.

He had been an orphan, raised by the church, and had shown great promise in Latin and the sciences, as taught in their limited fashion by a paranoid religion. It was after his lessons one day, almost eight years ago, that he was called into the Father's rectory and introduced to an imposing figure of a man with a gentle face.

He listened to the opportunities that would be afforded him, and with a nod and not a word spoken, had left hand-in-hand with the man, not to see the church or the Father again for five years.

And learned he had.

The knowledge bestowed him was wondrous, and frightening. The things that were possible he had had no concept of, and when asked if he would like to learn more, he jumped at the opportunity.

But the cost had been his soul.

He had sworn to remain a bachelor, to devote himself to the sciences, and to commit, for life, to The Order. Naively he had agreed, and the rest was history. And now that he was a doctor, and understood what The Order was, what the Circle of Eight were, and his future within that, and what the consequences were, he was filled with a horror of regret, not only at the cost he had already borne, but what his future of loneliness would bring.

And tonight, with the knowledge he had nothing to live for except The Order, he made one final commitment, then a silent prayer for his lost Heike.

He stepped through the entrance of his master's home, and resigned himself to his fate.

Westover Hills Blvd, Richmond, Virginia

Sylvia Dawson-Biggs entered the driveway and sighed. Every time she pulled up to her house lately it pissed her off. Things had been tight since her husband George had lost his job. He had looked for almost a year for something in his field, banking, but as their savings rapidly dwindled, and their house barely maintained a value above their substantial mortgage, he had finally announced he was going to take anything, even minimum wage, just to start bringing in something.

She had been the sole breadwinner that year, and for the past three years might as well have been. She had a decent paying job as a nurse, but their lifestyle demanded more, much more. They had cut back everywhere they could, including house maintenance. The lawn wasn't getting mowed by a service anymore, the weeds weren't getting sprayed, the gardening wasn't getting done, and the driveway hadn't been sealed since he had been laid off. They needed a new roof, the shingles curling badly, and the trim desperately needed a paintjob.

It was embarrassing.

They kept driving the same cars, the Jaguar already paid off, but the constant repair bills now that it was out of warranty were higher than the monthly payments they were supposed to be now saving. It was bankrupting them faster than the house, but George insisted on keeping it, wanting to maintain appearances. She begged him to sell the albatross to some other poor fool, but George wouldn't hear of it.

Instead he had set up an eBay account and was selling off everything that he could to try and make ends meet so they could pay their mortgage and keep food on the table. Neither of them had parents with enough money to help out, no rich aunts or uncles, no big inheritance that might be just around the corner.

They were screwed.

If George couldn't get a better job soon, they'd have to sell the house. She had long argued they should—it didn't matter to her. It was just a building they lived in. But to George it was a sign of failure to give up. To drop from high-middle income to low middle-income was just something he couldn't bear.

Eventually things will come to a head.

She reached up and pressed the garage door opener out of habit, then cursed as it did nothing. The opener had stopped working two weeks ago. No money to have it repaired.

She climbed out of her car, grabbed her gym bag from the backseat and released her nine year old Jenny from the booster seat. She followed Jenny up the front walkway, eyeballing the weeds and lack of flowers. No money for annuals this year. Or last.

She unlocked the door and went inside, Jenny sprinting up the stairs to her room, she entering the code in the unmonitored security system. The panel beeped twice, then she closed the door. The answering machine sitting on a console table near the door was flashing with several messages. She prepared herself for more bill collectors as she pressed the button.

The machine beeped and the misery began as she kicked her shoes off and made her way to the kitchen.

"This is Franco from Tim's Autopalace. The new ABS module for your Jag is in. Can you give us a call at 555-7838 to arrange an appointment to have it installed?"

George had learned how to do his own oil changes and basic maintenance like topping up fluid levels, rotating tires, and what not, but not the big things, which were constant. Her car needed new tires, his were probably on their last five thousand miles and with the damned Jag it was one thing after another. ABS module, new battery, alternator, electrical problems coming out of the woodwork. And a leaking roof. The thing that had finally told her the Jag people hadn't a clue was when they said all convertible roofs leaked in car washes. She had screamed at them. "This is our fourth convertible, and it's the only one to have ever leaked! And you're telling me that's normal?"

George had had to lead her out of the dealership before she started throwing things.

"Argh! That *stupid car!*"

She opened the fridge and pulled out the casserole she had prepared the night before during a few minutes of lucidity.

"Sis, it's me, Burt. You there? Pick up if you are, it's important."

Sylvia paused. *Burt? He never calls during the day.* Her thoughts immediately went to her mom and dad. *Something's happened!*

"Okay, well, as soon as you get this message, I want you to take George and Jenny to the nearest police station, okay. Don't stop to pack, just go. Once you're there, call me and let me know where you are. This is urgent, Sis, it's important. Please don't ignore it. Love you."

The casserole was forgotten in her hand. Sylvia simply stood, frozen, as she repeated the message in her head. Her brother wasn't a practical joker, not in his business. She knew he was army, in logistics, but with the amount of times she had called him where he wasn't home for extended periods, and the fact he was stationed at Fort Bragg, she had put two and two together years ago.

He was Delta Force.

She had confronted him on it once and he had denied it.

"I wish!" was his response.

Yeah, right!

She knew from the look he had given her when she pushed him that she was right, and when she mentioned it to her husband that night, he had told her to back off.

"The less we know the better. It's for his protection, and ours."

She put the casserole down on the counter, left the kitchen and went into George's study. She pulled a hinged painting from the wall, keyed in the security code of the safe, and removed a Glock 22 then loaded a clip, stuffing another in her pocket.

Her hands shaking, she headed for the stairs, for the first time noticing that Jenny wasn't making any noise, which was rare for her.

Please, Lord, let her be okay. Please let this be Burt just being paranoid.

But she knew the truth. Burt had *never* called her with something like this during his entire career, never even said a word about being careful. This was an out-and-out warning, and as she climbed each step, wincing with each creak of the wood, the gun grasped in front of her, ready to blow away anything that came around the corner, she realized she had to calm down. Her heart was slamming so hard and so fast that she couldn't keep her hands steady, and could barely focus.

And if Jenny were to come around the corner, she'd blow her away by accident, she was so wired.

She dropped her hands, the gun now at her side, slightly behind her in the hopes her brain would have the time to recognize her daughter before she could raise the weapon to shoot.

The final step.

She looked to her right, down the hallway toward Jenny's room but saw nothing. Her door was closed, which was unusual. The rule was the door stayed open. She heard a whimper to her left and spun.

Then nearly vomited.

A man in a black suit was standing in the hallway, Jenny beside him, her face red, tears streaking her cheeks, the man's hand firmly on her shoulder, holding her back as she tried to run to her mother.

"Mrs. Dawson. Let me tell you why I'm here. Your brother—"

She didn't care. She raised the weapon, single handed, took a quick bead on his chest, the laser sighting making it dead easy as the red dot bounced on the man's crisp white shirt, her hands still shaking.

She didn't see his eyes bulge as she squeezed the trigger twice. He fell backward, two fresh red stains rapidly expanding from his chest as he hit the floor, his hand letting go of Jenny, the little girl racing toward her mother the moment the hand gripping her had fallen away.

"Mommy, look out!" she cried before she reached her.

Sylvia spun around, squeezing off round after round before even seeing her target, another suit coming out of Jenny's room. Her last shot caught the man in the shoulder, sending him spinning to the floor.

Picking up Jenny, she raced down the stairs, grabbed her purse off the console table and rushed out the door toward her car. She pulled the fob out of her purse, unlocked the doors, and pushed Jenny into the backseat, slamming the door behind her.

She climbed in the driver's seat, jamming the keys in the ignition and started the car as she closed the door. She began to back out when Jenny's face blocked the rearview mirror.

"But, Mommy, you forgot to strap me in!"

"Do it yourself please, you know how. We need to get out of here now," she replied, trying to keep her voice as calm as possible.

"But, Mommy!"

"Jenny, just do it!" she yelled, immediately regretting it as Jenny began to bawl. Her head disappeared as she climbed over to the booster seat, Sylvia revving the engine and backing out of the driveway, cranking the wheel to the left, then putting it in drive and flooring it, praying her tires would hold out. She checked her rearview mirror and could see Jenny buckling herself into her seat, still sniffling.

"That's good, baby. Just as good as Mommy or Daddy could do!"

Her voice was shaking, but Jenny didn't seem to notice, instead beaming in pride at her successful attempt. As Sheila's eyes shifted from Jenny to the road ahead, she saw something in the rearview mirror.

The man she had shot stumbling toward a black SUV parked on the road, its passenger door already open.

God please help us!

The Unit, Fort Bragg, North Carolina

Dawson gave his Godson Bryson Belme a hug, then pushed him toward the other children who were now playing outside, the families safely moved onto the base, a squad of military police surrounding the area for additional security. He turned to Bryson's father, and Dawson's best friend, Mike "Red" Belme.

"He seems to be handling it well."

"He's got no idea what's going on. Shirley on the other hand is a mess, but is hiding it well."

"She's a brave woman. She'll be fine."

Dawson's phone rang and he grabbed it, looking at the call display.

His heart leapt as he took the call.

"Sis, are you okay?"

"No! Oh God no! There were two men in the house, they had Jenny! Oh God, you've gotta help us!"

"Where are you?" asked Dawson as he motioned for Red to follow him.

"I shot one of them! Oh God, I don't know how you do it! I shot one of them! I killed him! And I shot the other one too but he didn't die."

"Are you out of the house?" asked Dawson as he sprinted toward the Op Center. Red pulled his pass out and ran ahead of Dawson, clearing a path for them, occasionally none too gently.

"Yes! We're in my car, but they're following us!"

Red slid his card through the security scanner and the door beeped, Red pulling it open. Dawson ran inside, followed by his friend.

"Trace this call!" yelled Red, pointing at Dawson's phone, shouting the number to the room of techs manning terminals. The Ops Center Chief, Sarah Michaels, pointed to one of the techs.

"You take it." She turned to Red and Dawson. "We're in the middle of an op, Alpha Team. What do you need?"

"Do you know where the nearest police station is?" Dawson asked his sister.

"Yeah, yeah, I think so. I'm not sure."

"Okay, head there now, but leave this call connected, okay?"

"Yes. Oh God, Burt, what have you done? Why are they after us?"

"Don't worry about that now, just let me do my job." He turned to Michaels. "I need this call traced, then geo tracked so we can get her to a police station. My sister is being chased by the same people responsible for Stucco's death."

Michaels nodded, pressing a button on the control panel in front of her.

"This is the Ops Center Chief. Send in the secondary team, I need more resources." She pressed another button. "Colonel Clancy to the Ops Center."

She turned to Dawson and pointed to the tech she had assigned.

"He will assist you. Anything you need."

Dawson nodded in appreciation as he and Red took up positions over either shoulder of the tech. On the screen they could see a map rapidly drilling down until it reached street level, a red dot indicating his sister's car.

"Put up the nearest police stations."

A flurry of keystrokes, and several police stations, all several miles away, appeared.

"Map the closest based on current traffic."

More keystrokes then a blue line appeared and a set of instructions appeared on the side of the screen.

"Sis, you still there?"

"Yes! Yes Goddammit! Where the hell would I have gone?"

He knew telling her to calm down would set her off even more, so he chose to ignore it.

"Take your next right at the intersection, okay? If you have to go through the red or take the sidewalk, you do it. Just make sure you don't get hit by any oncoming traffic, okay?"

"Okay." There was a pause. "Oh God, they found us!"

There was a crashing sound and the call went dead.

Hull Street, Richmond, Virginia

Sylvia Dawson-Biggs screamed as the SUV slammed into the back of her car, throwing her body back into her seat, then forward, the only thing saving her from slamming into the steering wheel her seatbelt. Jenny was screaming, but she didn't have time to comfort her as she looked in the rearview mirror to see doors open on either side of the dark black vehicle, it huge compared to her Mercedes C300.

Two men were now approaching, one on either side. A small group of onlookers had gathered on the sidewalk, lookie-loos who delighted in other's misery. She looked for the phone. It had flown out of her hand and was nowhere to be seen. She grabbed her purse and felt the gun inside as there was a tap at the window. An ID was being shown to her.

FBI? Were these the same people from earlier? Was it the same vehicle?

"Thank God!" she exclaimed, deciding it couldn't be, pushing the button to roll down her window. "You've got to help me. Two men tried to kill me and my daughter earlier."

"We're aware of what happened, ma'am."

"Did my brother send you?"

"Yes he did, ma'am. If you'll come with us, you'll be perfectly safe."

"Of course, yes, of course!" she cried, joy and relief spreading through her as the adrenaline high she had been on began to slowly subside. Her happiness seemed to extend to Jenny who smiled at her and handed over the phone Sylvia had dropped in the crash.

It rang.

She answered it as she unbuckled her seat belt.

"Hello?"

"Sis, are you okay."

"Oh thank God, yes. It was the FBI. They're here now!"

"What was the FBI?"

"That hit us from behind," she replied, then paused. "You know, you sent them."

"Sis, listen to me very carefully. Is the car still running?"

"Yes."

"Then I want you to put the phone down, put the car in gear, and get the hell out of there. Take the sidewalk if you have to!"

"Why?" she asked, her voice quavering as her fear began to build again.

"Because I didn't send any FBI to help you, and FBI don't ram the vehicles of the people they're trying to help."

The phone dropped from her ear and between the seats. She reached for the gearshift when she felt a hand on her left shoulder. She yelped, reached over for her purse and pulled the gun as the man on the passenger side pulled his. She raised the weapon, the loop of her purse draped over the barrel, and squeezed the trigger. The man flew backward, a new hole in his stomach as those gathered screamed, rushing in every direction but hers.

The hand on her shoulder slid up to her neck and squeezed. She swung the gun around but he grabbed the barrel, deflecting the weapon, his grip too strong for her to break. She let go of the gun and put the car in gear, hammering on the gas. The grip on her neck broke and several shots were fired, her rear windshield bursting as the glass was taken out.

A car in front of her blocked her way and she cranked the steering wheel to the right, hopped the curb, and raced down the sidewalk just as her brother had told her to do, all the while laying on the horn, pedestrians scrambling to get out of the way. She burst onto the road again and turned right, rushing toward the police station she knew was only two blocks away.

The phone rang but she couldn't reach it. Remembering the Bluetooth in the car, she hit the button on her steering wheel.

"Hello?"

"Sis, what's going on?"

"I shot another one, Burt. The other one got my gun. I did like you said and drove on the sidewalk. I don't see them anymore!"

"Okay. Just keep driving straight and you'll be at the police station. We've already called ahead. They're expecting you. Just stop in front of the station, get out of your car, and go inside, okay?"

"Okay, I see it. I see it!" she cried, the police station parking lot coming into view as she caught a green light on the final intersection. She screeched into the parking lot then hammered on her brakes as her ABS brought her to a shuddering halt. Turning off the vehicle, she jumped out of the car.

"Help us! Please help us!" she screamed as she opened the back door, unbuckling Jenny and pulling her into her arms. She rounded the back of her car and rushed toward the steps as several officers ran toward her.

"What's wrong, ma'am?" asked one in uniform.

"Some men tried to kill us!"

"Are you Mrs. Dawson-Biggs?" asked a man rushing down the steps.

She nodded.

"Let's get you inside right away," he said as he took her by the arm and led her and Jenny up the stairs. Within minutes they were deep within the building, sitting inside a stark white room, a mirror across one of the walls. She had a bottle of water, Jenny a chocolate bar and her own bottle, happily humming as she nibbled at her treat.

Nobody had spoken to them since they had been put in the room about fifteen minutes ago, and she was getting frustrated.

If only I had my phone!

There was a knock on the door then it opened quickly, the man who had brought them inside, a Detective Lewis, entering, followed by two men in dark suits. Her heart immediately slammed into her chest at the sight of them. She didn't recognize them, but couldn't be positive they weren't the ones who had attacked her earlier. She quickly ran through the events in her head. She knew she had put several holes in the first one, and he was definitely dead. The second had a bullet hole in his shoulder, and neither of these men appeared wounded. She shot one in the stomach at the crash site, so there was no way he was one of them. And then there was the one who had taken her gun. She had never seen his face.

"Sorry for keeping you waiting, Mrs. Dawson-Biggs. But I had to make a few phone calls to get things cleared up."

"Who are they?" she asked, motioning for Jenny to come over to her side of the table.

The detective frowned, his face grim.

"I'm afraid, ma'am, that I have some bad news. The men you shot, two of whom you killed, were FBI."

She felt herself gag, her mouth filling with bile as her stomach flipped. *It can't be!*

"But they were in my house, they had my daughter!"

"Ma'am, I'm Special Agent Nelson Harcourt"—he flashed his ID— "FBI. My men were searching your house as there was an incident involving your brother. We were there to take you into protective custody. According to my man who survived, you shot one of our agents without provocation, and without giving him a chance to identify himself."

"This can't be happening!" she cried, the room starting to swim as she put her arm around Jenny. "I didn't know! It's not my fault!"

76

"Ma'am, we then pursued you, stopped your vehicle, and identified ourselves, yet you then proceeded to shoot and kill another one of my agents." The man stepped forward. "Ma'am, can you please stand up?"

She rose, trembling, Jenny clinging to her leg.

"Sylvia Dawson-Biggs, I am placing you under arrest for the murder of two federal agents, and the attempted murder of two others. You have the right to remain silent…"

The rest simply became words among the fog of her misery. She had shot innocent FBI agents, men just doing their jobs. Her jaw clenched as she realized why.

"Burt!" she muttered. It had been his message that had caused this. His message that had caused her to panic, to get the gun, to shoot the strange men.

"Burt!" she cried as she was led out of the room, Jenny holding her pant leg. Dozens of faces, none with any detail, stared at them, voices murmured, the doors opened, sunlight glared down on them as they descended the steps and were helped into the back of a black SUV.

As the door closed, her mind suddenly cleared.

"Wait!" she yelled as the door slammed shut, her eyes pleading with the detective who turned and took the steps two at a time.

The FBI agents climbed in the front seats and the vehicle pulled away. She didn't know where she was going, but she knew who she wasn't going with.

FBI agents.

Her brother's voice echoed in her head.

I didn't send any FBI to help you!

Operations Center, The Unit, Fort Bragg, North Carolina

"Report!" barked Colonel Thomas Clancy as he burst into the Op Center, pencil clenched in his teeth. Red turned to explain as Dawson continued to try his sister's phone, the screen showing the phone stationary.

"Sir, Sergeant Major Dawson received a call from his sister. She and her daughter were being pursued by men posing as FBI agents. She shot several of her attackers and escaped. GPS in her phone has her at the police station, but we haven't heard anything since."

"The phone's moving!" announced the tech.

Clancy motioned toward a large screen on the right.

"Put it up there."

The screen flashed and suddenly they were all looking at the map of Richmond, Virginia, a red dot slowly moving away from the police station.

"Why would she leave?" asked Dawson, more to himself than anyone else.

"She wouldn't," said Clancy. "She'd call you first." He turned to the tech. "Can you get us eyes on target?"

The man shook his head.

"No birds are in that area right now. I need authorization to access traffic cameras—"

"Do it."

"Accessing traffic cameras," said the tech, his fingers flying over the keyboard. Moments later they had a shot of an intersection. "She should be coming through here any moment."

"What kind of car are we looking for?" asked Clancy.

"Silver Mercedes. C300 I think. Unless she's got a new car."

"I pulled her registration. She's still driving a 2008 Silver Mercedes C300. License plate—"

"There it is," said Dawson, pointing at a tow truck that had just entered the frame, the silver Mercedes hanging off the back of it. He punched the table, straightening up and spinning around as he tried to cool his jets. "We've been tracking a damned empty car for the past fifteen minutes!"

Another tech spoke up.

"Sergeant Major Dawson, I finally have Detective Lewis on the line."

Dawson grabbed the phone.

"Detective Lewis? This is Sergeant Major Dawson. Do you have her?"

"We did, Sergeant Major, but we had to hand her over to the FBI."

"You did what?"

Dawson could feel the rage build inside at the stupidity of what he had just heard.

"I had no choice. They had the proper credentials, claimed they had been at her house at your request when she shot and killed one of them. I'm afraid Sergeant Major that they arrested her for murder not even five minutes ago."

"Murder!" Dawson sucked in a deep breath in an attempt to calm himself. "Detective, I can assure you those men were not FBI. They were imposters."

"I can assure *you*, Sergeant Major, that they were. I checked their credentials myself."

"Detective Lewis, you said those men were at my sister's house at my request?"

"Yes."

"Well I never contacted the FBI. I didn't even contact *you* until after my sister was attacked."

There was a pause, and Dawson could only pray it was because something was finally getting through to the detective.

"Oh shit."

"When did she leave?" asked Dawson.

"Maybe five minutes," replied a more subdued and less dismissive Lewis.

"Details."

"Front steps of the building. There was a black SUV there. She and her daughter left with the two agents."

Dawson turned to the tech.

"Front steps, black SUV, about five minutes ago. Can you pull footage?"

"Not from any police cameras without hacking the system. What direction did they head?"

"Detective, what direction did they leave in?"

"East. I'm going to put an APB out on the vehicle and I'll get back to you."

"There!"

The tech was pointing at the screen. It was the same intersection they had been watching, the time code rolled back. A large black SUV passed through the intersection.

"Sergeants, please come with me."

Dawson looked at the Colonel.

"Yes, sir." He turned to the tech. "Find out where that vehicle went."

He and Red followed the Colonel out of the Ops Center then to his office in silence. Dawson's mind was racing and suddenly realized that Sylvia's husband George didn't even know what was going on. And that he didn't even have his brother-in-law's number.

They entered the Colonel's office, Red closing the door as Clancy sat down behind his desk, tossing his chewed pencil where the humidor used to be. He motioned to the seats.

"Report."

Dawson let out the breath he had been holding.

"This morning just after our meeting Stucco called me and said he needed help." Dawson then gave the Colonel a full rundown on what had happened. "After the residence was destroyed, we found a secondary device attached to a piece of paper stuck to a telephone pole. It had a symbol on it that was the same symbol I saw in Lacroix's hotel room in Geneva."

"So it definitely ties back to him."

"Most likely. I don't believe in coincidences."

"Well, how's this for coincidence," said Clancy, leaning forward and opening a file on his desk. "We just received word that your hotel night manager is dead. Stepped in front of a bus."

Dawson's eyes closed as he shook his head, images of the happy young girl pushed away and replaced by the severely beaten girl he had seen lying in the hallway.

"And that's not all."

"What the hell else could go wrong?" asked Red. "They killed Stucco and his family! They've kidnapped BD's sister and niece!"

"They slaughtered Inspector Laviolette's family."

Dawson gripped the arms of his chair, his knuckles turning white.

"They need to pay."

"Who is they?" asked Clancy.

"This isn't one man. And this isn't about a rape. This is about anyone who might have seen what was on that table."

"The files with the symbol embossed on them?"

Dawson nodded.

"Unfortunately the State Department has made it crystal clear they don't want us involved in this case, so there's nothing Delta can do," said Clancy.

Dawson was about to protest, when Clancy held up a finger.

"But, I think you and your team are due for some vacation. You're not scheduled for any op, so I suggest you all go somewhere nice. I hear Switzerland is beautiful this time of year."

Dawson shot to his feet.

"That sounds like a fantastic idea, sir."

"And if you happen to need anything for training purposes, or should you decide to go hunting, you know how to equip yourselves."

"Thank you, sir," said Red as he headed for the door. "Some light reading for the flight might be good. Perhaps intel on Lacroix, case files. I'm an eclectic reader, so the more the better."

Clancy stood and headed for his door, pointing at the folders on his desk.

"Can you shred those for me on the way out?"

"Yes, sir," said Dawson as he waited for the Colonel to leave, then with a smile at Red, he grabbed the stack of folders. "Let's get back to Ops."

Red put his hand out. "Let me put those in my car. You don't want to be seen carrying them around."

Dawson nodded, handing the files over, then headed for Ops. Swiping his pass, he entered the secure room and joined the tech who had been working his sister's abduction.

"Any progress?"

"I'm afraid so, sir. And you're not going to like it."

Hull Street Road, Richmond, Virginia

Sylvia Dawson-Biggs stroked her daughter's hair, her hands thankfully cuffed in front of her for the drive. She still didn't know where they were going, except that it appeared they were leaving town. She knew once they were on the highway there was no way they'd be able to escape. She had to get them to stop somehow.

"Mommy, I need to pee."

Oh God bless you!

"Can we pull over somewhere?" she asked.

"No."

"She has bladder problems. If we don't stop soon, she'll pee all over herself."

Jenny was about to protest this grave insult when Sylvia put a finger over her mouth and prayed she'd figure it out.

"Shit!" muttered the driver.

"Language! I've got a kid here!"

"Not for long, lady."

The reply cut to the quick, the sudden realization that this wasn't a kidnapping at all hitting her. At the house they were going to kill her, but she had got the drop on them. At the car accident, it was too public. They couldn't do it at the police station obviously, so now they were taking them somewhere to finish the job.

Bile filled her mouth and she knew she didn't have time for games. She had to get her and Jenny away. She started to look around the back of the SUV, looking for anything that could be used as a weapon.

Nothing.

She looked at her hands. Useless. She was in shape but not enough to take on two men, especially in handcuffs.

Handcuffs!

She looked at the passenger, his eyes on the road ahead as were the driver's. They were turning onto the highway now, and there was no time to waste. She raised her hands, pushing forward, and dropped her cuffed wrists in front of the passenger's neck then pulled back fast and hard before he could get his own hands in the way. She pushed her knees into the back of the seat as she pulled with her back muscles, far stronger than her arms.

The man gasped, choking for breath as his hands tried to pry at the chain linking the handcuffs, but it was no use. The headrest was raised, and her arms were skinny enough to fit in the gap meaning there was no room for him to grasp.

"Let go!" yelled the driver as he swerved, trying to maintain the high speed turn he was in as he was about to merge onto the highway.

Sylvia pulled harder.

The man grabbed at her fingers but she clenched them into fists, tucking her thumb inside leaving nothing for him to grab. His slaps were getting weaker as the driver still fought for control.

"Buckle up, honey!" she yelled and Jenny immediately grabbed the lap belt of the center seat, snapping it securely. "Make sure it's tight!" Jenny pulled on it then looked at her.

"It's tight."

She kicked out with her left foot and clocked the driver in the side of the head. His hands flew from the wheel leaving it to immediately spin and straighten out. Realizing his mistake, he grabbed the wheel again, quickly turning it to regain control, but instead caused the SUV to tip onto the driver's side wheels.

She kicked again.

The vehicle tipped over, skidding on its side until it hit the edge of the road where the pavement lip of the highway caught the edge of the SUV and overturned it, the momentum causing them to flip several times, how many Sylvia couldn't count. She simply closed her eyes, maintained her grip on the man's neck with her cuffed hands, and shouted for Jenny to hold onto her.

Her head smacked the side window and she felt herself begin to black out, her arms still outstretched, strangling one of those who would kill her and her baby. She felt something give on the handcuffs, as if the man's neck had finally broken, or something was crushed. What, she didn't know, her mind now a fog.

All she knew was Jenny was still alive because her screaming hadn't stopped.

Operations Center, The Unit, Fort Bragg, North Carolina

Dawson watched the traffic camera footage of the SUV losing control, then flipping over several times. The fact there was no movement afterward gave him mixed feelings. If the abductors were alive or mobile, they'd have climbed out by now. But so would have his sister.

"I'm heading to Richmond. Call me if you find out anything on my sister or niece."

"Yes, Sergeant Major," replied the tech, his voice subdued.

All eyes were on Dawson as he left the room, marching toward his Mustang, ignoring all those around him. He rarely got emotional, rarely shed a tear, but this was his little sister. This was the little girl who had looked up to him her entire childhood, who had cried when he left to join the army, refusing to let him go, who had given him a niece that he adored, and still called him once a week to make sure he was okay.

Calls he was usually unable to take, and failed to return far too often.

It's when you lose someone that you realize how you had taken them for granted, mistreating them through inattention. The assumption was that they would always be there, that there was always time to tell them how much you appreciated them, how much you loved them. But once gone, torn from your life unexpectedly, it was too late. You prayed they knew how much you really cared despite your actions, but it left you wondering if they died thinking of the phone call you didn't return, or the phone call you ignored when they knew you were home.

He climbed into his car, revved the engine and squealed from the parking space, a single tear rolling down his cheek, unnoticed.

I swear to you, Sis, that whoever did this to you will pay.

Red stepped out from between two cars, holding his hand out. Dawson slammed on the brakes and Red climbed into the passenger seat.

"Where we going?"

"Richmond."

"Figured. The guys are waiting at my place for your orders."

"Call them, put them on speaker."

Red dialed his home number and immediately it was answered.

"This is Niner."

"Let me put you on speaker." He hit the button then held the phone between him and Dawson as they both rolled up their windows.

"Who's there?" asked Dawson.

"Everyone."

"Good. Here's the sit rep. The colonel has said we all need some vacation time and suggested we go hunting in Switzerland. I think it's a fantastic idea. Agreed?"

A round of agreements burst through the phone.

"Good. Now here's the immediate situation. My sister and niece were kidnapped by men posing as FBI agents. They were just in a car accident, I don't know the situation yet but I'm heading to Richmond with Red. We liberated some files that I'm going to need someone to copy for us."

"I'll meet you outside," said Atlas, his impossibly deep voice not so deep on the tiny phone speaker. "I've also got your 'go' bag here for you."

"We found yours too, Red," said Niner.

Red turned the phone slightly toward himself. "Good. ETA three minutes."

"I'll be outside," said Atlas.

Dawson spun the wheel as he gunned it out of the parking lot.

"Jimmy, Niner. You two find out where Professor Acton is. This has something to do with that damned symbol. I want to know what the hell it is, and he's the man most likely to know."

"Will do."

"Spock, pick three men, meet us in Geneva. I want all the traffic camera footage you can find of Maria's supposed suicide, and all the data you can find of the murder of the Inspector's family. Keep an eye out for that symbol. They don't know to look for it."

"Got it, boss."

"The rest of you I need here. Casey, I assume you're going to want to work on the funeral arrangements for Stucco. The rest of you help him when he needs it. But I need you guys to be our Ops Center. Set up in a secure location, tap into anything you need to tap into. I want to find this bastard Lacroix, what kind of connections he has, what his game is. We're taking him down. Understood?"

A cacophony of replies came back, the individual responses hard to hear, but their meaning clear.

"Good. Atlas, you're in charge here. Red and I are going to secure my sister then we'll join Spock in Geneva. Good hunting gentlemen."

Red ended the call as Dawson screeched to a halt in front of Red's house, Atlas waving them down. The massive man tossed the two go bags in the trunk then took the files from Red.

"Red filled us in earlier so we took action. Charlie's plane is waiting for you at Fayetteville Regional with instructions to get you to Richmond ASAP. I'll copy these then have a set waiting for you when you land. Thor will meet you with a vehicle."

Dawson shook Atlas' hand then floored it, pleased that Brad "Thor" Inglethorp, a retired member of The Unit from about ten years ago was their point man in Richmond. He was a good man who had lost part of his

88

foot on an op when a stray 50 caliber round had found him. Dawson wondered if his thick mane of long blonde hair that had earned him his nickname was still as golden as it once was.

Or as grey as he now felt.

He glanced at Red.

"Call the Op Center and see if there's any word on my sister."

Chippenham Parkway, Richmond, Virginia

Sylvia groaned, her head pounding, the taste of iron on her lips. She opened her eyes and blinked her surroundings into focus, and as she did so, realized why she felt so disoriented.

She was hanging upside down. There was no movement in the vehicle, their two abductors still in their seats. Her hands were still hooked around the passenger seat occupant's neck, her wrists aching from the strain.

"Mommy?"

Her heart leapt as she heard Jenny's voice. She looked to her left and Jenny was still belted in, her two hands hanging onto her mother's seat belt to stop herself from falling down to the roof of the upturned vehicle.

"Are you okay, honey?"

"Yeah. Are you?"

"I'm fine."

"But you're bleeding."

"I just bumped my head, that's all. I'll be fine."

"But you're bleeding from your arm too."

She looked and saw a lot of blood on her left arm, dripping down onto the clothed roof liner. Something was sticking out of it, a piece of wood or something. She followed it and realized it was a piece of a traffic sign that had punctured the front window, the shredded end where it had broken in half now partially stuck in her arm.

This isn't good.

She examined the wound as best she could with her hands cuffed. It was bleeding, but not profusely, suggesting it had missed the artery. A moan from the driver seat made her decision for her. They had to get out of here, which meant the pole had to be removed.

"Mommy needs your help, okay?"

Jenny nodded.

Terrified.

"I want you to take the piece of wood that's in Mommy's arm, and pull it straight out, okay?"

Jenny nodded, letting go of the belt with one hand, then unbuckling her own belt, flipping head over heels and landing on her knees as only young children could without hurting themselves. She grasped the pole and Sylvia nodded.

Jenny yanked and Sylvia screamed as the pole came out.

"Don't stop!" she yelled as she felt Jenny hesitate.

She continued to pull and Sylvia felt the pain immediately ease. She opened her eyes and saw her arm was free of the pole. It looked like a broken shard had embedded itself about two inches. She knew enough to know that her brachial artery wasn't severed—if it were, she'd be dead—but it might be nicked.

"Can you reach Mommy's belt buckle?"

Jenny nodded, her face tear stained.

"Unbuckle me."

"You'll fall."

"It's not far."

She heard shouts outside then saw feet and legs through the window.

"Are you okay in there?"

"Help!" she yelled. "We're trapped in the back!"

She saw two people at her window and heard the door being yanked on. Suddenly it opened, fresh air and the evening sun pouring in.

"I'm wounded in the arm," she said. "I'm a nurse, I'll need—"

"I'm an off duty EMT. Don't you worry, ma'am. I'll have you out of there in a few seconds. Can you move your arms and legs?"

"Yes."

"Any pain anywhere?"

"Just my head from where I hit it, and my arm where the traffic sign punctured me."

"No pain when I do this?" he asked as his hands went over her body, feeling for broken bones.

"No."

"But you can feel it?"

"Yes."

"Okay, we're going to get you out of here now."

He unclipped her seatbelt, his arms gently lowering her. He freed her of the belt and she was able to reposition herself so she could free her cuffed hands from around the throat of her abductor without anyone noticing.

Two sets of hands lifted her out then lay her on the pavement. Jenny scrambled out on her own, holding his mother's hands.

"Hey sweetheart, how are *you* feeling?" asked the EMT.

"Fine," replied Jenny, looking away.

"Hey, this one's dead!" called another voice. She looked to her right and saw someone had the passenger side door open, shaking his head at what he saw.

She felt the EMT tie off her arm with a tourniquet, wincing as he did it.

"That should hold until the ambulance gets here. She could hear sirens in the distance.

"Hey, what's with the handcuffs?"

Her heart raced and her eyes flooded with tears.

"Are you a prisoner?"

The EMT seemed to back off a bit, his face one of shock.

"We were kidnapped," she said.

"Uh huh."

It didn't sound like he believed her.

"This one's alive!" called the other voice, sounding more distant. She looked to see several people gathered on the other side of the vehicle.

"Help Mommy up," she whispered to Jenny. Jenny pulled on her good hand so that she was now sitting up. She rolled onto her knees, Jenny pushing with all her might to keep her from falling forward, then between the two of them, she managed to sit up right on her haunches. One final push and she was on her feet, rushing across the road, Jenny in tow, toward a row of thick trees.

"Hey, where are you going?" yelled someone.

She didn't look.

"Keep going!" she said to Jenny in a harsh whisper. "Don't look back!"

They made it to the trees and through an opening revealing some sort of abandoned construction or demolition site, packed dirt and rubble strewn about. The trees continued to the left, blocking their view from the road they had just crossed. Ahead she could see a house and other buildings they might be able to hide in.

Fortunately her legs were working fine, but she was weak. She couldn't raise her cuffed hands to apply pressure to her wound, the blood still dripping from her elbow onto the ground.

A trail!

There was nothing she could do about that. She needed to get to a phone and call Burt. That was her only hope. She reached the house, the driveway empty save a covered car that looked like it hadn't been moved in years. She hammered on the door, but the only answer was the bark of what sounded like a huge dog. She knocked again, and there was no retort of an occupant telling the dog to be quiet.

And with the dog, there was no breaking in.

They rounded the house, a quick glance behind her showing no one pursuing them. Behind the house was a large yard then open space, a few cars parked to the side of a thin paved portion, this obviously meant to be used as a parking lot, for what she didn't know.

Then she gasped as she saw the spire proudly thrusting into the air.

A church!

She ran as fast as she could toward the carport at the front, then leaned on Jenny's shoulder with her elbow to climb up the few steps to the large front doors. As she entered, she heard a shout and she looked to her right to see the driver of their SUV stumbling past the corner of the house.

He raised his weapon and fired, the bullet slamming into the brick railing sending shards of sharp rock blasting in all directions. Sylvia pushed Jenny inside then jumped across the threshold as another bullet tore into the door.

"Somebody help us! Please!" she yelled as the few inside turned toward the commotion. She stumbled forward, down the aisle of the church toward the altar, her body weakening rapidly, the adrenaline she had been running on waning in its effect, forcing her to lean on Jenny more and more, Jenny's tiny body struggling under her mother's weight, the little champion not saying a word in protest.

A man near the front, kneeling deep in prayer, looked then jumped up as fast as his old bones could manage as the pastor ran toward them from a side room. There were only a few worshippers here, it not Sunday, and almost all were retirees well into their final years.

But every one of them moved to help.

The pastor quickly took control.

"Was that gunfire I heard?"

"Yes," gasped Sylvia as she finally fell to her knees, her body too weak to continue.

The pastor turned to his parishioners.

"Call nine-one-one, tell them we need police and ambulance, shots have been fired."

One of the women pulled her phone out of her purse, dialing as she walked away from the commotion.

"Kurt, you were a medic in the war, weren't you?"

The first man to have reacted nodded as he struggled to kneel on the floor. The pastor helped him then ran for the doors. Sylvia heard the clicking of locks as Kurt quickly looked at her wound, then noticed her cuffs. Loosening the tourniquet, he quietly said, "Who's after you?"

"Some men pretending to be FBI. They tried to kill us. It's something to do with my brother's work."

"What's he do?"

"I'm not allowed to say. It's military though."

"Ahhh, one of our Special Forces boys. Enough said."

"I need to call him."

"What's the number?" he asked as he tore her sleeve off. She gasped in pain and passed out as hammering could be heard at the doors.

St. Paul's University, St. Paul, Maryland

"Let's talk the Black Death."

Professor James Acton sat perched on the edge of his desk, legs extended out in front of him, crossed at the ankles. He faced a class of over one hundred students, most of whom actually seemed to want to be there. Eager heads popped up at the mention of one of his favorite topics in history.

"Who can tell me why it was called the Black Death?"

A hand shot up.

"Wasn't it something to do with these black things growing under their armpits?"

"Very good. One of the symptoms was the infection collecting in the lymph nodes, some of which are located under the arm pits. These would swell, filled with a black puss that would darken the skin. The doctors at the time would slice them open, letting the infected blood out. It would be this nasty thick, black, horrible smelling ooze that would cure you of eating anything for a few days."

There was laughter from the students, and a little queasiness.

"But, keep in mind that's a new term. At the time it was called many things such as The Pestilence or The Great Mortality." He paused and took a sip of water from a glass on his desk. "So, where did it originate?"

Silence.

"It was thought to have originated in the Orient, probably China, then made its way along the trade routes, and eventually to Europe. Any idea when it hit Europe?"

"Wasn't it in the dark ages? Like thirteen hundred something?"

"Yes. The first case was believed to have happened in 1328, and the plague ravaged Europe until 1351. Over the next sixty years there were additional outbreaks, but none like the first. Some estimates put the death toll at as much as sixty percent of the European population, most of that toward the end."

That got a reaction.

"Now imagine a plague hitting us, killing off half of America in just a few years. What kind of impact would that have on us?"

"Our economy would be screwed."—"We'd be open to invasion." — "China would take over."

Acton nodded.

"I hear mostly negative things. In fact, I think everything was negative unless you really like Chinese food." Laughter. "How about we learn from history? It's hard to believe that having half your population die horrible agonizing deaths in a few short years could produce anything good, but it did. In fact, the Black Death eventually led to many advancements that still impact us today."

"You mean like how war spurs technological progress?"

"Yes, in some ways, but also in others. The obvious was advancements in science in general. Once cases started to show up, doctors were trying to figure out ways to cure it. They experimented on patients, and in doing so, came up with the scientific method. Before that, most experimentation was haphazard guesswork with no method. But by the end of the Black Death, many new methods of experimentation were developed that evolved over the centuries into our modern scientific method."

"What caused it?"

"Great question. For centuries no one knew. There were crazy theories out there. Wrath of God, bad air being released by earthquakes. As well, Jews were often blamed."

"Man, can't those dudes ever get a break?"

More laughter, and Acton smiled, but became serious.

"Jews were tortured into confessing that they had caused the plague to destroy Christians, then were put to death or expelled by the thousands. In Strasburg, Germany, they gave Jews a choice. Convert to Christianity, or be burned at the stake. Thousands chose to die rather than give up their religion."

The laughter was gone.

"The Black Death was a period of fear. Much of it fear due to ignorance. Back then they encouraged people not to bathe for fear it would open up the pores on the skin which would let the plague in."

"Very Klingon!"

Acton chuckled. "Very! So, guess what came into use around that time?"

"Deodorant?"

"Close. Perfumes and colognes to cover up the stench. But we've since determined that the disease was carried by infected fleas on rats. The rats were aboard the ships that spread it to rats all along the trading routes, and eventually to Europe. It never occurred to anyone at the time that it was rats spreading it. The rats spread the fleas to other rats, the fleas jumped onto the people and bit them, infecting them."

"Besides questionable advances in medicine and stench maskers, what possible good could killing off half of the population have brought?" asked a skeptical voice from the back of the room.

"Well, for one thing it loosened the grip religion held over the population. First, there were a lot less worshipers, second, those worshippers were being blamed for the plague, saying it was punishment for their fornicating and blasphemous ways, and when people did what the church told them, and nothing changed, they began to question things. It took time, but over the centuries that followed, it led to the reformation, and eventually the separation of church and state."

"But how can we learn from that now? We already have a separation of church and state."

Acton nodded.

"True. *We* do, but much of the world doesn't."

"Who?"

"Pretty much any country that isn't a democracy. Outside of Western democracies and officially atheist countries like China, there is no separation of Church and State."

"So what they need is a good plague?"

Laughter filled the room and Acton held up his hand to stop it.

"No, I wouldn't say that. I'm just saying that a plague was one of many things that helped *us* progress. For those who still haven't figured out how to separate religion from their government it may be any number of things, but until they figure out how to separate the two, there will always be conflict between those who want to cling to the old ways, and those who want to move forward. But we're getting off topic." He clapped his hands together. "So, what else happens when you wipe out half your population?"

Silence.

"Well, wouldn't your workforce also be cut in half?"

Nods.

"So, if your workforce is cut in half, what do you think would happen?"

"There would be more demand for workers?"

"Exactly. So what would happen then?"

"Umm, wages go up?"

"Yup. And if you remember from last week's class, what type of system did they have in England and much of Europe at the time?"

"The feudal system."

"Exactly. Subsistence farmers working the Lord's land in exchange for a share of the crop and a roof over their heads. But if the worker can go into the town and get a reasonable wage and buy his own food, what do you think happened?"

"The Lords had to pay more for someone to work their lands?"

"Correct. So essentially the feudal system began to slowly break up as the availability of people willing to work for slave wages dried up, especially after the Peasants Revolt in 1381. Farming techniques were changed to less labor intensive forms, the migration to the cities began, and the reformation eventually occurred with the church having lost much of its influence."

The door to the back of the room opened and Acton nearly fell off his perch as he recognized Niner and Jimmy sitting down in the back row.

Something must be wrong!

"So, I want you all to think about what would happen to America, and the world, if half the population were to die off. Not from the negative side, but from the positive side. What *good* would come out of a mass die off in let's say five, ten, fifty and a hundred years out. Two thousand words on my desk by Monday, then be prepared to discuss it.

"And don't just go on the web and pull down a list. That's where I get all my information, so I'm liable to recognize it." Laughter and some averted eyes greeted his closing statement. "Dismissed."

The room emptied and Acton motioned for Niner and Jimmy to join him. They came down the steps toward the pit where he taught, and he knew something was definitely wrong. There were no smiles, none of the usual Niner joviality.

Acton extended his hand.

"Niner, good to see you."

"You too, Doc."

"Jimmy," said Acton, shaking Niner's traditional partner's hand.

"Doc."

"What can I do for you guys?"

"We need your help."

Acton's heart skipped a beat. The last time these guys had needed his help he had been flown halfway around the world in a race to find a nuclear weapon and save his fiancée, Professor Laura Palmer. Whatever had happened to his nice, cozy life as an archeology professor he had no clue. It seemed more often than not he was dodging bullets or worse from either terrorists or some ancient cult determined on maintaining a millennium long status quo.

But if it weren't for those adventures, he never would have met the love of his life, and his classes wouldn't have been half as popular as they were now.

"It's not another nuclear weapon is it?"

Niner shook his head.

"Sorry, Doc. This one's different." Niner and Jimmy then gave him the rundown of what had happened over the past week. The rape, the threats, the murder of Stucco and his family, the victim, the cop's family and now Dawson's sister and niece's kidnapping. But through it all, he failed to see anything he could possibly help them with, and said so.

Niner opened a file folder he was carrying, and placed it on Acton's desk. His eyebrows immediately shot up.

"Where did you find this?" he asked, his heart pumping a little harder.

"BD said he first saw it on a table in Lacroix's room. Lacroix got really pissed when BD looked at the papers," replied Niner.

"And this one," said Jimmy, pointing at the photograph, "was nailed to a telephone pole outside of Stucco's house."

"Clearly he was sending a message," commented Niner. "I'm willing to bet that symbol is at the other two murder sites, they just didn't know to look for it."

"Sounds probable," agreed Acton, his mind racing.

"So, Doc, what are we looking at?"

Acton crossed the floor to the door and locked it, pulling down the blind. He returned to the two soldiers and lowered his voice.

"*If* this is genuine, and I do mean *if*, you may be dealing with one of the most dangerous groups to have ever graced the face of this Earth."

Pentecostals of Richmond Church, Pickens Road, Richmond, Virginia

Something forced Sylvia to wake. She heard it again, a loud bang, screams, her daughter crying. Her eyes shot open and she found herself being dragged by the legs, Kurt and another man pulling her between two rows of pews, Jenny trailing behind her, shielded by an elderly lady, her hair so thin and grey it was almost a remembrance of what was, rather than a leftover. As she was pulled between the thick benches she saw the door swing open and the few that remained scattering for their lives as the driver limped in.

The pastor stepped forward, his hands held out wide to show he was no threat, but his voice stern nevertheless.

"This is a house of the Lord," he said. "How dare you fire a weapon here!"

A shot rang out and she heard a gasp, her view blocked, now all that was visible were feet. Then the body of the pastor collapsed onto the floor, his head twisted toward her, the look of horror on his face heartbreaking.

Why is this happening?

Several people cried out and she saw feet, fleeing moments before, rushing toward their fallen leader, cries and wails echoing through the large building. The hands pulling her legs let go and she looked to see Kurt stand, his teeth clenched, jaw tight as he stepped over her and put himself squarely between her and her abductor.

She watched the man's feet slowly make their way down the aisle, then looking over her shoulder from the floor, she could see him standing in front of Kurt, his weapon raised, the proud veteran not budging.

"Out of my way old man, or you die."

"If you want them, you have to go through me."

"Me too," said the other who was dragging her moments before. He stepped around her, standing shoulder to shoulder with Kurt.

"And me," said another, his footsteps echoing up the next aisle.

"How touching. Your war is *long* over. Go home and soak your tired bones in a hot bath, otherwise those bones are going six feet under."

Kurt took a small step forward.

"Sonny, we fought to protect the innocent and the weak. Our buddies died for a country that was better than those we fought. If I walk away today, I betray not only my country, but those men who died by my side, and my God who gave me the strength to get through that hell. There's no way I'm going to let you harm this woman or her child."

She heard a hammer cock, and she cried out.

"No, wait!" She grabbed Kurt's pant leg, pulling at it. "No, I won't have anyone die because of me." She tried to look at her abductor, to make eye contact with him. "Just let them take my daughter. Whatever this is about, it can't involve her. She's just a kid!"

She felt Jenny squeeze on her leg, but remain silent as she lay on the floor at her side.

The sound of sirens and the squelch of tires on pavement distracted everyone, their accoster rushing for the front doors to prevent anyone from leaving, slamming shut the doors he had shot open only minutes before.

"Mommy?"

She looked at Jenny and felt the world swim as her grip on Kurt's pants loosened and her head, held above the floor through sheer willpower, dropped with a thud, the world a blurred mass of confusion as she passed out yet again.

Chesterfield County Airport, Richmond, Virginia

The Cessna Turbo Skylane JTA bounced to a landing, their pilot, Charlie Wilson, a local "friend" of The Unit, guiding it expertly off the runway and toward the private terminal. Thor waved from the tarmac, a grim expression on his face. This wasn't a reunion, this was business. Personal business. One of the many unwritten rules in The Unit was 'don't mess with a man's family'. If Lacroix had killed Stucco, that would have been one thing. But to kill his family, to kidnap and possibly kill Dawson's family? That was personal. The gloves were off, and this would be ended, one way or the other, off the books.

Dawson had every intention of killing Lacroix and whoever had planted the bombs and even laid a finger on his sister and niece.

Charlie brought the plane to a halt near Thor and dropped the engine down to idle, his orders to immediately return in case any more of the team needed transport. Dawson and Red climbed down from the plane, Thor walking forward, his hair still gold, its luster a little dimmer than years ago.

"Good to see you, BD, Red. I wish it were under better circumstances," he said, shaking both men's hands then leading them toward a nearby black Ford Expedition. "I got you the biggest engine I could find just in case you need pursuit capability. Lots of cargo space, seats up to eight. She's topped up with gas, and I took the insurance option, so feel free to beat the shit out of her if needed." He tossed Dawson the keys, who flipped them to Red.

"You drive; I'm going to be making phone calls."

They both climbed in the SUV, Red firing up the engine and Dawson rolling down his window.

"One more thing," said Thor, leaning on the truck. "Just as you were landing I got confirmation that Niner and Jimmy are with that Professor of yours now. They were able to charter a jet—a little faster than your Cessna."

"Thanks for the update. We've got your number if we need anything else."

"Don't hesitate to call." He motioned to the rear seat with his chin. "I put together a care package for you. Now go get your sister."

Dawson's lips pursed and he nodded.

"Thanks." He turned to Red. "Let's go."

Red peeled off the tarmac and toward the side road of the airfield as Dawson punched the location of the crash where his sister and niece were last seen into the GPS. It had been less than ninety minutes since the crash, his team efficient to say the least. There had been no word from the Richmond police since he had left, Detective Lewis merely saying he was on his way to the crash site to check on Sylvia and Jenny.

"According to this we'll be there in less than ten minutes," said Dawson, glancing at the map on the navigation display.

"Really?"

"Stop."

Red hit the brakes and Dawson opened his door, stepping out onto the running board, pushing himself to his feet as he looked about the airport. Red did the same.

"What's on your mind, BD?"

"I'm thinking they were headed here."

Thor pulled up in his Honda Civic, his wife in the passenger seat.

"What's up, BD?"

"I think they may have been on their way here," he said. Dawson scanned the tarmac filled with a mix of Cessna's and other similarly sized airplanes—one stood out.

A Bombardier Learjet 45 XR.

"Any idea who owns that?" asked Dawson.

Thor took a look and shook his head.

"No, but it's not unusual to have them here. Want me to check it out?"

"Yeah. Get the details to the guys. If it's in any way connected to our situation, I want that plane stopped, understood?"

"Consider it done."

Dawson climbed back in the Expedition as did Red, and they were underway again, Red flooring it, shaving a couple of minutes off the NAV computer's estimate.

What they saw when they arrived cleaved a hole in Dawson's stomach.

St. Paul's University, St. Paul, Maryland

Niner frowned, Jimmy bit his lip, neither saying anything. Professor James Acton had the distinct impression that what they had just heard wasn't something they had wanted to hear.

And he didn't blame them.

"Who are they, Doc?" asked Niner finally. "Who are we dealing with here?"

"They're known by many names. Most people that have heard of them have heard them referred to as the Rosicrucians."

"Rosicrucians?" asked Jimmy. "Can't say as I've ever heard of them."

"Me neither," agreed Niner.

"Not surprised. Little is known about them due to their founding being near the end of the dark ages. It's believed that they were founded around 1407 by a German doctor named Christian Rosenkreuz. In German, Rosenkreuz roughly translates into 'rose cross'."

"That would seem to match this symbol," said Niner, shaking the printout.

"Indeed," agreed Acton.

"So what makes them so bad?"

"You've heard of the Black Death?"

The two soldiers nodded.

"Well, at the time, Europe was just coming out of the Black Death. Nearly half their population had been wiped out, and over the next fifty to a hundred years, tremendous progress was made in science, medicine, personal freedoms, and in overthrowing the almightiness of the Roman Catholic Church.

"Dr. Rosenkreuz grew up during this era. The Rosicrucian's own manifesto, Fama Fraternitatis, gave his birth date as 1378, and said he lived to be one-hundred-and-six years old, nearly unheard of in those days. It is said that he travelled to the Middle East and beyond to study under the masters there, but when he returned to Europe to spread his medical and scientific knowledge, he found none of the aristocracy willing to learn from him. So instead, in 1407, he gathered a group of men willing to listen, doctors who were sworn to uphold his ideals, and remain bachelors until their death. And before their deaths, they were required to find their own replacements, so the order could survive. It was called the Rosicrucian Order or Brothers of the Rose Cross."

"What happened to them?" asked Jimmy, now sitting at one of the desks.

"They practiced their craft, said to be some sort of mystical forgotten science, and used it to try and advance mankind. They were willing to teach those who would listen, but few did, and after several centuries they were rumored to be alchemists and sages—so not very well respected. They released several manifestos, written almost as parables, demanding change in Europe that were widely spoken of, and taken quite seriously at the time by some. They believed that through their science and teachings, they could advance mankind to a higher level of being, closer to God, and through their ancient knowledge, create a better world."

"Sounds like hocus pocus to me," muttered Niner.

"Eventually most tended to agree, and they seemed to have disappeared over the years, but not before a set of beliefs attributed to them were made known. These beliefs have been refined over the centuries to more accurately represent the modern world, but their spirit remains the same. Who has refined these is unknown. It was always thought it was people who had taken the Rosicrucian beliefs and adopted them as their own, without any of the rumored ancient science the beliefs were founded upon. But if what you have here is true, and I really do mean *if*, then it would tend to suggest that the *real* Rosicrucian Order still exists to this day."

"Real?" asked Jimmy.

"There are a lot of wannabe's, none genuine."

Niner leaned forward.

"How were they dangerous? It sounds like they were just some whack-jobs spreading mystical stories."

Acton smiled.

"True. Their beliefs were summed up in ten guidelines. One of which, and the most important of which, is population control. This is thought to have come from the times Dr. Rosenkreuz was raised in. After the Black Death came many advancements for mankind, and it was an era of increased prosperity and decreased misery. It could be likened to after World War Two. Think of the fifties and how everybody has this nostalgia for it being one of the greatest eras in history.

"The same could be said for this period of rebuilding after the Black Death. Things were better for those who were left, better than they had ever been. Were they fantastic? Of course not, but that's all relative. You can't compare their living conditions then to ours now. But after that horror, and the changes that were brought about as a result of it, there was renewed optimism in Europe, and this would have infected Rosenkreuz' beliefs, and he would have wanted to maintain that progress.

"And in his mind, maintaining a smaller population rather than letting it get out of control as it had in the past, would be a central pillar to any belief system. Some who interpret their beliefs think that it wasn't necessarily a specific number of people, such as five hundred million, but rather a number that would be in harmony with what the Earth could provide for naturally, without having to rape the land. This number might indeed be five hundred million, or a billion, or even more.

"One thing is for certain, our current population level is not sustainable without damaging the environment, which would mean it is too high for those who follow the Rosicrucian beliefs."

"Meaning what?"

"Meaning that if the Rosicrucian Order does exist today, it is their mandate to reduce the population of the planet to a number that they believe is ecologically sustainable."

Chippenham Parkway, Richmond, Virginia

Dawson jumped from the SUV before Red had brought it to a complete stop, running over to a gurney holding a body, the sheet draped over the victim's face. He pulled the sheet aside and sighed in relief when he saw a man, his neck obviously broken by what looked like handcuffs or some other metal chain.

Way to go, Sis!

"What do you think you're doing?" asked a uniformed officer.

Dawson turned to him, changing his body language to defer to the officer, his shoulders slumping slightly, turning inward to make him seem shorter and less of a physical threat, his arms at his side, his hands empty, and a worried expression on his face—that part not needing any faking.

"Is there a Detective Lewis here? He told me to meet him here, something about my sister?"

The cop shook his head.

"Naw, he *was* here but there's something going on up the road. Shots fired so most everybody redeployed." He paused. "Was your sister in this vehicle?"

Dawson shrugged.

"I don't see why. She's a nurse. The detective didn't say why he wanted to see me, just that this was where he'd be. I don't think it's related."

"Uh huh."

"Why, was there a woman in the accident?"

"Yes, but she ran away before paramedics could get here."

"That's strange."

"Not if you're a fugitive."

Dawson smiled.

"Now I *know* we're talking about two different people." Dawson turned to Red. "Let's go see if we can find the detective up ahead." He turned back to the officer. "Thanks, Officer, you've been a big help."

"No problem, just keep out of the way when you get there. Last thing they need is amateurs backseat quarterbacking."

"Good advice on any day," said Dawson with a grin.

He and Red returned to their vehicle, slowly passing through the accident scene, the upturned SUV unsettling, but the large pool of blood near the rear passenger side door even more so.

"She's injured."

"I saw that," agreed Red as he cleared the scene. "But if she were able to run away, we know your niece is okay as well—she'd never leave her."

"True. But that was a lot of blood and she couldn't have gotten far."

"I know you're thinking what I'm thinking."

"That what we're rolling up on involves her?"

"Yup." Red pointed with his chin. "There it is."

Along the highway were several police vehicles, then on the other side of the grass berm were another half dozen or so vehicles in a church parking lot.

"There's no way in there," said Dawson, scanning the road ahead. "Just park up there by those trees, far enough so they don't feel like walking and checking us out."

Red parked as close to the guardrail as he could and put his flashers on then popped the hood. The traffic was light as he climbed out to prop the hood up, hoping anyone passing would simply think they were a broken down vehicle with an owner who went to look for help.

Dawson unzipped the loot bag in the backseat that Thor had left and smiled. Pretty much everything from hand guns to hand grenades was inside. If they were pulled over, they'd have one hell of a time explaining it. He pulled the bag out of the backseat, closed the doors and climbed over the guardrail, disappearing into the trees with their supplies. He heard the vehicle chirp as Red locked it up. Just before the edge of the trees opened up into a cleared area that appeared to be part of the church property, Dawson dropped the bag and began to gear up, as did Red.

Body armor, Glock 22 with a few clips, and shades. Nothing more. Shotguns and submachine guns might attract the attention of the gathered law enforcement. Body armor hidden behind civilian jackets, clips in the pockets and a piece tucked into the waistband didn't.

Dawson and Red casually walked across the clear area to a large tree standing in the middle, several cars parked around it to take advantage of the shade it provided, no longer a concern this late in the evening. Dawson wondered if they belonged to potential hostages inside.

Dawson took a knee behind the tree and pulled out his cellphone, dialing Detective Lewis' phone.

"Lewis."

"Hello, Detective. This is Burt Dawson, Sylvia's brother. What can you tell me?"

"Not much, Mr. Dawson, except that the vehicle your sister was taken in was in an accident. One man is dead, your sister and niece ran away and were pursued by another occupant of the vehicle. We've had a report of shots fired at a nearby church and believe she and at least a dozen others are being held hostage inside."

"Has he made any demands yet?"

"No. One person who managed to escape through a back door said he kept checking his phone, as if he were expecting a call."

"He's awaiting instructions," muttered Dawson.

"What was that?"

"Nothing."

"I'll call you as soon as I know more, Mr. Dawson."

"Thank you."

Dawson killed the call and turned to Red.

"They're inside, one gunman apparently awaiting instructions from his handlers. My guess is those instructions will be to kill Sylvia and Jenny, then try to negotiate his way out. If I were them, I'd be bringing in a clean-up crew, at least one sniper in case he gets captured. They won't want him talking."

Red nodded in agreement.

"How do you want to handle this?"

"He won't get his instructions until the sniper is in place, but once they're in place, it's too late. We can't outrun a phone call. I say we go in, take him out now, get Sylvia and Jenny out of there, worry about the sniper later."

"Okay, I'll go get the truck."

"Good. Grab some door busters for us, we'll probably go through the back. And a couple of flashbangs."

Red nodded, strolling across the covered area and disappearing into the trees as Dawson walked toward a building to the left. A quick survey of the area showed only two police officers covering the back, one at the two-three corner in the back closest to him, the other at the three-four corner, but both were moved toward the front number one wall, distracted by all the action.

If we play our cards right, we can enter and no one will ever know.

St. Paul's University, St. Paul, Maryland

"All I know is we've got one guy, some high up snob who thinks he's above the law and is killing our people. We're going to take him and his organization out—six hundred years old or not, I don't care," said Niner.

"You should," said Acton. "We have no idea who they are, where they are, or what they're capable of. You may just piss them off and they come after all of you. Or worse, you advance whatever plans they might have."

Jimmy sighed.

"Why does everything have to be so difficult with these guys? That's why I prefer attacking government or terrorist targets. It's nice and easy. You know what their agenda is, you know what they're capable of, and with so much infighting amongst themselves, killing a bunch of them usually wins you tacit thanks from their rivals, or empty threats."

"So how big is this group, you figure?" asked Niner. "Are we looking at something massive like those Triarii guys, or something nice and small?"

"No way to know for sure. I'd suggest that they would have kept their structure over the centuries, so there will be one at the top, another seven senior brothers, all in the medical profession, all bachelors, all probably over fifty years of age. Each will have an underling they are training to replace them, then any number of operatives helping them accomplish their goals.

"And don't forget, these guys will be extremely well funded. They will have pooled the resources of eight doctors for centuries, all working toward a common goal which would require massive amounts of financing."

"In other words they'll be well equipped and well protected."

"Extremely." Acton clasped his hands, leaning forward slightly. "Listen, if you've found them, and they're genuine, we need to stop them."

Niner crossed his arms.

"Why now? What's so important about stopping them now and not ten years from now? They've been around for hundreds of years; why would you think they're about to act?"

"Because there's never been a time in history where it was possible to enact their plan."

"What do you mean?" asked Jimmy.

"We have never been more connected as a society than we are now. We have three billion people flying a year. That's almost ten million people a day. Put a virus on one of those flights, it's spread around the world in days. Our food supply is global now, our populations live in cities that can't feed themselves, we are so dependent upon computers that EMP weapons could wipe out our economies—there's an infinite number of things that could be done that would have global repercussions and result in massive die offs. Fifty years ago we weren't globalized, now we are. *This* is when they would act, because they *can* act. And the reaction you've had to just *seeing* some folders on a desk tells me they're up to something."

"So you're in?" asked Niner.

"Huh?"

"You said 'we' need to stop them."

Acton smiled.

"I meant the collective we, as in the societal we."

"We could use your help, Doc."

"Use your help in what?"

They all turned to see Professor Laura Palmer enter the lecture hall from the rear door—a door Acton realized he had forgotten to lock—her auburn hair down around her shoulders, lightly curled, her alabaster skin as perfect as the day he had met her. She never ceased to make Acton's heart skip a beat every time he saw her, which it did just now. He held out his hand and she joined them, grasping it and giving it a squeeze.

"There's a situation," said Acton.

Laura placed a kiss on her fiancé's cheek, then turned to face the two soldiers she had come to know over the years.

"What kind of situation?"

"With the Rosicrucians."

Laura's face slackened, her skin paling several shades.

Elk Road, Richmond, Virginia

Dawson's phone vibrated with a text message.

Walk south.

He strolled from the scene of the standoff and walked down a small road past the cleared side parking lot and a minute later saw Red and the truck parked, facing the opposite direction it had come for a quick exit.

Red stepped out, handing a flashbang to Dawson along with some detacord and detonators.

"I called Ops. They can't task a bird obviously, but one is over our area for the next fifteen minutes." He handed him a comm unit and Dawson hooked it over his ear, Red hooking his own on.

"Overseer, Bravo One. Do you read, over?"

"Bravo One, Overseer. Reading you five by five, over."

"Overseer, watch for a lone target, hidden. We're expecting a sniper and cleanup crew at any moment, out."

They made their way along the side of a nearby house then on the left side of a row of trees that ran behind the several buildings making up the church complex. Dawson motioned to where the first cop was, and noted that he was now almost all the way to the front of the building, his corner now uncovered.

They stopped directly behind a rear door. Dawson looked to their left but couldn't see the other officer. He quickly prepped some detacord to breach the door if necessary, then sprinted across the twenty feet of dry grass, unseen. He tried the doorknob and it turned. He pushed gently and the door opened.

No blowing up shit today.

He motioned for Red to join him, and moments later his friend was inside the building with him, the door closed, the police "covering" the back none the wiser. They were in some sort of utility room with another door at the opposite end. Dawson tried it, and it too was unlocked.

Trusting lot.

He pushed the door open enough to find a well-lit area behind it. Poking his head out, he found an empty hall and continued forward, Red closing the door behind them. As they advanced Dawson heard something through a door on his left. Taking a quick look he spotted a terrified woman huddled in a corner of what appeared to be a kitchen or food prep area. She nearly yelped at the sight of him but Dawson had his finger to his lips before she even saw him. Nodding, she covered her mouth and they moved on, around a corner where the hallway revealed several doors, but only one seeming to lead toward the front of the church.

The door was ajar, and sounds of general human suffering could be heard on the other side. Dawson dropped to his knees and pulled an extendable mirror from his utility belt. Pulling on the arm he extended it enough to stick it past the door, slowly angling it. He could see one man standing with a gun pointed at a group of people, a cellphone in his other hand and his back to their position, his attention focused on the front door where a voice was blasting on a megaphone, asking him to please take their call. A lonely phone rang in an office somewhere in the complex.

Dawson took a chance the man was acting alone and pushed the door open enough to fit through.

It creaked.

The man's head swung around as Dawson tossed the mirror aside, raising his weapon. The man began to spin around, wincing with the effort, his gun rising, Dawson's left hand grasping the butt of his own weapon as he took aim then squeezed the trigger.

120

The man's eyes bulged and he gasped in pain as the round shattered his right shoulder, his weapon dropping uselessly to the ground as he lost control of the hand gripping it. Dawson and Red rushed forward as the man stood in shock, then suddenly there was a shattering of glass followed immediately by the explosion of the man's head, a bloody, pulpy mass sprayed over the crouching parishioners.

The distinct clap of a round fired from a sniper rifle echoed outside.

"Sniper!" yelled Dawson. "Everyone down!"

He hit the floor, crawling toward the now dead man and pried the cellphone from his hand. He looked to his right and saw Sylvia lying on her back, covered in blood, too much of it her own. He scrambled to her side and took her hand.

"Sis, it's me."

"I know, I'm not blind," she said, her voice weak, but a look of relief on her face.

"Let's get you out of here, okay?" She nodded as he tousled Jenny's hair. "Ready to be brave princess?"

She nodded.

"Good." He turned back to his sister. "This might hurt like a mother. Ready?"

She nodded.

He put both arms under her, one under her knees, the other under her shoulders, then lifted her from the floor, still on his own knees, crouching, his muscles screaming at the unnatural position. Several elderly men helped by putting their hands under her, supporting her body as he advanced, their help relieving some of the weight he was carrying. As he cleared the pews, there was another clap and the corner of the last one shredded.

"Keep your head down, princess," he said to Jenny. "Crawl on the floor like a snake, okay?"

The little girl dropped to her belly and pushed herself with her elbows. As they cleared the pew Red reached forward and grabbed Jenny by the blouse, yanking her forward, then pointing to the door they had come through.

"Go toward the door, just the way you're doing it."

Another shot tore into the floor about five feet away. Outside shouting could be heard as the police assembled tried to figure out what the hell was going on.

"Overseer, Bravo One, we're taking fire from a sniper, over."

"Bravo One, we're trying to pinpoint him now, over."

"He's got a bead on us through the south side window. Look for him south of our position, less than a mile, then phone it in to the locals outside, over."

"Roger that, Bravo One."

He stepped forward on his haunches, his upper body lowered over his sister to protect her and his own head as he inched forward, his thighs burning with the effort as the parishioners crawled for the door and hopefully safety, Red guiding them along. These were all elderly people, people who had been through hell, people whose joints and muscles were no longer meant for this level of exertion.

But none said a word of complaint, and it wasn't until several minutes of crawling that he realized three of the men had intentionally positioned themselves between his sister and the window, providing cover for her with their own bodies. He met the eyes of one of the men, his expression grim, and gave him a nod of gratitude, the man returning an expression that immediately told him he was dealing with a vet.

They reached the altar at the front of the church and another shot rang out, blasting apart one of the pews behind them.

"He's got no angle, BD!" yelled Red, standing by the altar, pulling up the people as they reached him.

"Let's go!" yelled Dawson as he pushed to his full height, every muscle in his body screaming for relief as he sprinted the final few paces toward the door. He burst through it, little Jenny standing on the other side rushing forward and hugging his leg. He placed his sister on the floor and examined their surroundings. Where they were assembled had no windows so they should be safe, but his sister was pale, far too much blood having been lost. He knew she only had minutes before she would die without a paramedic.

"Bravo One, Overseer, we've got him located. He's in a grove of trees south-east of your position, on the move. Locals have been informed but they're taking their sweet time responding, they're just taking cover, over."

"We'll take care of it. Tell them to get paramedics inside now, over!" He turned to his sister. "I'll be back."

"I know."

Dawson sprinted for the rear entrance, Red hot on his heels. Reaching the door to the outside, Dawson activated his comm.

"Overseer, report!"

"Still on the move, now swinging south-west of your position, advancing. Locals are starting to redeploy as we update them, over."

"Roger."

He pushed open the door then rushed for the trees, taking a knee behind the thick trunk of one of them. If he were the sniper, he would take the same route as he and Red had taken earlier. He couldn't spot him, the tree cover and fences blocking the view, but if they acted quickly, they could get the drop on him. He turned to Red, pointing at a large building south of the church.

"Let's end this thing. You take position at the three-four corner there, I'll hold this position. Whoever gets the shot, takes it. I want him alive though."

Red nodded then sprinted toward the corner, taking cover, the cop covering the south side of the church long gone. Dawson watched several police cars pulling away, racing toward the road their SUV was parked on.

"Overseer, report."

"We've got you and Red in view now. He's coming right toward you, hundred yards. You should see him when he clears the next fence, over."

Dawson shifted farther behind the trunk and into the shadows, only a slight bit of his profile showing as he waited for his target to come into sight. Suddenly a head leapt into sight as a pair of hands grabbed the top of the fence and a set of very fit legs swung over in a smooth motion. The man's feet hit the ground and his MAC 10 was at the ready nearly instantly.

This guy's a pro.

The man advanced cautiously, but blindly, the eye in the sky not helping him. Suddenly he raised his weapon and fired at the very corner Red was behind causing Dawson's friend to leap backward as the man's weapon swung toward Dawson. He could feel the tree vibrate as the trunk was torn apart by perfectly placed shots.

Dawson held his position then noticed the sound changing as the man repositioned toward the building Red was using for cover. Shifting to the left, Dawson tried to maintain the angle between him and the shooter so the trunk would continue to protect him.

He knows exactly where we are.

"Overseer, he's got a spotter somewhere, over!"

Dawson glanced over his shoulder and saw Red falling back, taking up position behind a large HVAC unit attached to the building. The bullets stopped slamming into the tree and Dawson took the time to flip around so his stomach was now against the trunk, then switched his Glock to his left hand. He poked his head out just as the gunfire resumed, the man having reloaded quickly.

This guy is definitely Special Forces trained.

Dawson got a bead on where the man was heading by the sound of his shots, the shooter angling toward the same line of trees Dawson was using as cover, increasing the angle he would have to engage Red with.

"Red, get ready. He'll be in your sights any moment."

He watched Red take a knee, poking out from behind the metal HVAC unit.

"Don't worry about taking him alive. Just take him," added Dawson.

"Roger that."

A shot every couple of seconds continued to slam Dawson's position, keeping him pinned down and helpless to return fire.

"Got him."

Red opened fire, rapidly emptying his clip at the target as Dawson jumped out into the grass, rolling and firing at the same time, coming to rest with a clean shot.

He squeezed.

The man dropped to his knees, then forward onto his face. Red rushed him as did Dawson. Red, arriving first, disarmed the man just in case he wasn't as dead as they assumed, then Dawson quickly began to search his body for anything that might be of use. He found nothing but a cellphone. He stuffed it in his pocket just as several police officers rushed their position, weapons raised.

"Freeze!" yelled the first. "Don't move a muscle or you're dead!"

Dawson lowered his left hand to the ground, placing his weapon on the grass, then slowly raised his hands, clasping them on top of his head, Red doing the same.

"Is there a Detective Lewis with you?" asked Dawson.

"I'm Lewis," said a voice Dawson recognized from the phone conversations he'd had. "Are you Dawson?"

Dawson nodded.

"I think you have some explaining to do."

St. Paul's University, St. Paul, Maryland

Niner's phone rang and he answered it, walking away from the two professors and Jimmy. Laura's heart was pounding a little harder than normal now that she had been brought up to speed on what was happening. And once again she knew they were going to get caught up in something as usual. *What is it about us?* She had thought about it once and realized it wasn't her and James that were the problem. It was the people they had met during the incident with the Triarii and the crystal skulls.

They were the ones attacked, and in the process met their now friends from Scotland Yard, DCI Reading and DI Chaney. Her mind flashed to Chaney, still in a coma, wondering if he'd ever come out.

And what was his message?

They had also met these Delta Force soldiers and the rest of their unit, under orders to kill them, being told they were on a termination list of terrorists. It wasn't until after they realized what had been happening and how they had been manipulated that these men had become their closest allies over the years, going out of their way to help them when needed, in their minds perhaps atoning for the horrors they had committed during that mission.

The Brass Monkey incident she certainly couldn't blame on Scotland Yard or the Delta Force, but they had dragged James into it, albeit willingly when he found out what had happened to her. *The Broken Dove incident was pure Chaney! Same with that Templar relic.* Now China, that was nobody's fault. *We were on vacation!* Same with Egypt, though it was a dig.

She sighed.

Maybe it wasn't always someone else's fault. Maybe they were cursed to live this life.

And she had to admit it was thrilling every time it was over, but terrifying while it went on. She sometimes debated whether or not she would rather lead the nice, simple life she had before—a mega-millionaire archeologist teaching eager students and funding various digs around the world—or her current lifestyle, which was much the same, except for the number of bullets, grenades, fighter jets and tanks.

And nuclear weapons.

And James.

If it weren't for all this, they never would have even met.

And she loved him with all her heart, more each and every day. She had popped in on a private jet a few days ago to surprise him, their dig in Egypt put on hold due to the upheaval there. And they had celebrated.

She tingled.

"And what do you intend to do about it?" asked Acton.

"We've been suspended and are all on vacation," replied Jimmy.

Laura smiled slightly.

"Meaning?"

"Meaning we're going hunting."

Laura bit her lip then looked at her fiancé.

"And what do *you* intend to do about it?"

"Well, I was thinking of going with them to help. Just in case they need my advice on anything else that might help track down where the Rosicrucians have been hiding."

Laura shook her head. She knew James. Knew him far too well. He was a fabulous archeologist, fabulous teacher, fabulous fiancé, and he had a penchant for doing the right thing, even if it meant risking his own life to save others', including her own.

And she knew there'd be no talking him out of it, because he secretly loved the adrenaline rush the action brought.

The professor in her also understood the intellectual intrigue. To find the Rosicrucians, to prove they still existed, would be incredible. But once found?

"So you're going to kill them?" she said, turning to Jimmy.

"Yes."

"All of them?"

"I'm thinking just the head is all that's necessary. Those eight doctors you mentioned might be a good place to start."

Niner returned.

"BD's sister's family is secure. He wants us to join Spock and his team and head to Geneva." He turned to James. "Are you coming?"

James nodded.

"Yes."

"And so am I," said Laura. She expected objections perhaps from the Delta team, but she knew her love wouldn't bother. It was an argument he would never win.

"Happy to have you aboard," said Niner, "I've seen you shoot. This should hopefully be a little tamer than China was."

"God I hope so," said Laura and she felt James take her hand and squeeze.

Köln, Germany
1472 AD

"Do you require time, or are we finished with this evening's business?"

Dietrich stood in his master's chambers, his head bowed, his eyes almost closed, his hands clasped tightly behind his back, and though he knew it was impossible, he could still feel Heike's soft fingers between his. *This evening's business?* Is that all it was to him? A little bit of business? The death of an innocent woman whose only crime was to love a man in The Order?

His blood boiled.

"No, it's over," he replied, his voice calm, cold, his emotions held in check by the knowledge there was nothing he could do to bring her back.

"Excellent." His master stood from the chair he had been occupying, his arm extending, quickly finding its way across Dietrich's shoulders. "I have tremendous news."

"What news, my master?"

The hint of excitement in his master's voice had him intrigued. He was usually devoid of most emotions, as were most in The Order that he had met that weren't young like him. Those who had been in for decades like his master seemed strangely subdued. It was as if emotion were the enemy, something to be purged from your soul so you could function better, could understand the forgotten sciences better and fulfill the goals of The Order to one's fullest potential.

"We have been bestowed a great honor," said his master as he led his apprentice down a hall toward the stairs that led to the basement, and an area all were forbidden to enter except for he and his master. His master produced a key from around his neck and unlocked the door, then, taking a lantern from the outside wall, he descended the stairs into the darkness, the sole light the flickering flame from within its glass enclosure.

Dietrich followed, trying to keep within the circle of light so he could maintain his footing on the tight stairs. A sigh of relief escaped his lips as he felt the floor under his feet. His master struck a flint hammer to his right, igniting a thin trail of black powder that ringed the basement. As the trail burned along its route, various torches sprung to life, and within minutes the entire basement was bathed in light.

It was impressive, but it meant that Dietrich later would be required to replenish the black powder for the next time his master deemed it necessary to use.

He thanked God every day that it was a rare occurrence to visit the basement.

At the end of the large room there stood an ornate cabinet, its hard oak impossibly old and impossibly solid, the walls on it so thick that when tapped, there was little if any echo from inside. Dietrich had never seen it opened, having only admired its craftsmanship when attending to his duties in the basement.

His master produced a key from his robe he had never seen before. A previously unnoticed cover was slid aside revealing a keyhole. His master inserted the key and twisted, a heavy mechanism echoing as what must be a substantial lock was opened.

Silence.

A door was pulled open revealing a dark hollow inside. His master reached into the dark and pulled out a cube shaped box that Dietrich had never seen before, but knew immediately what it was.

"The Catalyst!" he gasped.

His master held the cube out in front of him as he walked to a table on the right. He gently placed the Catalyst on the empty table, then stepped back as Dietrich advanced in awe.

"I never thought I would see it in my lifetime," he whispered.

"If you are to be my replacement, you will see it many times. But it will be rare that you have the honor of being its keeper. This is only the second time I have been given the honor. The Founder is traveling to the Holy Lands again to seek council with the elders. It is essential that we determine how the device works so we can unlock its secrets and fulfill our destinies."

"May I?" asked Dietrich, his hands tentatively reaching out for the cube.

"Yes."

Dietrich's hands caressed the cube, his fingers tracing along its smooth edges, his fingertips outlining the strange markings that adorned its entire surface.

"Is this writing?" he asked.

"Yes, but we've been able to translate very little. The Founder has taken pressings and will be attempting to find someone who knows the ancient tongue this was written in."

"How do we know it's genuine?" asked Dietrich. "I mean, how do we know it does anything?"

"Because the Founder saw it demonstrated and claimed it held a great power, a forgotten power, that once unleashed, could shape matter into all things and control the thoughts of man."

"How did the Founder come to possess it?"

"He liberated it from heathens during his travels as a young man through the orient and the Holy Lands."

"He stole it?"

"Crudely put, but yes."

"And what is our job while he is gone?"

"To secure it at all costs. There will be extra guards at the house until the Founder returns."

"Where? I did not see any."

"They are about. Inside and out. They will make their presence known if necessary." His master stepped forward, retrieving the Catalyst and returning it to its hiding place. Dietrich watched as the key was carefully returned to the small pocket on his master's robe. "And now I think it is time for bed."

"Yes, my master."

Dietrich followed the man up the stairs, his mind racing with what he had just witnessed.

Virginia Commonwealth University Medical Centre, Richmond, Virginia
Present Day

"The FBI has no clue who these guys are."

Dawson looked up as Detective Lewis entered the hospital room. Dawson's sister was hooked up to a few machines, her surgery complete with a full recovery expected and little Jenny was sitting in a corner chair, fast asleep, refusing to leave her mother's side.

"Oh my God, Sylvia!"

Dawson looked past the detective to see his brother-in-law George appear in the doorframe then rush toward his wife.

"Is she going to be okay?" he asked, searching the room for an answer, his eyes settling on Dawson.

"She'll be fine," replied Dawson. "We just need to let her rest."

"What happened?" he asked, holding his wife's hand and pushing some stray hairs from her face.

"She was injured in a car crash and lost a lot of blood."

"But she'll be fine?"

"Yes, don't worry, George. She's tough, she'll get through this."

"I don't understand, there were police at the house and there was a body being taken out." He stopped, then turned to face Dawson. "What the hell are you doing here? Does this have something to do with you?"

Dawson nodded slowly, a frown creasing his face.

"I'm afraid it does. I can't get into it, it's classified, but there will be a twenty-four hour guard placed on all three of you, and as soon as she's strong enough, you'll all be brought back to Bragg until this is over."

"So this has to do with"—he lowered his voice, glancing at the detective—"you know, your, umm, job?"

"Yes." Dawson gave him "the eye" and George backed off, returning his attention to Sylvia.

Detective Lewis cleared his throat.

"I've got two of my best outside the door, plus another two on the floor. Hospital security has been notified to be extra vigilant as well. According to the doctor she should be safe to transport tomorrow."

"Good," said Dawson standing. "I'd like you to have a unit escort George and Jenny to their house so they can pack, then return here. When they're ready to transport, call this number"—he handed a card to the detective—"and within an hour a team will arrive to transport them. Please provide them with an escort to the airport."

Lewis nodded.

"And these men are yours?"

Dawson nodded.

Lewis pursed his lips then put the card in his wallet.

"Listen, I think I know who and what you are. Officially, I can't sanction what you did, unofficially, I think you did a hell of a job and I thank you. The official report will have to be written up a little differently. Don't worry about it, I'll figure it out and keep your names out of it. I'm thinking a couple of bystanders got involved then disappeared before we could secure the scene."

Dawson smiled as he stepped over to his sister's bedside.

"I'm sure you'll think of something."

Detective Lewis left the room, closing the door behind him. Dawson noted the head of a uniformed officer as he moved in front of the door. Dawson leaned in and gave his sister a kiss on the forehead, then turned to George.

"I have to leave, but some of my men will be here tomorrow to pick her up, okay?"

"Where are you going?"

"To put an end to this, once and for all."

He stepped out into the hall and found Red waiting, a concerned look on his face.

"What's up?" asked Dawson.

"You know that private jet you wanted Thor to look into?"

"Yeah."

"Well, it just took off, unauthorized."

"What?"

"Yeah, the tower was stonewalling them, delaying them as long as possible, and finally they just taxied onto the runway and left."

"What's happening now?"

"Nothing. We could have them intercepted and forced down."

"No, that's too public. Any idea how many are onboard?"

"Apparently another jet arrived and was met by a vehicle, then immediately departed. Two people got off that plane, then the same vehicle returned just after our incident, and three people got aboard the original jet—one looked wounded."

"So the cleanup crew came in, removed anybody that could damage them, then left in a hurry. Where to?"

"Looks like they're landing on a private strip in New York."

"Any chance we can get there beforehand?"

"Funny you should ask," said Red, grinning.

Adirondack Regional Airport, New York

Spock and his team watched as the Bombardier Learjet landed then taxied toward the tarmac. Prearranged with the tower after some arm twisting and fake credential flashing, the plane was now holding position awaiting permission to approach the small terminal as the runway was inspected for debris seen falling off the plane upon landing.

The idea was Zack "Wings" Hauser's, their resident expert in flying anything that could fly. They just hoped it would work on their target.

"Any pilot worth his salt is going to be concerned if something fell off his aircraft," Wings had said.

But this pilot had proven to be someone willing to break the rules, so they weren't going to wait too long to test him. Spock looked at Trip "Mickey" McDonald, his prominent ears tucked behind a bandana today and nodded. Mickey pulled their airfield maintenance vehicle out of the hanger and toward the runway. Within moments they were driving from the opposite end. About two thirds of the way down Mickey directed the vehicle to the left and stopped. Wings jumped out and pretended to pick something up on the blind side of the vehicle. He held up the piece of palmed plastic and waved toward the tower.

He jumped back in the vehicle and Mickey gunned it toward the taxiway the Learjet was idling on. Mickey brought the vehicle to a stop behind the private jet where there was no way for anybody onboard to see them, this the ultimate blind spot. Wings and Jagger jumped out, rushing up to the rear landing gear and under the wings. Mickey moved the vehicle alongside the plane and stopped, climbing out and making certain he was seen by anybody who happened to be looking. Spock joined him, making a show of examining the decoy they had "retrieved" from the runway. Spock saw the pilot looking out the cockpit window and he gave the man a wave, then pointed at the engine, slicing his hand across his throat, indicating he wanted the engines cut. The pilot gave a thumbs up and immediately the engines began to power down. Spock then ducked under the fuselage as if to inspect the aircraft, instead joining the rest of his team as they readied their weapons.

The door opened and the steps lowered to the taxiway, two men in crisp white shirts, captain's bars on one, quickly descended the steps. Spock kept his eyes on them as all four of the Delta team pretended to inspect the landing gear, their weapons hidden from sight.

"What's going on?" asked the captain as he approached, his accent a thick German but perfectly understandable.

"We think something fell off your landing gear assembly," said Wings. The two men were only feet away when Spock nodded. Mickey and Jagger whipped around, their MP5K's raised, the startled men left with nowhere to run as Spock and Wings rounded the pair, blocking their escape. Mickey quickly zip tied the two men, covering their mouths with duct tape. A pat-down revealed each had a Beretta.

"Now, what would a pilot need with this?" asked Spock as he ejected the clip and any chambered round, tossing the weapons aside. The two uniformed men were placed against one of the massive tires then their ankles were bound.

"Let's go."

Spock stepped back into view along with Wings, their bright orange vests indicating their official airport titles, and quickly climbed the steps, pulling their weapons as they entered the cabin. Spock went left, clearing the cockpit as Wings took right, his weapon still behind his back. The cockpit empty, Spock turned and found two men near the rear of the plane, chatting. They stopped as they finally took notice of the two new arrivals.

"What the hell do you want?" asked one of them, rising and reaching for what was certainly a weapon in a shoulder holster.

Spock and Wings raised their weapons, taking aim at both men. The second man, not yet standing, dropped to his knees, hidden behind his seat. A MAC 10 appeared over the seatback, firing blindly as the other man dove.

Wings took him out with two shots to the midriff, Spock dropping to a knee as the shots went over their heads. He put half a clip from his MP5K into the seatback, the MAC 10 silenced. They dashed forward as Mickey and Jagger rushed into the cabin. Spock checked his target and confirmed he had no pulse. Wings did the same.

"Clear!" called Spock. He pointed at the rear. "Check the bathrooms and any other compartments." Mickey and Jagger jumped forward.

"Got a body!" called Mickey. Spock followed the voice to find Mickey standing outside a small bathroom. Spock poked his head in and found the body of a man sitting on the lavatory, his shoulder wound not the cause of death; the bullet through his head apparently more lethal.

"Must be the one she wounded at the house," he said.

"Clean-up crew, indeed," muttered Mickey.

Spock stepped back into the cabin. "Sweep for intel, anything we can use."

The four began to search the cabin, several briefcases found in the overhead bins, wallets from the shooters, but not much else.

Until Mickey cursed.

"What?" asked Spock, joining him in the rear, a storage compartment opened in the galley.

Mickey pointed.

"We've got company."

Spock dropped to a knee and looked.

At the pile of C4 bricks neatly joined together with detonators, and a countdown timer showing less than five minutes.

"What the hell is this?" asked Wings as he joined them.

"If we hadn't delayed them, they'd have refueled and been well over the Atlantic by now. Bomb detonates, no evidence, completely clean operation."

"Jesus. Whoever is behind this is ruthless," said Mickey.

Spock rose. "Okay, everyone out. Grab the intel, we've got four minutes."

Suddenly the distinct rattle of gunfire from outside had them hitting the deck as the fuselage began to take fire, several windows hit, the bullets tearing into the cabin. Spock scrambled to the door, taking a quick look and saw a black Lincoln parked less than fifty feet from the plane, four men spraying weapons fire on them.

"Four shooters, left side, behind a town car," yelled Spock.

"We've got three minutes until this thing lights up!" reminded Wings.

"And they know it." Spock knew all these guys had to do was keep them holed up in here for a few more minutes and the bomb would do their job for them.

"Got an emergency exit over here," said Mickey. Spock glanced and saw Mickey pulling on the mechanism. Spock turned back to the door and sprayed some fire blindly in the direction of their attackers.

"Got it!" announced Mickey. Spock fired again then took a look as the window fell outward, leaving a gaping hole in the right side of the cabin. Mickey went first followed by Wings.

"Let's go!" yelled Jagger, firing out one of the shattered windows. Spock fell back toward the emergency exit, then slapped Jagger on the back. Jagger turned and dove out the hatch. Spock fired several more rounds then grabbed the briefcases piled in the middle of the plane and threw them out the emergency exit. He stuffed the wallets in his jacket then jumped through the hole, landing on the wing and sliding down to the ground. He felt a hand grab him, pulling him behind the landing gear.

Spock flipped to his belly as Mickey and Wings made quick work of the four men still firing. He scrambled forward and found the two prisoners they had bound earlier dead, shot by their own men.

The gunfire stopped.

"Let's get the hell out of here!" he yelled as he jumped to his feet, grabbing one of the briefcases. The others each grabbed a case and sprinted away from the plane. Spock was out front slightly and glanced over each shoulder to make sure no one was being left behind when the plane suddenly erupted from within, the bomb tearing at the air, the sound horrifying, the plane suddenly bulging, bursting its seams as the fuselage tore apart.

"Keep going!" he yelled, the worst yet to come. The sound of the fuel igniting and erupting in a massive blast sent Spock diving for the ground and covering his head. The others dropped around him as the shockwave rolled over them, the heat licking at them as if it had a taste for flesh, then within moments it was over, the blast collapsing back in on itself.

Spock pushed himself to his feet to see the passenger cabin torn open as if clawed apart by an angry beast hell-bent on escaping. The entire plane was now aflame, the dark black smoke billowing into the evening sky as the airfield's disaster response team raced toward the smoldering mess. The Lincoln with the four new arrivals was no more, merely a twisted seething mass of metal, its occupants charred to the point no useful intel would be found on their bodies.

"Everybody okay?"

Three acknowledgements and he began to walk toward where their plane was waiting.

"I've got a hankering for chocolate. Switzerland anybody?"

"Forget chocolate. I want one of them fancy knives that MacGyver uses," said Mickey. "With that, some twine and a box of toothpicks we could get out of pretty much anything."

Spock smiled as the theme song for one of The Unit's favorite shows played through his head. They hadn't watched it in at least a year.

"Whose got the DVDs?" he asked.

"I think Stucco had them," said Mickey, his voice suddenly subdued.

Spock nodded.

"Then in his honor, I say when we've put these bastards six feet under, we buy the collection again and start watching from Season One, Episode One."

"Sounds like a damned good idea to me," replied Jagger.

The group became silent, Spock was sure with the same thoughts of Stucco flashing through their minds. He was a good man, a good soldier, and a good husband and father. He had only been with them a few years, but had become one of Spock's best friends.

A friend who would now be avenged.

Köln, Germany
1472 AD

Dietrich lay in his bed, staring at the ceiling above, his mind sharp, fatigue a faint memory that had yet to arrive, his mind consumed with thoughts of Heike and how her family must be so worried. He ached to go tell them what had happened, that their baby would never be home again, that her life had been snuffed out by a madman whom he was essentially bound to in servitude until death.

But whose death?

The thought had him bolt upright in his bed, the slats underneath protesting loudly, filling the room with their angry creaking. He froze, hoping he hadn't woken the household, then carefully swung his legs out of the bed and stood, realizing the noise couldn't have been as bad as he feared since even his breathing seemed loud.

He tried to calm himself, to resolve himself to the decision he had just made. He looked out the window, the sky clear now, the rain's only evidence the glistening stone below. He stared up the road to the top of the hill and could see various houses still well lit, and he knew it was most likely Heike's family and the neighbors beginning a search.

A search that would lead to nothing, for there was nothing to find unless her body had snagged on a tree root or something. If it hadn't, it would be far from here by now, not to be fished from the river until a passing boat spotted her in the daylight, if at all.

He dressed himself properly, ran his fingers through his hair to try and straighten it, then flipped up the hood of his robe. He knew there were others about the premises now that the Catalyst was here, but that shouldn't matter. This was his house, not theirs. *How would they know what is normal routine and what isn't?*

He opened his door carefully, thankful the old hinges didn't squeak. He had rubbed goose fat on them just this week to keep them quiet so he didn't wake the master when he woke to prepare the master's breakfast. He knew as soon as he officially became the apprentice tomorrow, or rather today, he wouldn't need to perform any of the menial tasks again—his entire life would be devoted to learning, rather than proving humbleness in the eyes of his master.

He walked with purpose down the hall toward his master's chambers lest anyone be watching and a furtive gait arouse suspicion. He reached the end of the hall and turned right. He saw something in the shadows and he nodded at it, not even knowing if it was a person or a trick of the shadows, but he continued and moments later was at his master's door.

What if he's awake?

The thought hadn't occurred to him. He would have to fight him, and the master was a powerful man. Dietrich had little doubt he'd be made quick work of, his frame comparatively tiny.

The black powder!

He hadn't yet replaced it and knew his master would want to admire the Catalyst when he awoke, so retrieval of the basement key was the perfect excuse.

He pressed down on the handle, and the door opened silently. He stepped inside, the chambers lit gently with several candles, enough for his sensitive eyes to see clearly. His master's steady yet gentle snoring could be heard from the bed, the curtains drawn around it as he had left him.

The dagger his master regularly carried would be on the dresser at the opposite end of the room. He slowly crept toward it, cautious of one area of the floorboards that had a tendency to creak, and arrived without incident, the loudest noise the pounding in his ears.

He glanced over his shoulder at the bed. There was no movement to be seen through the thick curtains, however the steady breathing continued. He reached for the gold plated dagger, grasped it in his now shaking hand, then turned toward the bed.

He stepped forward slowly, the snores getting louder the closer he got.

They stopped and he froze, as did his heart.

Had he made a noise?

Had the master sensed his presence? After all the man seemed to be able to read minds.

There was a snort, then a shift behind the curtains, and the snoring resumed.

Dietrich almost let out a sigh of relief, but stifled it. He stood frozen for several more minutes, his muscles aching as he held the slightly crouched position, terrified to move.

He willed himself forward.

The dagger was at the ready in his right hand, the blade turned downward so he could plunge it into the man's chest. He reached forward with his hand, grasping the curtain, then slowly pulled it aside, the wood hooks sliding silently along the polished mahogany rail above.

He let go, the man's back revealed to him.

He hadn't counted on this. He would either need to roll him over, exposing his chest, or thrust from behind, through the back. Confusion began to consume him.

Then he paused.

The key for the basement sat where it always sat when not around his master's neck, on the nightstand to his right. But the key used to open the cabinet where the Catalyst lay hidden had slipped out of his robe pocket and lay on the bed not an arm's length from where Dietrich stood, poised for his kill.

And he smiled as a new plan formed.

Martin Lacroix Residence, Republic of San Marino

"What are we looking at?"

Number One's voice rumbled through the room, Dr. Martin Lacroix using the speakers this time instead of headphones. The room was soundproofed from eavesdroppers, and shielded from electronic surveillance. He was alone save his apprentice, both robed for the formality of the meeting with The Circle who were dialed in from around the world.

"Footage from our cleanup efforts," replied Lacroix. "The woman at the hotel has been eliminated. The Public Prosecutor has dropped the case without even filing the charges. This means there will be no negative publicity."

"Assuming the others remain silent," interjected one of The Circle.

"I have had one of the Delta Force members eliminated with his family. He was the one that assaulted me."

Lacroix's blood boiled at the humiliating memory. It was one thing to be beaten, an entirely different thing when you were naked and too drunk to defend yourself.

Then to be put in a cell at the police station in nothing but a robe, mixed with hard core criminals and junkies—he shivered at the memory. His robe hadn't remained on his person long before it was "borrowed" by someone far bigger than him. He had sat curled in the corner, covering his genitalia until his lawyer had finally arrived.

Which was why Inspector Laviolette had to pay.

"Was that wise?" asked a voice.

"He was a witness. One of the ones in the room who could have seen our material."

"Yes, but now you've pissed off the most highly trained military unit in the world."

Lacroix nodded.

"Yes, but they have no way of finding us."

"They can find you."

"I'm far too public for them to do anything to. Besides, with today's events we've proven we aren't to be trifled with. One family is dead, another was nearly successfully kidnapped—"

"By 'nearly' you mean the mission was a failure and resulted in us having to clean up the mess so none of our operatives could be captured. A complete fiasco!"

"Piss off!" exploded Lacroix, the voice of Number Three, a constant thorn in his side, grating on his nerves. "If you don't have anything useful to contribute to this conversation, then shut it!"

"Enough!" roared the voice of Number One. Silence followed. He finally spoke after there was no noise coming from the speakers. "I was particularly intrigued by what you did to the detective's family."

Lacroix smiled.

"My idea. I wanted a message sent that this should never be pursued, lest it happen to someone else's family. The fact the inspector reacted the way he did—well, I was pleasantly surprised at that."

"Can we consider this matter closed, then?"

Lacroix wished they could, prayed he could hide the latest information that had just arrived, but he knew the same resources used by him to garner the intel could be used by them.

And knowing them, somebody was probably back checking everything he did.

"No," he finally said. "My sources inform me that at least four Delta Force members are on their way to Geneva. The same four that assaulted our plane in New York."

"And the rest?"

"We're not certain, but we're monitoring all inbound Geneva traffic. We think as many as four more may be on their way. We should know more shortly. We suspect they'll rendezvous with the first group that should be landing in the next couple of hours."

"And what do you intend to do about it?"

"Make sure they never see the light of day again."

Köln, Germany
1472 AD

Dietrich had a new plan. A bolder plan. One that would not only give him his revenge, but torture and destroy the man who had killed his beloved Heike. And it didn't involve anyone's death except perhaps his own, which he could live with should he succeed.

He slowly reached forward, his heart slamming against his chest, his pulse roaring in his ears as he tried to make no sound, not even the creak of his own bones. His fingers grasped the small chain the key was on and he pulled. It didn't move.

He pulled slightly harder, and he felt a tug on the master's robe, it obviously clasped to something inside the pocket.

He felt sweat forming on his forehead as his plan hit its first literal and figurative snag. He gently tugged on one end of the chain, slowly pulling it through the small pocket that lay partially hidden under the master's sheet, and was rewarded with the clasp. He squeezed the tiny device and unhooked the two ends.

His master snorted and began to roll toward him.

Dietrich panicked and yanked the now divided chain just as his master rolled completely over, now facing him.

But he had the key in his hand.

He quietly turned, the blade hidden behind his back, and clasped the other key and its chain from the nightstand. He stepped back as his master's breathing readjusted with several snorts, then gently closed the curtain. Stuffing the cabinet key into his pocket, he firmly held the basement key in his left hand, the dagger in his other, hidden away in a deep pocket in his robe.

He inched his way from the bed, then at the door, prepared himself for looking purposeful again.

He was so tired now, the fear that had been fueling him no longer able to keep up, that he could feel himself fading. Too much had happened, and he had given himself no time to recover.

Only ten minutes more, if that!

He opened the door, stepped out into the hall, then closed the door silently behind him. A quick glance and a wipe of his forehead, and he was walking toward the basement, key in hand. The door wasn't far, and he reached it in moments, encountering no one.

The key slid in the lock, the mechanism creaked gently and the door unlocked. As he pushed it open he felt a hand on his shoulder, pulling him back.

He nearly urinated on the spot.

He turned his head and found a robed figure behind him.

"Good morning," he whispered, his voice wavering in fright. "You startled me," he said, placing his hand on his chest. "I didn't realize anyone was up."

"What are you doing?" asked the man, his voice low but not the whisper Dietrich would have preferred.

"Shh," admonished Dietrich, holding a finger to his lips. "We don't want to wake the master." He held up the key to the basement. "My master and I were in the basement earlier and he lit the room with the black powder. I have to go replenish it before he wakes up, as I'm certain he will want to check on the *item* immediately." Dietrich looked at the hand still on his shoulder. "Now if you'll excuse me? I'd like to get this done so I can go to bed. Tomorrow I become a full apprentice, and do not want to be tired."

At the mention of becoming an apprentice the hand darted away from the shoulder. Though an apprentice had little power, especially early on, the power within the organization they would command after their master's death was only rivaled by that of The Founder.

The man disappeared into the shadows, saying nothing.

Dietrich pushed the door open, took a lantern from the wall, and entered the basement, closing the door behind him. When he reached the stone floor below he paused for a moment, leaning on a table as he caught his breath and tried to steady his shaking hands.

He eyed the cabinet at the far end of the room, but resisted. If someone were to check on him, he would need to be seen doing his job. He retrieved a small barrel of the black powder and scooped a generous amount out, then poured it through a funnel as he let it fill the tiny groove carved around the room, carefully filling the side channels leading to the various torches to be lit.

He did the job a little quicker and a little sloppier than he normally would, this merely his cover should someone come down, and only his master would know if it wasn't up to his usual standards.

Finished, he rushed toward the cabinet and slid aside the lock cover. He pushed the key in the hole and turned, swinging open the door. Reaching inside he grasped the Catalyst and pulled it out, placing it on the nearby table. He locked the cabinet again, stuffed the key in his pocket, then looked about the room for something to hide the cube in. It wasn't large, perhaps from his wrist to his elbow in length, width and height, and it wasn't heavy beyond feeling solid and substantial.

But it wouldn't fit under a robe without an obvious bulge impossible to explain.

His eyes travelled the room and came to rest on the powder barrel. He rushed over, tipped it and emptied the black powder into a corner. Then, prying off the top, he placed the Catalyst inside, the fit nearly perfect, then put the top back on, hiding it from sight.

Now he merely needed to act as if it were empty.

He was about to climb the steps when he had one final idea. It was bold, crazy, and potentially deadly. If there were any delay on his part whatsoever, he might die.

Again, something he could live with.

Laura Palmer's Private Jet, Over the Atlantic Ocean

"Sorry, BD, no luck. We just don't have the intel feeds we need here to do it, and we can't ask the Colonel."

Dawson was frustrated, but he knew it wasn't Atlas' fault. They were running this op off the books, privately financing it with their own savings, and calling in every favor they could. The plane and rental in Richmond were donated by friends, the first flight to Geneva donated by a corporate honcho whose daughter they had rescued years earlier from Yemen.

And this flight, donated by Professor Palmer. He wasn't too proud to accept funding from someone who was filthy rich. He had read her dossier when she had been first identified during the Triarii incident, and knew her late brother had left her over one hundred million when he died. He had often wondered what he would do if he were to suddenly find himself rich. It was hard to think of doing anything beyond The Unit. He knew eventually he'd be too old for it, but then he figured he'd still be involved, probably training the new recruits, or becoming one of those "go to" guys like Thor had become.

If you need me, I'll be there.

The Unit was his life and he didn't want it any other way. Which was why he never bought lottery tickets. There was too much of a risk he might win. And it was also why he was determined to avenge Stucco's death. This was his family.

And you don't mess with my family.

Spock and his team had already landed in Geneva and were arranging quarters and supplies. He and Red, along with Niner and Jimmy, as well as the two professors, would be arriving within a few hours, but they didn't have enough intel. He had hoped the cellphone they had retrieved from Sylvia's abductor in the church might have led to something, but it had come up empty due to a lack of resources. The briefcases and wallets retrieved by Spock's team had proven dead ends, the wallets merely filled with cash and fake ID's, the briefcases holding weapons and clothing, the only thing of value were that their clothes were made in Italy.

"Time to call in another favor."

Dawson hung up and dialed a number he had been given only for emergencies. A number he had never thought he'd have to call.

The CIA makes me nervous.

Namale, Fiji

CIA Special Agent Dylan Kane sat in a very feng shui chair, his back to the wall, all the entrances and exits visible, the lighting subdued due to the unscrewed bulb in the light hanging from the ceiling. It had been a fabulous dinner with equally fabulous company. The young lady that had sat across from him as they had their Kobe beef steak had shifted to the chair beside him, one hand on her Chalk Hill chardonnay, the other on his leg, squeezing life into an adjacent appendage.

He sipped his Glen Breton Rare, a scotch that was hard to find but worth the effort. All of his regular haunts across the world had a case stored away in the event he might show up. He felt the tingling numbness begin to take over, the warmth spreading through his body with each sip.

He leaned back and sighed, pulling Talei's chair a little closer then putting his arm around her. He was about to plant a kiss on her that he knew would lead to something even better than a fine scotch, when his phone vibrated.

"Just a second, darling," he said as he fished the phone from his pocket. He answered, not recognizing the number. "Go ahead."

"Hi, it's me," said a voice Kane didn't recognize.

"That's nice, this is me too."

"You had that same damned sense of humor every time you got a finger or two of scotch into you after training."

Kane smiled, the voice now clearly recognizable as his old Sergeant Major and Delta buddy Burt "Big Dog" Dawson.

"Hey! What can I do for you old buddy?"

"I need a favor."

"Name it."

"I need a cyber-asset."

"I know just the man for the job. I'll have him contact you shortly."

"Thanks, my friend. Now make that call before you take another drink."

"You know me so well."

Kane ended the call then fired a message through his phone to an untraceable relay, the encoding on his text message directing it to the correct recipient more securely than any other method available to him in Fiji.

The message sent, he cleared the phone of any record of the message or call, then pocketed it, turning back to Talei.

"Now, where were we?" he asked, his mischievous smile awarded by a heart quickening kiss from a woman so gorgeous, she'd piss off super models.

The perfect distraction for trying to forget New Orleans.

Chris Leroux Residence, Fairfax Towers, Falls Church, Virginia

CIA Analyst Chris Leroux sat on his couch, sipping a Diet Coke and grasping at air, the bag of Cheetos empty.

"I ate the whole thing?" he asked aloud, examining the bag. He turned to scold his girlfriend Sherrie for allowing him to eat the entire bag when he remembered she wasn't here. She was off on some op in God knows where. She was an agent, he was an analyst, and he wouldn't have it any other way. At least in that there was no way in hell he wanted to be an agent. He knew the gonads for that belonged to her.

Which was totally cool with him.

She was like his own personal Lara Croft, a superhero off fighting for duty and honor, then the best damned girlfriend a guy could ask for when back home.

Damn, you're hopeless.

He knew he was damned lucky. Until he had met her he was chronically shy. Still was. He was on his way up at the agency, at least in the analyst pool since the Brass Monkey incident he had figured out for them, and he had the ear of the Director now. But all of his current confidence he owed to Sherrie.

God I miss you!

His phone vibrated on the table, the dull rumble causing him to nearly shit his pants.

Definitely not agent material.

He checked the message and jumped from the couch, turning off the TV and calling his escort team that had been assigned for security purposes, his current assignment considered too important and too risky for him to be left unguarded.

"We're leaving in five."

"Yes, sir."

Dylan Kane had been his friend since high school. Kane had gone army then CIA, Leroux had gone academic then CIA. Neither had known the other had ended up at the agency until a chance encounter that had rekindled their friendship.

Kane had saved his life, had given him the courage to go after Sherrie, and had been a good, albeit infrequent, friend.

And he'd do anything for him.

Köln, Germany
1472 AD

Dietrich pushed open the basement door and stepped into the hallway, closing it behind him. The barrel was tucked under his arm as he tried to make it seem as light as he could. He returned the lantern to the wall, then locked the door, stuffing the key back in his pocket. He turned and the robed figure was again there.

"What is that?"

Dietrich looked at the barrel.

"What, this? It's an empty powder barrel. I need to put it out with the others so they can get refilled when our supplier gets here in two days."

"Let me see it," said the man, his voice at least a whisper this time.

"Of course," said Dietrich, his hand still in his pocket from depositing the key. He gripped the dagger handle, shifting his body to the left to transfer the barrel to the man's outstretched hands, then swiftly pulled the dagger and plunged it into the man's belly.

He dropped with a groan that echoed through the halls, his body sliding off the now bloodied dagger.

There was no time to waste as the shadows seemed to be moving.

He rushed down the hall, away from the basement door and toward the front of the house. He passed the master's room, the door still closed. He saw a hand reach out from the shadows but he darted to the left, avoiding it, the dagger still in his hand, the barrel uncomfortable under his arm.

He reached the front door and turned the latch then pushed open the door. A hand grabbed his left shoulder and he spun, driving the dagger between the man's ribs and into his heart. He dropped to the ground in a pile of moaning flesh as his blood spurted out over his robes and the floor.

"Alarm!" yelled a voice from deep within the house, and immediately he could hear the pounding of footsteps.

He ran down the steps, out the front gate, and raced up the hill toward Heike's house. They deserved to know what had happened to their daughter, and he was determined to tell them should he be successful. Footfalls echoed through the dark streets behind him, his exhaustion and the barrel slowing him down. He knew he wouldn't make it, the guards undoubtedly well rested and strong.

As if to prove his thoughts, he was suddenly overtaken by several of them who blocked his path, their arms outstretched, the ghostly figures of the baggy robes terrifying in the moonlight. He dodged to the right but it was no use. A glance over his shoulder showed more coming. To the left was the ledge Heike had been thrown over, to the right the wall of a house. He made for the ledge, but was blocked, forcing him to retreat to the house.

He sensed a shadow to his left and spun to see the imposing figure of his master standing before him, how he had managed to get there so fast Dietrich did not know.

"What are you doing, Dietrich?"

The voice was again emotionless, barely questioning, as if he already knew the answers to the questions he was about to ask, having already read his subject's mind.

"I'm just disposing of the empty barrel, my master," he gasped, stunned he had been able to form the words.

"Then why do you run?"

Dietrich slipped the dagger into his right pocket and shifted the barrel from his left to his right arm, shaking out the left arm and playing for time.

"I'm sorry, master, but somebody grabbed me and I defended myself. I forgot you had extra guards, and in my horror, I stabbed one. Then more came, and I panicked. I thought they would seek revenge before I could explain myself, so I ran."

He pushed away from the wall several feet as his breath slowly steadied. The group still surrounded him, his master at an even height with him as he was several feet farther down the road, his imposing stature making the difference.

Dietrich kept his side to him, the barrel under his right arm, then flashed him a smile he hoped would disarm the man.

"I don't believe you," said his master. "I believe you were more affected by the death of the girl than you admitted to, and that your misguided emotions are leading you astray."

"No, master, I would never let my emotions affect my judgment."

"And yet again, I don't believe you."

His master flicked his wrist, and the robed figures surrounding him began to advance.

Dietrich swung his body to the right, grasping either end of the barrel in his hands, then swung back, pivoting his entire body to the left, releasing the barrel at the apex of the swing. The advancing robes stopped as all heads followed the barrel as it flew over their heads. Dietrich held his breath, praying his throw was long enough, but his heart sank as the barrel fell short, hitting the stone wall and bouncing back.

"Pathetic," said his master as he turned back toward Dietrich. But Dietrich smiled and watched as the barrel began to roll down the steep road, the cobblestones unforgiving, their firm surface causing the barrel to bounce higher and higher as it gained speed and caught on the various imperfections in the road.

"Get it!" yelled his master as the robed figures scrambled after the barrel, now bouncing as high as a man.

Dietrich took the opportunity to turn toward Heike's home but he felt an iron grip on his left arm, dragging him down the road. He reached for the blade in his pocket with his free hand and swung it toward his master, but it was easily intercepted, his wrist caught by the left hand of his captor.

Who then squeezed.

The pain was unbelievable, his grip like the jaws of a lion. Within seconds the blade clattered to the pavement as his master continued to run down the road, undeterred. As they came around a bend to the right, Dietrich laughed as the barrel bounced over the wall on the left and hit the side of a building, falling out of sight and into the roaring river below.

"No!" screamed the master, the sound unbelievable, inhuman. Dietrich felt the grip on his arm loosen and he prepared himself to break away, but instead the hand quickly let go and gripped his neck. He felt his entire body lift off the ground as he was carried toward the precipice he had last seen his beloved from. The grip was crushing and he couldn't breathe. He clawed at his master's hands but it was no use.

He felt his legs hit the waist high wall as his master held him out over the river below.

"You will pay for eternity for what you have done," growled the man, his eyes flaring in the moonlight as if a demon.

The grip loosened and Dietrich felt air surge into his lungs as he plunged to the river below.

But he didn't care.

He smiled as his mind filled with thoughts of Heike, and how they would be together soon, the bliss he felt enough for him to ignore the harsh shock of cold that enveloped him, then the snapping of his back on a rock below.

Heike!

Laura Palmer's Private Jet, Over the Atlantic Ocean

The phone vibrated on Dawson's chest. He was drifting in and out of sleep as he lay back in the ridiculously comfortable Gulf V seats. He answered.

"Go ahead."

"Mr. White, a mutual friend wanted me to contact you."

Dawson recognized the voice of the young CIA analyst he had dealt with several months ago during the New Orleans crisis, Chris Leroux. He was trusted by Kane and had come through in a big way. He also had it on good authority this young man had figured out the Brass Monkey incident long before anyone else.

"What have you got for me?"

"Do you have access to a laptop and the Internet?"

Dawson looked at Professor Palmer.

"Doctor, do we have a laptop with Internet access?"

She nodded, pointing at the laptop on her pullout desk.

"Go ahead," she said as she shuffled out of her seat. He took her place as the two professors stood behind him, the rest of the team gathered around. He put the phone on speaker.

"You're on speaker. I've got a laptop with Internet access."

Leroux quickly gave him a set of login instructions and moments later they were looking at a secure briefing the CIA analyst had put together.

"I've put together everything we have on Martin Lacroix. He's a medical doctor, apparently brilliant when he worked publicly, but he's gone more into the political side of things now, directing third world funding for various programs the World Bank supports. He's a big proponent of family planning programs, woman's rights in the third world—"

"That's ironic," commented Niner.

"—birth control, population control programs, conversion of traditional farming to larger corporate based farming using genetically modified grain and rice. He seems to be a crusader to bring the third world into the twenty-first century when it comes to reducing poverty and improving food supply."

"I'm guessing he has ulterior motives," muttered Acton.

"What?"

"Nothing," said Dawson. "Continue."

"Well, it's all in the file, but if he's not off on a World Bank junket, he's usually found at his home in San Marino."

"San Marino? Never heard of it," said Jimmy.

"The Most Serene Republic of San Marino," said Acton. "It's a microstate within Italy, about twenty-four square miles, maybe thirty-thousand people."

"Jesus, I've dropped deuces bigger than that," muttered Niner who then looked at Professor Palmer. "Umm, sorry ma'am, I was born crude."

"Call me ma'am again and you won't need to worry about how the next generation turns out."

Jimmy punched Niner in the shoulder as Acton gave his fiancée a thumbs up then continued.

"On a per capita basis it's one of the richest in the world, very stable, very safe, no debt, budget surplus, little unemployment. It's a leftover from the fourth century that managed to survive the turmoil around it. The rich love it because they can live in Europe, live their lifestyle, come and go as they please, and have all of their money sheltered from the idiocy of the European Union."

"So it's a tax haven," said Niner.

"Pretty much."

"Do we know if he's there now?" asked Dawson.

"Intel has him arriving there two nights ago," said Leroux. "Also, we've traced the calls to and from that cellphone you retrieved. It was a burner. All of the calls were to and from the same number. The number was a repeater that bounced around the world a few times, but I managed to track it down."

"Where?"

"San Marino."

"Anything on his movements over the past few years? We're thinking he might be linked to seven others in his organization."

"It's difficult to say. Passport records show him travelling all over the world, almost a different city every week."

"Any pattern?"

"Well, I cross referenced these trips with World Bank business and was able to find one anomaly."

"Yes?"

"Four times a year he goes to France almost like clockwork, only missing a few times in ten years. Each solstice and equinox, he's in France. Sometimes there is World Bank business, but never on the day before or the day of."

"That's odd," commented Acton. "Almost pagan. The Rosicrucians were Christian, but they did embrace all belief systems that were thought to better themselves."

Palmer cleared her throat.

"You gentlemen do realize the next solstice is in three days?"

"He could lead us right to them."

"If he thinks we're after him, do you think he'd be stupid enough to go?" asked Jimmy.

"Not stupid enough, but he just might be arrogant enough," replied Dawson. He picked up the phone. "Sir, thank you for your assistance. We'll contact you if we need anything else."

"My pleasure, Mr. White."

Dawson ended the call, looking at those gathered around him.

"We may just have what we need. Let's get to Geneva, gear up, pre-position in France, then find out where this bastard goes. With any luck, we take these guys down by season's end."

Geneva Cointrin Airport, Geneva, Switzerland

Customs was usually cleared quickly on private jets. Private terminals, a separate customs gate for the few passengers that came through that particular terminal, then you were free and clear to enjoy whatever city you had just flown into.

Acton had only been to the Swiss city of Geneva once before. And he loved it. The history, the architecture, the people. It was small for such an influential city, it carrying a lot of responsibility internationally, reflected in its multinational population, fully half of its nearly 200,000 residents foreign. With its neutral status, Switzerland had managed to avoid almost two centuries of neighboring wars, and was able to play arbiter to many conflicts and international projects. Recognized worldwide as a center for diplomacy and international finance, its bank accounts were still legendary, if not as secret as they once were.

But this time he was here for anything but pleasure. He had been filled in on what had happened to Stucco and his family, to the Geneva police detective's family, and to Dawson's family as well. It was unbelievable. It was horrifying. He glanced over at Laura and gave her a little smile.

If anything ever happened to you, I don't know how I'd go on.

He had never been truly in love before in his life. He had thought he was several times, but it wasn't until Laura had come along, and they had fallen in love, that he realized all the previous times had been nothing. *This* was *true* love, *this* was what life was about. Imagining life without her was something he couldn't fathom. They had had a lot of close calls since they met each other, and every time he had thought he had lost her he had felt empty, hollowed.

Sometimes he wanted to become a hermit, settle down in some small college town somewhere and teach, her in the town's other college—a nice, safe, predictable routine. No dangers, no secret cults, no bullets or rockets flying by their heads.

But that wasn't them.

Being out in the field at a dig site with their students, that was what they lived for. Holing up, leading a sheltered life, wasn't for either of them. They'd go shack-whacky within weeks if they couldn't get their hands dirty. And if that meant grenades and ninjas, then so be it.

Ninjas?

A quick mental rerun of the last few years and he confirmed Ninja's hadn't made an appearance.

Yet.

Too cliché!

As they exited the terminal, the familiar face of Spock greeted them along with Mickey, both standing in front of SUVs.

Why are they always black?

He didn't see any rental stickers as they loaded their luggage in the backs in silence. He and Laura were in the same SUV as Dawson, Red and Spock, the rest in the other with Mickey. Spock began to immediately bring them up to date.

"I've secured rooms in a busy part of town so our comings and goings shouldn't be noticed. Wings and Jagger are securing supplies now. Comms have been set up with Atlas already. I've already tapped into the locals and got their files on Maria's rape case and the suicide, along with the Inspector's family's murder. Not much in the details. There's no forensics, nothing to lead to the killers, but you'll find this interesting," said Spock. He pulled a file folder off the dash and handed it to Dawson. Dawson flipped it open as Acton leaned forward to see what it was.

Dawson shifted in his seat, holding the contents higher so the backseat could see. The first was of the suicide scene where Maria had been hit by the bus.

"See anything unusual?" asked Spock.

"No," replied Dawson. Acton stared at it and admitted he didn't see anything either.

"Don't look at the accident site. Look at what has nothing to do with the accident."

Acton leaned in even closer, still seeing nothing. An intersection, a stopped bus, a chalk outline where Maria's body had come to rest, painted lines, a pool of blood, a pole covered in bills in the foreground, occupying the right-hand side of the photo, slightly out of focus.

"Holy shit!" he exclaimed as it finally jumped at him.

"Ah, the Doc has it," smiled Spock as he made a turn. "I haven't had time to retrieve it yet, so we'll go there now. Only about two minutes from here."

"I must be dense because I still don't see it," said Dawson.

"Neither do I, Sergeant Major, and I *know* I'm smarter than him," said Laura with a wink at Acton's feigned wounding.

"Ouch," he said. "That's it, we're done. Spock, I insist on separate rooms."

Spock cocked an eyebrow and looked at him through the rearview mirror.

"Doc, I like you and all, but I insist on separate rooms as well."

Laura giggled, whispering, "burned!" as they came to a stop.

"This is it."

They climbed out and walked about fifty feet to the intersection. Acton immediately saw what they were looking for and walked up to the lamppost. Dawson, still holding the photograph, held it up once he saw where he was supposed to look, and cursed.

"How the hell did I miss that?"

Posted on the pole was a black sheet of paper with a bright red rose filling most of the page, and a golden cross in the center.

Proof that Maria Esposito's death was no suicide.

It was an assassination.

Lacroix Residence, San Marino

Dr. Martin Lacroix's time was being eaten up by this entire fiasco. If it wasn't for his apprentice, he wouldn't even have time to eat or sleep. He certainly wouldn't have time for his daily stem cell harvesting. At the moment he was hooked up to a machine that was drawing his blood, extracting stem cells, and reintroducing the blood, freshly oxygenated, back into his system. It was a daily ritual when at home, and it made him feel terrific, and it prepared him for the future when he would need the cells to reverse any damage to his body from heart attacks, strokes, his drinking—whatever might ail him.

It was the future. Forget fetal stem cells. They were a dead end—there simply weren't enough, and science had moved beyond that, discovering stem cells were in everyone's body their entire lives, not just in the fetus. There were just far fewer of them, and they were harder to get, but the beat of science drummed on, soldiering forward, and adult stem cells were getting easier and easier to harvest, and store, to ultimately be used when needed.

His intent was to have these cells injected into each of his organs to repair any damage caused by age and a libation filled life. Stem cells had already restored sight to the blind, repaired damaged heart muscle and more. It was the future of medicine, and would ultimately lead to the extension of useful human life far beyond anything imagined today.

And he was alive at the right time to take advantage of it. In his mind 150 years old was a reasonable life expectancy, and by then, he was certain nanotechnology along with computer and cloning technology will have progressed enough for science fiction like possibilities.

The thought was what kept him going.

Soon it would be time for him to exit the public eye, and move into the shadows. Already he looked ten years younger than he should, and in another ten or twenty years, it would become far too obvious unless the technology they now used went mainstream. But if their plans were to succeed, that mainstream would be far smaller than anybody today could imagine.

Earth will be the Eden God intended, once again.

The machine beeped indicating the end of the procedure. His private nurse entered the room immediately and removed the needles. Lacroix hurried to his study and found his apprentice huddled over a computer. He turned to face him.

"Master, you won't believe what I've found!"

"What?"

"I've had the first team tailed since they arrived. About an hour ago two of them went to the airport to pick up a new set of arrivals. Four of them we knew about, Delta Force, but they had two other people with them—a man and a woman. I ran their faces and found out they are two archeology professors—a Professor James Acton from St. Paul's University in Maryland, and a Professor Laura Palmer from University College London."

"What would they be doing with the Delta Force?"

"Classified files indicate these two professors have been involved in a few incidents lately, but that doesn't matter. What matters is this." He pointed at a photo on the screen and Lacroix felt his knees about to give out in excitement.

Rue du Mont Blanc, Geneva, Switzerland

Acton pushed away the photo showing the Laviolette family crime scene. It was disturbing, a clear message being sent to any who would understand it.

Don't mess with us, or this could be your family.

He squeezed Laura's hand.

"What now?" he asked. "We've got the evidence to prove they are behind the killings, but since nobody knows who *they* are, and nobody knows that Lacroix is one of *them*, it's pretty much useless."

"Not true," said Dawson. "We now know that the Rosicrucians are real and that Lacroix is high enough in the organization to warrant this type of effort to protect. We know where this man lives, we know that he goes to France in the next couple of days for what is most likely some sort of Rosicrucian meeting or ritual, and we know that this meeting will most likely attract the rest of the leadership. I think we know a lot more than what we did before we arrived."

"Okay, again I ask, what now?"

"When the others get back we pre-position in France and get a team on Lacroix in San Marino. When he goes to France and this meeting starts, we hit them with everything we've got."

"Which isn't that much," said Niner, looking about the room. Acton actually thought they had enough to start World War III, but perhaps it was only enough to start it, not win it.

"We'll make do," said Dawson.

"Aren't we forgetting one thing?" asked Laura.

All eyes turned to her.

"What's that?" asked Acton.

175

"While I understand your desire for revenge—blast, even I want to stomp on their bollocks until they die—don't we have a responsibility to find out what they are up to?"

There was silence for a moment, then Acton nodded.

"She's right. You heard what that CIA guy said. All of these programs he supports are aimed at reducing the population of the third world through reducing the birthrate. They seem innocuous enough, but it just fits too nicely into their desire to cap the planet's population. What if there are other plans they have, already set into motion? Shouldn't we try to find out what these are and stop them?"

"Isn't a reduced population not necessarily a bad thing?" asked Niner. "I mean, they keep saying we're running out of resources and killing the planet. Maybe a few less births are a good thing."

Acton pursed his lips, nodding slowly.

"Yes, but remember, those are all aimed at slowing down population growth, which I agree is an excellent thing. But what next? Reducing the population through birth control is a laudable and plausible goal, but would take centuries to accomplish any significant population *reduction*. We're already seeing it in countries like Japan and most of Europe. The only thing sustaining European populations now is immigration, and that has proven to be a disaster. Their cultures are being overwhelmed by incompatible cultures, and if they keep trying to solve their demographic problems by bringing in cultures from around the third world that don't share their belief systems, they'll lose the very culture they're trying to preserve.

"Europe and the other Western societies plagued by low birth rates need to embrace these rates and recognize that they aren't a negative thing. The problem is we have massive pension liabilities and debts that were designed around the thinking that our societies would continually grow so that there would always be more workers than retirees. That simply isn't true anymore without immigrants, but now with our social safety nets, many immigrants simply arrive and become a burden on society rather than a contributor. The West needs to rethink how it's going to survive in a one point five birth rate world.

"Incentives to increase the birth rate, incentives for people to stay at home and raise kids rather than treating it as some horror that one spouse inflicts on the other, increased automation, reduced pension expectations, revamped health care aimed at prevention rather than treatment, allowing people to work longer, allowing people to continue working part time without clawing back pensions and entitlements. Treat our seniors as an asset rather than a liability. There are many solutions beyond opening the floodgates to fill jobs that perhaps just aren't necessary or needn't be thought of as beneath us.

"Take a maid for instance. Nobody wants to be a maid; it's considered a subservient minimum wage position, so nobody in our society wants to do the job unless they're desperate. So what do we do? We bring in an immigrant who is more than happy to do the job, doesn't think it's beneath them, and happily takes that minimum wage job so they can have a better life. Laudable if they then integrate into our society, support our constitution and institutions the way we do, and a generation later their offspring are as American as we are—or British!" he added with a wink at Laura. "But those immigrants aren't available anymore for the most part. We're bringing in people who don't like our ways, so keep their own.

"But what would happen if we shut that down? Would everybody have to clean their own houses? No, it would be just like after the Black Death. In Europe, half the population died within a few years. Did that mean that the work didn't get done? No. Before the Black Death labor was plentiful, jobs weren't necessarily so. This meant low wages and an inefficient work force. After the Black Death, when labor was scarce, but jobs still needed to get done, those who wanted it done the most, paid the most. Those who worked the hardest, or the most efficient, commanded even more pay, and those who wanted the same, had to work harder and more efficiently to get it as well.

"It revolutionized the work force. If we didn't have people to fill the menial jobs, but the menial jobs still needed to get done, those who didn't have work today because they weren't qualified for the good paying jobs, and just didn't see the point of toiling for minimum wage, or were too ashamed to take minimum wage jobs, would start jumping at those jobs because the people who wanted the work done would need to pay more. Instead of paying six bucks an hour for a maid, suddenly you'd have to pay fifteen or twenty. Being a maid would become a well-paying job, a job that Westerners wouldn't feel is a sign of failure. The work would get done, those who fell through the cracks of our own society would be lifted up, and everybody would benefit."

"How the hell did we get to talking about this?" asked Niner, a grin on his face.

"My other half has a habit of ranting about things he feels passionately about," said Laura, holding his arm.

Acton felt his cheeks flush.

"I'm sorry, she's right. I flip into professor mode too easily, and start to lecture. Just stop me whenever I do that."

"You had a point," said Dawson diplomatically. "We were discussing why it was important to determine what the Rosicrucians were up to, because reduced birthrates wouldn't accomplish their goal." He paused for a moment, then looked at Acton. "To me it seems they would need a Black Death type event to accomplish their goals."

"That's disturbing," said Niner to which the rest of the room agreed. "I think Professor Palmer is right, we need to figure out their endgame, and stop it."

"I agree," said Dawson, "but no matter what we find or *don't* find, we are taking them out at their meeting."

"Which means we don't have much time," said Acton. "And I can't even begin to think of where to start."

"There is one place," said Dawson. "His office right here in Geneva. There might be files."

"We'll leave that to you," said Acton as Dawson and his men rose. "We'll do what we do best."

"And what is that?"

"Research."

There was a knock at the door.

They all spun toward the sound.

"That wasn't the code," said Niner as they all jumped to their feet. Dawson pointed toward a rear corner of the room on the same side as the door. Acton took Laura by the hand and headed for the corner, but not before Laura grabbed two Glocks off a nearby table and several clips. By the time they reached the corner they were armed, with Niner and Jimmy on either side of the door, Spock and Jagger at the corners near the windows, Red and Dawson kneeling behind furniture with their weapons trained at the door.

"Who is it?" asked Niner.

No response.

Acton could feel the entire room tense up.

"Anything on the street?"

"Nothing unusual except somebody exited the building a moment ago and got in a black van. They left right away," replied Spock.

"Open it," ordered Dawson.

Niner pressed against the wall then reached over, unlocking the deadbolt, then turned the knob and pulled the door open.

Nobody.

Niner peered down the hallway to the right, then stepped out with his weapon gripped tightly in front of him as he made a semi-circle around the door, clearing the area, ending at the frame on the other side.

"Clear!" he announced. "But we've got a package."

Dawson rushed forward, probably thinking exactly what Acton was thinking.

Bomb!

Suddenly Dawson picked it up, stepping back into the room with a smile on his face.

"Pardon me, Sergeant Major, but are you nuts?"

It was Niner who asked what they were all thinking.

Dawson put the package on a nearby table. It was about the size of a briefcase, but twice as thick as usual. As Acton approached, holding Laura slightly behind him with his outstretched arm, his eyebrows climbed.

"It looks like one of those legal briefcases," he said.

Red stepped over.

"Okay, BD, spill. Why are we not running like pansies?"

"It came with a note," said Dawson, pointing at a bright yellow Post-it note stuck to the top.

"What's it say?" asked Laura.

"*A gift from Langley,*" said Dawson, "with the initials D.K."

"Who's that?" asked Acton, then it dawned on him and his jaw dropped. "Dylan!"

Dawson's head whipped around at Acton.

"You know him?"

Acton was taken aback.

"*You* know him?"

Dawson's eyes narrowed, but he remained silent.

Acton shook his head.

"Either we both have to break promises of secrecy, or this question goes unanswered." He looked at Dawson. "Do you really need to know how I know him?"

Dawson frowned.

"He's a national security asset that you seem to know about."

"He was my student. I helped him with his decision to join the army."

Dawson visibly relaxed.

"We'll leave it at that," he said. "So, yes, we're talking about your former student, who miraculously knew we would be here needing toys."

"He's who you contacted on the plane!"

"No comment," said Dawson as he opened the case, revealing a contraption unlike anything Acton had ever seen. It was a combination of composite fibers and metal, probably making it fairly light for its size. Dawson unfolded the device, revealing what looked like a metal frame on one side, with a series of round metal feet, a glass surface within the frame, and circuitry behind that. Dawson placed it face down on the feet, revealing a control panel and a screen.

"Is that a computer?" asked Laura, taking a nearby seat. Acton sat on the arm, overcome by a sense he shouldn't be seeing this piece of technology.

"Is that what I think it is?" asked Red, stepping forward.

"Yup," replied Dawson.

"I've only ever read the briefing notes on that thing. I never thought I'd get to see one."

Dawson leaned over the device, running his hand over the surface. He pressed a green button and the device powered on. His fingerprint was scanned, and the display popped to life.

"Christ, he's even got it programmed for you," said Red.

Dawson pressed a red button, then motioned for Niner to come over.

"Try it."

Niner pressed the green button, his thumb being scanned as he did so. The device activated.

"Good. Everyone check themselves so we know who can use it," said Dawson, stepping aside. "This"—he pointed at the machine—"ladies and gentlemen, is a file scanner. And I do mean that literally. The base has magnets. You simply mount the device to a drawer of a filing cabinet, activate it, and it scans the entire contents, separating everything into individual pieces of paper. No longer do you have to open cabinets and photograph every sheet of paper, you just attach the device, hit the button, it scans in about a minute, then you move on to the next drawer."

"How the hell does it work?" asked Jimmy as he tested his thumb. The machine activated.

"I have no freakin' clue, but all I know is it does. This will come in extremely handy when we hit the World Bank tonight."

"It's like he knew," said Red.

"He probably just put two and two together," replied Dawson. "He knew we would be seeking intel, he knew who Lacroix works for, so he figured we'd be hitting his office."

"I don't buy it," said Niner. "I don't care what any of you say, the guy's magic. Pure, dreamy magic."

Spock's eyebrow shot up.

"Dreamy?"

"Have you seen those abs?" asked Niner. "If he was on the other team, I'd switch for a shot at those."

Acton shook his head, laughing.

"You have no idea how far away Dylan is from that team."

"I know," sighed Niner, walking over to the window and looking down at the street below. "Always the bridesmaid, never the bride."

Jimmy threw his knife at him, embedding it in the wall by Niner's hand.

Niner gripped his chest.

"Oh, another dagger through my heart. You men are so"—his voice cracked—"cruel."

Dawson's eyes popped open and his lips pushed out. "Oookaaay, and on that note, how about we get to work?"

Martin Lacroix Residence, Republic of San Marino

Martin Lacroix was so excited he had almost forgotten to put his robe on, the impromptu meeting he had called of the Circle of Eight about to start. Fortunately his apprentice still had his head in the game, and he was properly cloaked just as the computer beeped to indicate the final Circle member had logged in.

"What is the purpose of this interruption, Number Eight?"

He could hear a slight tinge of annoyance in the usually monotone voice.

"I assure you honored members, that once you hear what I have found, you will remember this day for the rest of your lives. Lives that may, perhaps, be far longer than any of us had ever anticipated possible if the legends are true."

"To what legends are you referring?"

"To the legend that the founder, Dr. Rosenkreuz himself, lived a healthy lifespan three times that of which he should have."

"We are decades away from those types of advancements," said one of the others. "Has there been some new breakthrough?"

"No, nothing of the sort," replied Lacroix. "Something far more spectacular." He paused for effect, then resumed. "But let me start at the beginning."

"Must you?" asked his most regular detractor.

"If you have no desire to hear what will undoubtedly be our generation's greatest contribution to The Circle, you are welcome to crawl into some lonely corner somewhere and die a natural death."

"Proceed," rumbled Number One, this time clearly annoyed.

"Thank you, Master. As you are aware, we have had the first Delta team under surveillance, and as a result, discovered the arrival of a second unit several hours ago. With them were two archeologists."

"Archeologists?"

Number One sounded surprised; something he had never sounded that Lacroix could recall.

"Yes. Professor James Acton, and his fiancée, Professor Laura Palmer. I had a background check done on both, and in reviewing the information, we found this."

He motioned to his apprentice to transmit the image.

"Oh my God!" exclaimed one, then others with their own reactions, all of which were flabbergasted.

"Could it be?"—"It has to be!"—"But we thought it was gone forever!"

"Do we have any idea where it is?" boomed the voice of Number One, excitement lacing his voice, even he unable to apparently control his emotions, some even beginning to sob in excitement.

"No, but this professor must, and he's in Geneva right now."

"Pick him up immediately."

Lacroix smiled.

"I've already given the order."

Chemin des Colombettes, Geneva, Switzerland

Wings sat at the controls of the Agusta Westland AW109, its rotors pounding the air overhead, the roar unbelievable compared to the Ghost Hawk "Jedi Rides" Dawson had been riding in lately. How the guys in Vietnam with those Hueys ever survived an insertion he'd never know. It was almost as if they made them loud on purpose, as if it would intimidate the enemy rather than let them know exactly where they were.

Stealth back then was for the soldier already on the ground, not in the air.

"Sixty seconds!" announced Wings.

Dawson pulled open the door and put a foot out on the skid. At this altitude it was fairly dark, the glow being emitted by the city almost unnoticeable if he looked up. But down, the streets and buildings were well lit, if not busy. It was a little after two in the morning, and the streets were fairly empty, Geneva turning into a sleepy town at night in this area.

"Ten seconds!"

Dawson leaned forward and saw their target, a large tower that housed the World Bank offices in Geneva. They didn't have the entire building, only one floor about a third of the way down. Security would be a obstacle from a technological standpoint—security passes and cameras, as well as armed guards, the only challenge they would provide would be to not kill them.

The point of this operation was to get in and get out with nobody ever knowing they were there.

"Go! Go! Go!" yelled Wings.

Dawson jumped out, hitting the roof with a roll as Red, Niner and Jimmy followed. Dawson waved at Wings who immediately banked, dropping out of sight as the team sprinted for the door nearby.

Dawson activated his comm.

"Bravo Six, Bravo One. We're in position, over."

"Roger that, cutting power now." The block went dark as a pre-positioned Mickey did his job, emergency lighting kicking in almost immediately. "Overriding security system, now." Fire alarms began to beep and the red light on the pass control turned to green. Dawson pulled the door open and the four of them entered the stairwell, closing the door behind them. "Camera feeds are tapped and stairwell feeds are looped all the way down to the twelfth floor. Count them off as you hit the landings, and I'll loop them. Keep tight, I don't want your asses getting caught on camera as I reactivate, over."

"Roger that, out."

Niner led the way, Taser extended in front of him should they encounter anyone. The building should be mostly empty, but with the fire alarm going off, any poor souls still there should be heading for the stairwells to evacuate. Mickey was in position nearby, tapped into all the security feeds, the emergency call for the fire service intercepted.

There would be no one coming to answer the call.

Outside communications should also have been cut, now all that was needed was for them to get to Lacroix's office without being detected.

Niner's fist shot up and they all froze. A door one flight down opened, a man and a woman, the woman giggling as she tucked her blouse in, he still struggling with his belt, stepped out onto the landing, then with one more passionate kiss, rushed down the stairs.

"Mickey, we need some warning on these things," said Niner over the comm.

"Sorry about that, I'm having trouble maintaining the overrides. Someone is trying to reboot the system, over."

"Bravo One here, how long have we got, over?"

"You better hustle, BD, this isn't looking good. It's this damned equipment, it's too old, over."

"Shit!" muttered Dawson. "Let's go!" he said in a harsh whisper that sent Niner sprinting to the next landing as the two office lovers continued their descent, giggles continuing, the sound of other doors opening below them as cleaning staff and those pulling all-nighters evacuated.

They continued their descent, Niner whispering each floor number, Mickey hopefully flipping the cameras, hiding their advance. A door above them opened and Dawson looked back to see a pair of feet through the railing. They kept moving, pacing themselves between the lovers and the descending feet above.

Fifteen.

They cleared the landing, only three flights to go.

"What's the status on the twelfth floor, over?"

"All clear so far, BD. But hurry. We've got security coming up from the ground floor. I think they might have caught a break in the feed, over."

Niner continued forward.

Fourteen.

The footsteps behind them were getting closer, the lovers not keeping pace. Dawson caught up to Red a bit, tightening up the team slightly, Red carrying the CIA scanner on his back.

The footsteps continued to get closer.

Dawson pulled a flare off his utility belt and removed the caps, grinding the striker against the top of the flare. It immediately sparked, a red glow filling the dimly lit corridor, a trail of smoke now being left behind them.

A women yelped above them, the footsteps stopping. Dawson could hear her run back up a flight then open the door to the fourteenth floor, his fake fire having its desired effect.

"We're here!" whispered Niner. "Mickey, report!"

"You're all clear, but security is on the eleventh floor, going office to office. You've got maybe three minutes to get inside, over."

Niner burst through the door, sprinting to the right then coming to a halt at a large glass wall in front of the elevators, "The World Bank, Geneva" frosted into the glass in large letters. He immediately dropped to his knees, his lock picking kit already in his hands and opened.

Dawson covered him, his back to Niner while he did his work, mentally counting the seconds in his head. When he reached two minutes he began to get antsy.

"Mickey, report."

"They're coming up the stairwell, you've got about fifteen seconds."

Dawson heard a click behind him.

"Got it!" Niner rolled aside as Red and Spock entered through the now open door, spreading out. Dawson followed, Niner bringing up the rear and closing the door behind them.

"They're on the floor!" hissed Mickey through the comms. "Five seconds and they're looking in that fishbowl!"

"Everything's locked!" said Spock as he and Red tried several doors at the rear of the reception area.

"There's no time to pick another one," said Niner as Dawson looked around.

"Everyone behind the reception desk," he said, his team immediately rushing toward the only substantial piece of furniture in the waiting area that could provide cover from the hallway windows. Dawson dropped, pulling the late arriving Spock under the cramped desk.

"They're right on you, keep still."

Dawson looked over his shoulder and cursed. The back of the desk, providing them with the only cover they had, was made from a single piece of gently curving frosted glass.

He clenched his fist and could see everyone tense up, freezing. A rattle at the front door had Dawson thanking God that Niner had the presence of mind to lock it behind them. Niner cleared his throat.

Dawson looked over at him, moving only his eyeballs, and could see Niner staring at the wall that backed the waiting area. Dawson looked to his left and nearly shit.

It was wall to wall glass. Mirrored glass. And sitting right where they should be, were four Delta team members huddled under a desk, as plain as plain could be.

The door rattled again.

Rue du Mont Blanc, Geneva, Switzerland

Acton rubbed his eyes, the jet lag hitting him hard, and the screen he had been staring at for hours not helping. Laura had already given up, curled in a ball beside him, gently breathing, gorgeous as ever.

His eyes drooped.

On the other side of the room Jimmy was asleep, lying on a cot, the space Spock had rented for them definitely commercially oriented as opposed to residential. It made sense, comings and goings at all hours were less noticed in a commercial district. They had equipped it with cots and sleeping bags, lots of bottled water and food that didn't need to be cooked like protein bars and dried cereals.

It was adequate for their purposes, and being used to living at dig sites in the middle of nowhere for weeks or months on end, it didn't bother him at all.

Because there was a bathroom.

A clean bathroom with running water. No shower, but they could wash themselves enough to not stink in a crowd. There was a sound at the door and Jagger rose.

"Could they be back already?" whispered Acton, reaching for the Glock 22 that sat on the table in front of him.

"Only if they had to abort," said Jagger, shaking his head. He kicked Jimmy's cot and the man bolted upright, immediately alert. "We've got company," whispered Jagger.

The door suddenly burst open, men in what looked like military or police gear bursting through, one of them yelling, "Police!" along with something in French.

"Stand down!" yelled Jimmy as the room quickly filled with armed men, their automatic weapons raised. Acton raised his hands, the Glock still gripped tightly, and positioned himself in front of a startled Laura.

"Take it easy," said Jimmy, trying to calm the room. "Professor, Jagger, just lower your weapons very slowly, let everyone know we're friendly here."

Acton changed his grip, pinching the weapon between his thumb and forefinger, slowly lowering it to the table he had just picked it up from. Once laid down, he raised his hand back up, then stepped away from the table.

"You are all under arrest for the possession of illegal firearms," announced a man in plainclothes. He looked around the room. "Where are the others?"

"What others?" asked Jimmy.

"There are six other men with you. Where are they?"

"I think you have bad information there, officer, there's just the four of us, and those two"—he nodded toward Acton and Laura—"are our prisoners."

"Yes, I too give all my prisoners their own semi-automatics."

Jimmy shrugged and gave Acton an "it was worth a try" look.

Handcuffs were slapped on all four of them, then they were patted down, Laura and Acton clean, but several knives and other accoutrements of the trade discovered on the Delta operatives.

They were led out and down the stairs to the street below. Acton and Laura were loaded in the back of a paddy wagon with metal seating along the sides. Two officers joined them. The doors closed and the vehicle began to roll.

Suddenly the two men leapt forward. The one nearest Acton pressed his service weapon against Acton's temple, the other doing the same to Laura.

"Don't move!" ordered Acton's man. Something jabbed in his thigh. He looked down to see a needle stuck in his leg, the plunger being pushed by his captor, and as he spun to see the same thing being done to Laura, his world faded to black, only one thing clear in his mind.

These are not police.

Chemin des Colombettes, Geneva, Switzerland

Dawson held his breath, praying the dim lighting and the fact nobody was looking for them would trick the guards into not noticing the four figures reflected in the mirror, huddled under the reception desk. Every muscle in his body tensed as he tried to freeze, and he could tell the others were doing the same, terrified a single movement would be noticed and they'd be forced to engage these two innocent men.

Suddenly, after what seemed an eternity but was only seconds, the guards stepped away from the door and continued on. Dawson watched the shadows move away, the pounding in his chest easing as they eventually disappeared.

"You're all clear," announced Mickey.

Dawson scrambled out from under the desk and pulled Red out as Niner did the same for Spock. Niner raced for the first locked door and jimmied it.

"Bingo!" he hissed. They all quickly entered the office area and closed the door behind them, momentarily safe from the guards. A hallway stretched in three directions, with no indications on where to go except for red exit and blue bathroom signs.

Dawson used hand signals to send the other three down each hall, and within seconds Spock's voice was heard over the comm. "Got it."

Footfalls filled the hallways as they all converged on Spock's position, the opened door labeled "Dr. Martin Lacroix, Chief International Funding" and translated into French and German underneath. Dawson waited for everyone to enter then he closed the door. Niner dropped into the bastard's chair, inserting a device into one of the USB slots and booting the computer.

Dawson helped Red unpack the cabinet scanner from Langley and within moments the first cabinet was being scanned, page after page flipping by on the display.

"Remarkable," muttered Red. Dawson and Spock began rifling through drawers and other personal belongings, looking for anything useful.

"I'm in," said Niner. "I'll just download everything from his local hard drives, pull all his emails, contacts and calendar; anything else will be gravy."

"Do it," said Dawson, kneeling to Niner's left as he went through the last drawer in the desk, having found nothing so far but office supplies, and a few bottles of scotch. "Hello." Dawson held up a Glock that had been stuffed in the back of the drawer, hidden behind several boxes of Cuban cigars. He quickly removed the firing pin, Niner grinning as he did so.

"Mickey, status."

"They're about to find your flare," replied Mickey. "That should set off a shit storm."

"Roger that." He looked up and saw Red already moving on to the final cabinet. "Red, time?"

"Three minutes."

"Niner?"

"On to the gravy already."

"We're out of here in three," said Dawson to everyone including Mickey.

"Not sure if you're going to get it. The woman you scared off with the flare is talking to the guards in the lobby. The guards will find the flare in about five seconds"—he drew out the word—"and they just spotted it. They know someone's here."

"How long can you maintain control?"

"I've already lost it. I'm just an observer now, they've rebooted their system and now have complete control. You might not have noticed but the fire alarm hasn't been going off the past minute."

Dawson paused to listen and realized Mickey was right.

"Options?"

"Plan B."

"Plan B it is."

"Done!" announced Red, packing the machine back in his bag and slinging it over his shoulders. Niner yanked the USB scanner from the slot and zipped it in one of his pockets. Dawson opened the door then waved his men through.

"Status!"

"You're clear on the twelfth floor for the moment, but guards are converging from upper and lower floors. They'll know for sure where you are once you enter the hallway."

"Left or right."

"Left. Get to the stairwell and haul ass down."

"Roger that."

They entered the outer office and Niner tossed a spray paint can to Spock who quickly laid down a little art.

World Bank = New World Order!

Dawson opened the outer door as Spock discarded the can. They exited the office, sprinting toward the stairwell doors at the end of the hallway.

"You're still clear," said Mickey.

Dawson pulled the door open, letting the other three go by, then followed. He popped a smoke grenade and tossed it onto the landing, then dropped another down the gap between the railings, the metal casing clanging against the rails, a trail of smoke obscuring its final resting place. He pulled a face mask down that would filter his breathing from the nontoxic smoke, then pulled a rifle scope from his pocket with a thermal imager. Holding it up to his goggles, he was able to see clearly through the smoke, quickly rushing after the others who were now a flight below him, their own scopes out.

"You've got company coming from two floors below, but they're confused. Exit on the next floor then cut across to the opposite stairwell."

Niner pushed through the door to the eighth floor, the others disappearing through the doorway. Dawson took a peak down and could see the guards waving at the smoke and coughing. He went through the door and gently closed it, then sprinted after the others.

"You've been spotted," said Mickey. "Two guards are crossing from the seventh to the same stairwell you're about to hit."

"Roger that," said Dawson. "Keep going."

A little more gas was applied and Niner reached the door, pulling it open then racing down the stairs, the others close on his heels. Dawson hit the door, his foot bracing in the jamb, then pushing off toward the stairs, he dove through the air, his left hand grabbing the railing then pulling his body so his feet hit the landing below, then swinging around to the next flight of stairs with his momentum carrying him.

His foot hit a step about half way down and he jumped again, releasing his grip on the railing above and dropping his hand, grabbing the next railing below. Just as his feet hit the seventh floor landing the door opened. Dawson twisted and grasping the railing hard enough to let his hand slide down it, he swung his feet out, planting them hard against the door, slamming it shut, then pushing off to resume his descent. He tossed a smoke grenade behind him as the door opened again.

"You've gained a level on them," announced Mickey. "You've got four waiting for you in the lobby, armed. One is at the security desk monitoring the cameras, the other three are at your door, weapons drawn, over."

"How many above us?" asked Dawson as they passed the third floor landing.

"Two."

"Red, hold up," ordered Dawson as he spun around, drawing his Taser. He took a knee as Red joined him on the landing, his own Taser out. "I'll take the left, you take the right." The footfalls above them neared and Dawson spotted the boots of the first one rounding the landing, then their owner's face gasping in surprise as he tried to hold up, the other rounding the railing with him.

Dawson squeezed the trigger, the probe firing, embedding itself in the first man's chest, the wires conducting the 50,000 volts to the man's body.

He dropped, tumbling down the stairs as Red fired into the second target. Dawson grabbed the first man, throwing him over his shoulder and carrying him down the remaining flights as Red did the same with his. Niner was at the door with Spock.

"Status?"

"You've got them confused," said Mickey. "They know you've got two of their guys."

"Okay, meat shield time," said Dawson, handing his spent Taser to Niner who reloaded it, handing it back as Spock reloaded Red's. Dawson swung his man's feet to the ground as he slowly began to regain control of his body, then looked at Niner. "Ready?"

Niner nodded then pulled the door open. Dawson pushed his man out in front of him, Red following, quickly advancing toward the three guards now joined by the fourth. Red was beside him, his man barely able to walk as Niner and Spock ducked behind them.

Dawson whispered into the comm. "By the numbers, left to right. Three…two…one…execute." He squeezed the trigger on his Taser and the probe burst from the tip, hitting the man second from the left in his chest.

Red took out the man immediately to the right as Niner and Spock leaned out and incapacitated the two on the ends. All four men dropped to the floor, shaking. Dawson shoved his man on top of the mass of electrified flesh, then ejected his cartridge, his feet already pounding toward the front doors.

"You're all clear from here, but police are on the way, ETA one minute," said Mickey.

Dawson pushed through the first set of double doors, then the next, the crisp night air a welcome feeling. He checked left and right, a single car heading the opposite direction the only traffic, no pedestrians in sight. He sprinted across the street, fishing a fob from his pocket and pressing the button. A van pre-positioned earlier for their Plan B option chirped as the doors unlocked. Dawson jumped in the driver's seat, Red the passenger as the other two climbed in the back.

"Go! Go! Go!" yelled Spock from the back as he closed the door. Dawson hit the gas, pulling out from the curb and gunning it toward the intersection ahead just as the flashing lights of a police car swung around the corner. Dawson eased off the gas but didn't hit the brakes, the harshness of brake lights perhaps arousing suspicion. He came to the intersection just as the lights turned green and immediately made a right, heading away from the building and the source of more police cars in the distance.

"There's Mickey," said Red, pointing. Dawson pulled over and the side door slid open. Mickey jumped in and Dawson gunned it as Niner closed the door.

"Wings?" asked Dawson.

Mickey leaned forward between the two front seats. "Already returned the chopper and on his way back to paradise."

"Good. You guys change back to civie clothes," said Dawson as he made another turn, easing off the accelerator now that they were far enough away. Grunts and curses from the back made him smile as the men changed their clothes, packing their gear in large duffel bags.

Spock seemed the most efficient.

"Whenever you're ready, BD," he said. Dawson pulled into a parking spot and stripped out of the most obvious gear, tossing it into the back for Niner and Mickey to deal with. When he wouldn't attract attention, he stepped out of the vehicle and switched off with Spock, the van underway moments later as Dawson continued to change along with Red.

"BD, put on your comm, Wings says we've got a problem."

Niner handed him his headset and mike. Dawson inserted the earpiece and held the mike up to his mouth.

"This is Bravo One, go ahead."

"Bravo One, we've got a problem. I just reached our rendezvous point and it's crawling with police, over."

"Are you clear?"

"Yeah, I was able to duck down an alleyway. It looks like they hit our rooms."

"Any sign of the others?"

"Negative. Suggest you avoid this area."

"Understood. Spock, take us one block south. Wings, meet us there."

"Roger that. ETA?"

"Three minutes," said Spock as he eyed the GPS mounted on the dash. Red reached forward and reprogrammed it to the next street just in case there were any one way surprises, and they drove the rest of the way in silence.

"You're gonna want to see this," said Niner, handing a tablet computer to Dawson as Spock pointed.

"There's Wings."

He pulled to the side, Wings climbing into the vacant passenger seat, motioning for Spock to move on.

Dawson eyed the footage of the camera they had planted, its feed transmitted and stored on a secure Internet site. It showed the professors on a couch, Jimmy sleeping, Jagger on watch, then suddenly the door bursting open and police rushing in. They were led out in handcuffs, the remaining footage of no concern.

"Shit!" cursed Dawson, handing the tablet back to Niner. "They've been arrested."

"Now what?" asked Niner.

"Now I call in another favor."

The Wellington Hospital, London, England

Interpol Special Agent Hugh Reading sat at the bedside of his former Scotland Yard partner, Detective Inspector Martin Chaney. He had been shot almost two months ago in Egypt when Professor Palmer's dig site had been attacked. It was supposed to have been a vacation, friends joined together in the camaraderie of doing something with your hands other than firing a weapon.

It had been anything but.

And now his friend battled for his life, stuck in a coma the doctors said he may come out of today, or never.

When his job didn't take him out of the city or out of the country, Reading tried to visit his friend every day. He'd read him the paper, insult his favorite football club, and relay emails from the two professors, and on the bad days, he'd curse him out for being so stubborn. Today was a bad day.

"Listen you selfish bastard, if you don't snap out of this right now, I'm not coming back. I'm sick and tired of wasting my time hanging around having one way conversations and reading out loud as if to a three year old. Now wake up you prick!"

He waited, watching for an eye to flicker, a lip to curl, a finger to twitch.

Nothing.

He sighed.

"Don't worry you selfish prat, I'll be back tomorrow." He yawned. "Perhaps at a better hour." It was after two in the morning and he was exhausted but restless, this late hour visit designed to make him tired, entertained by the staff here only because he was a charmer who brought coffees and biscuits for the nurses.

It had worked.

He gave his friend a pat on the shoulder, then headed for the door. His phone vibrated in his pocket. He pulled it out and didn't recognize the number, but recognized the country code.

Switzerland.

Who the blazes do I know in Switzerland?

He took the call.

"Reading."

"Hello Special Agent. This is Agent White. We met in London and recently in Egypt. Do you remember me?"

Reading didn't recognize the voice at first, but with all the cloak and dagger those few words exuded, he quickly realized it was the head of the Delta Force unit that had tried to kill him a few years ago. Unlike Jim who had chosen to forgive them, he hadn't. He didn't hold a grudge per se, but he wasn't willing to completely let them off the hook. He understood they were following orders, but that excuse had been used too often in history. He accepted that they were told the people they were after were identified as terrorists, and after 9/11 and England's own 7/7 everyone was paranoid.

But it was their attack on Scotland Yard that he couldn't forgive. Good men had died that day, but even then he had to give them credit. They hadn't killed any of his fellow officers until one of their own had been killed.

Argh! It's so bloody convoluted!

He had been trying to push it out of his head since the day it had happened without much success. And today apparently he was going to be reminded of those events.

"Yes, I remember."

"Good. We have a problem I can't get into over the phone, however two of my friends, and two of yours, were just arrested in Geneva. We need your help."

"Two Professors I assume?"

"Yes."

"I'll call you back in one hour at this number."

"Thank you, Special Agent."

The call ended and Reading turned back to his silent partner.

"Back into the thick of it, my friend," he said, then walked out the door.

And a finger twitched.

Unknown Location

"No! No! No! No! No!" sobbed Acton, his voice fading as his head dropped to his heaving chest, his sobs harder than anything he could remember, worse even than the sight of his students massacred in Peru only days before he had met the love of his life. It was overwhelming, it was heartbreaking, it was more than he could take. Their plans, their future, all gone. They were going to be married, build a family together. And now it was all gone.

And it was his fault.

If he hadn't of insisted on coming to Geneva to help the Delta Team, she'd still be alive, and their future plans would still be intact.

He felt his stomach wretch and he turned to the side, vomiting on the floor, the harsh liquid burning his mouth and esophagus as his sobs continued. He spat to clear his mouth then stared into the darkness.

"You'll pay, you bastards! You'll all pay!"

The rage began to build, to take over, to fill him with a warmth as he imagined gutting those responsible.

They're all dead. If it isn't me, the Delta guys will finish the job.

Suddenly the light went out.

He bit his lip, trying to ease his sobbing, and listened.

Nothing.

He peered into the darkness but could see only black, telltale random dots of grey, almost like static, filling his field of vision as his eyes tried to make sense of what it was seeing, which was nothing, there being no light whatsoever. The pounding in his ears overwhelmed any sound that might be present, so he closed his eyes and busied himself with trying to control his racing heart. For there was one thing that he was determined to prevent, and that was being killed before he avenged his fiancée.

A foot scraped behind him, then footsteps, slow and deliberate, crossed the floor to his right, seemingly in a semi-circle, coming to rest in front of him, perhaps where Laura had been.

"Who's there?" he asked, his voice tinted with hatred, soaked with sorrow.

No response.

"I'm going to kill you for what you've done."

The footsteps retreated, then the sound of a door opening, a hint of light silhouetting a robed figure.

"Not, I think, today, Professor Acton."

The door closed with a click that echoed through the room. He listened again. Footsteps retreated from the door, then nothing. He shook in his chair, straining at his bonds, but again, nothing.

It's hopeless.

He forced himself to take deep, slow breaths, calming himself. He had to think, otherwise he'd just be wasting time and energy. With his eyes closed, he sucked in a breath through his nose, down into his stomach, and held it, the pounding in his ears slight now compared to moments before. The breath escaped through his mouth, and he repeated the process, his mind beginning to work the problem.

He was bound to a chair by the ankles, his hands bound behind his back, in a completely dark room. Whether he was alone or not, he did not know, and whether or not there were cameras for surveillance, he did not know. As well, there could be a guard on the other side of the door. He frowned. He didn't even know if there was one door or ten.

Work the problem.

How many doors, guards or eyes on the room were irrelevant. He had to first free himself of his bonds. His hands were too tight, so there was no point in cutting himself further. His feet however were individually bound to the chair legs. If he could free himself of the chair, he'd be able to walk.

He tried to stand.

No luck. His hands were bound behind him, but were tugging on something else, probably one of the spindles he could feel against his back. He leaned forward and to the left, hard, trying to put all the weight on the one leg.

Nothing.

He repeated it with the right front leg, leaning as far over as he could, lifting his feet and toes as much as possible.

He felt it give slightly.

He sat back down on all four legs, repositioning himself to the front right as much as he could, then pushed himself up, dropping all the weight he could on the one leg.

It creaked, then suddenly snapped, sending him tumbling to the floor. He closes his eyes and turned his head before smacking face first into the cold, hard floor.

With one free foot.

With his right foot free, he was able to stand a bit more and his left foot popped free, the zip tie sliding off the leg. This left him hunched over with a chair still attached to his back, but at least he was slightly mobile. He stopped to listen, and there was no evidence of anyone coming to stop him.

Perhaps I'm not being watched.

Or they were just laughing since he had in fact accomplished little.

Feet freed. One problem down.

Next problem. Free self from chair.

His hands were tightly tied and attached to probably a single spindle. The chair felt fairly solid, so trying to break the spindle was out of the question, he'd simply slice his wrists open further. Separating the spindle from the top of the chair would be difficult since he had no leverage there, but the bottom might be possible. He stood up as straight as he could, pushing against the seat of the chair with his legs.

It gave a little.

Or perhaps it was his imagination.

He tried again but too much of the pressure was transferring to his wrists. He stopped, still hunched, part of him missing that fourth leg.

Pain?

He nodded to himself. He had to risk it, there was no other choice. He balanced on the front left leg, and with some effort it snapped as the chair and he fell to the side and on the floor, wincing as he barely avoided bouncing his head off the unforgiving surface. He rolled over then pushed himself to his feet, his muscles and wrists screaming in agony. Stumbling forward, he tried to maintain a straight line until he felt himself run into something. Exploring it with his shoulder, he determined it had to be the wall. Turning around and placing the rear chair legs against it, he walked forward ten paces then took a deep breath.

Now or never!

He rushed backward, still hunched over so the legs were at about a sixty degree angle with the floor, then suddenly felt the jarring impact of wood against stone as he pulled forward with his upper body and pushed back with his legs, the momentum carrying him hard into the wall.

There was a snapping sound as the rear legs gave way.

He came to rest against the wall, gasping for breath as he now sat attached to a chair with no legs, held on only by a zip tie to a single spindle.

And still as uselessly trapped as he was before this all started.

He slid down the wall, his muscles screaming for a rest, when he felt his wrists slide up the spindle toward the top of the chair. He pushed himself against the wall, his back now free, and stopped his descent. Pushing himself back up, he lifted his right foot, bending his knees as tightly as he could, leaning forward. He felt the sole of his shoe grip on the seat of the chair and he stopped, catching his breath as he tried to balance on one foot.

He sucked in a deep breath then pushed back as hard as he could with his upper body, putting as much pressure as he could on the back of the chair, while pushing down with his right leg. He could feel the sweat popping from his pores, his muscles screaming, and nothing happening with the chair.

He groaned in agony, his body about to give up when finally a splintering sound erupted from the chair behind him sending a surge of hope through him as a second spurt of energy from his emergency reserve was released.

He strained harder, getting his wrists in the game, feeling the bite as the chair splintered some more then finally, suddenly, the bottom ripped free and fell to the floor followed by several of the spindles, including the one his hands were bound around. Shaking himself back and forth, he managed to rid himself of the rest of the chair and finally stand up straight.

And the first thing he wanted to do was sit down.

Instead, he pressed his back against the wall and caught his breath. He looked about the room and still could see nothing, the black he had been engulfed in taking on a distinctly red color with white spots, probably from his exertion.

And still no sounds beyond his beating heart.

Surely they would be coming now if I were being watched.

Now he needed to free his hands. With it being zip ties, it should be dead easy. He bent forward, sticking his butt out and lifting his arms behind his back as high as he could manage. Then, swinging his hips forward, then back, he dropped his arms as hard as he could to smack his wrists against his buttocks as his hips surged back.

The zip tie snapped with an agonizing scrape of his wrists, the training he had done with Laura's ex-SAS men always done with taped wrists.

But it was a small price to pay to be freed of his bonds.

He gingerly touched his left wrist with his other hand and winced, immediately regretting it. Next problem.

Prioritization.

Should he try to find a weapon in this room, which meant he needed light, or should he try to get out of this room, and find a weapon or some means of escape beyond the room?

If there were a light switch, it would most likely be by the door he would need to escape through regardless, so he gingerly made his way across the room to where he thought the door was. He found the wall with his outstretched hands, then began feeling up and down the wall from head to waist height, searching for the door and any switches as he moved to the right.

On the down stroke his left hand hit something and he paused. He moved his hand back up and knew immediately it was a switch. He closed his eyes and pushed it up.

The back of his eyelids turned bright red and he slowly opened his eyes, blinking them rapidly to try and adjust as he turned around, quickly scanning the room for any secret observers.

All he found was a lone bulb hanging from the ceiling, a broken chair, a knocked over lamp that had been shining in his face earlier, the bulb now broken and useless, scrape marks from where his beloved's body had been dragged out in her chair, and nothing else beyond a barred window.

He strode across to the blacked-out window and tested the bars to no avail. He could poke a spindle through and break the glass, but it would do him no good. He was certain yelling for help would only bring the guards. Stepping under the light, he examined his wrists. They were in bad shape. He yanked at his sleeve, tearing it off then ripping it in two pieces, each of which he then carefully wrapped around the wounds.

He grabbed two spindles from the floor for weapons, turned out the light, and tried the door.

It opened.

He stepped into a dimly lit hallway, and waited for his eyes to adjust. He was at the end of a hallway, it stretching out before him with doors about every twenty feet alternating on the left and right.

Time to explore.

Geneva Cointrin Airport, Geneva, Switzerland

Interpol Special Agent Hugh Reading cleared customs rapidly with his passport and police ID, Switzerland not being part of the European Union but still one of the founding members of Interpol. He hadn't bothered to go back to his office; he had immediately gone to his flat then the airport, calling in his requests and having them sent to his phone. It was now the morning after he had received the call, and his only communication with Sergeant Major Dawson had been through text messages.

I'm coming there, arrival 6:35am.

And the response.

Ok.

He had quickly found out about the arrest, but there was some confusion. The police raid showed four arrests, but they could only find two in the system. What had happened to the other two, a man and a woman, they didn't know. They assumed they were just lost in the paperwork, occupying a holding cell somewhere. The other two, whom Reading assumed were Delta Force members, were listed as John Doe's, refusing to give their names or any other personal information.

Reading had wrangled an interview with them, claiming they matched the descriptions of two men he was after.

They didn't worry him. They'd figure a way out of it eventually. What worried him was that his friends were missing, and no one knew where they were. He didn't believe for a second they were lost in the system. If those two were in Geneva with the Delta team, then they were involved in something, and it wasn't taste testing chocolate samples.

They're in trouble.

He briskly walked through the terminal and out the doors. He was about to get in the line for the cabs when he was bumped into. He felt a hand do a poor lift from his inside jacket pocket and was about to confront the man when he heard a whispered, "A gift for you." Reading resisted looking after the man, the voice familiar enough to know he had just been handed something by a Bravo Team member. The urge to check what was in his pocket was overwhelming, but he resisted, instead dragging his suitcase to the lineup for the cabs, and minutes later he was on his way to his hotel.

With the airport safely behind him, he reached into his pocket and pulled out a small envelope. Inside was a note and a tiny item that almost looked like a pill. He unfolded the note.

Give this to either of them.

Reading stuffed everything back in the envelope then into his pocket as he wondered what the pill could be. *It must be some sort of tracking device. But why would they need that? They're going to break them out! And now you're involved.* The situation was ridiculous. He couldn't help two American soldiers break out of prison. He'd lose his job and probably go to prison if he were ever caught. But then again, it might be the only way to find James and Laura. They still hadn't been found in the system, which meant they weren't *in* the system. They had either escaped, which was unlikely, or they were taken by some other party. And if he didn't help the Delta Force get their men back, they probably wouldn't help him find the professors.

Then again they had proven to be quite fair and reasonable since the events in London. Almost as if they wanted to make up for what had happened.

It wasn't long before he was at his hotel and checked in. A quick toilet and he was on his way to Bourg-de-Four Police Station. A flash of credentials and he was cleared to an interrogation room where he found a familiar face sitting, waiting for him, the other not so familiar. In fact, he couldn't be certain he had met the other, but there was no doubt it was Jimmy who was giving him a surly face.

"Good morning, gentlemen. I assume you speak English?"

Jimmy and the other nodded, still not making eye contact, their arms crossed, their legs extended far out, their butts pushed away from the back of their chairs.

A typical casual, 'I don't give a shit' pose.

"I'm Special Agent Reading, Interpol," he said, taking a seat across the table from them. "I have a few questions for you."

No response, except Jimmy leaned forward, putting his cuffed hands on the table not a foot from where Reading's hands were.

He ignored them, instead pulling out a pad from his briefcase, and a pen from his pocket, the cap very loose, the "pill" inside the top. He pulled the cap off the pen, letting the pill spill into the palm of his hand, out of sight of the cameras. He gripped it in his left hand as he picked up the pen with his right.

He looked at Jimmy.

"And your name is?"

Silence.

"Look, we can do this the easy way, or the hard way."

Still only silence.

Very well, the hard way.

He leaned forward quickly and grabbed Jimmy's hands, yanking them. Jimmy fell forward, his head smacking the table as Reading pushed the pill into the man's hand. Jimmy's fist closed over the device and Reading let go of the hands, leaning back in his chair as Jimmy recovered, rubbing his chin then licking his lips as if searching for blood. Reading saw the pill go into his mouth.

"What did you do that for?"

"To get your attention."

"Well you got it, and that's all you're getting. Save your questions for when our lawyer gets here."

Jimmy stood up, as did the other man.

"Guard! Take us back to our cell!" yelled Jimmy.

A moment later the door opened and they were led out, followed by Reading who yelled after them, "This isn't over!"

He went to the front desk to retrieve his belongings.

"Any luck?" asked the old officer at the desk.

"Nil. As expected I guess. But now that you've got them, I'll have them put under surveillance. They'll slip up at some point."

Reading stuffed the last of his personal items in his pockets, then gave the officer a final nod. He left, a cab already waiting for him, and returned to his hotel room, his mind filled with thoughts of his friends and what they could possibly have gotten themselves into now. As he entered he paused.

Something's not right.

Suddenly a head poked out from behind the wall of the L shaped room and Reading jumped, nearly filling his trousers.

"Good morning, Special Agent."

Reading shook his head then kicked the shoes off his aching feet.

"Good morning, Sergeant Major."

Unknown Location

James Acton reached for the handle in front of him, his ear still pressed against the door. And still he heard nothing. He gripped the knob and twisted, but it didn't budge. It was locked. *Shit!* He couldn't risk kicking it open—that would certainly bring everyone down on him. He had searched the only other room that had been unlocked and found nothing beyond an extensive wine cellar. There was nothing he could use as a real weapon and he knew he had to escape. Avenging Laura was of course at the top of his agenda, but in order to do that, he needed manpower and firepower, and that lay in Geneva. If he could escape from wherever he was, he could bring the Bravo Team back here and remove those responsible from existence for his beloved Laura's death.

They were going to die, even if he didn't get any help from the Delta team.

At the end of the hallway he had found a set of stairs leading up, at the top of which was this locked door. He examined the lock and decided lock picking would be on the agenda the next time he received training from Laura's security team, but for now, beyond fiddling with hairpins he didn't have, or jimmying it with a credit card he didn't have, he was stuck.

Time to try the locked rooms.

Forcing those doors hopefully wouldn't make enough noise to attract any attention. He was about to turn and descend the stairs when he heard voices. He pressed his ear to the door and could distinctly hear footsteps and whispering.

And they sounded like they were coming directly toward him.

He rushed down the steps and into the hallway just as he heard the door above being unlocked. His heart pounding, he scrambled down the hall and opened the door to the one room he had found unlocked, the wine cellar, as footsteps echoed on the stairs. He closed the door behind him, then pressed his back against it.

Two voices vibrated through the door as they passed. A key hit a lock and he heard a door open, the voices disappearing as it was then closed. He pulled open the wine cellar door, stepped out into the hallway, closed the door then ran as quietly as he could to the end of the hall. The door at the top was closed, but there was a chance they hadn't locked it. He took the steps two at a time, reaching the door and grabbing the knob. He twisted, and it turned, his heart slamming repeatedly against his ribcage as his adrenaline rush almost overwhelmed him.

He pushed the door open slightly and peeked out through the sliver. He could see what looked like a large foyer with a double staircase leading to a second floor, several suits of armor from the middle ages standing guard in the corners, but nobody in sight.

A door closed below and he jumped. He stepped into the foyer then closed the door behind him as gently as he could. Looking around for a place to hide, he could see nothing, donning a suit of armor in comedy movie style the only thing occurring to him. It unfortunately took more than the ten seconds he figured he had, and knights back then were far too short to be wearing armor that would accommodate him.

He moved along the wall, away from the basement door, but toward what appeared to be the front door. As he got a better angle he noticed the front entrance had closets recessed on either side. The door behind him opened and he darted into the nearest closet, pushing himself behind the coats that filled it.

The two sets of footsteps faded away, the whispered voices seeming to have never stopped, but were quickly replaced by another set approaching rapidly, with purpose. It was an older man talking to an underling, Acton could recognize the tone from anywhere. He pushed deeper into the corner, the view now blocked.

The footsteps stopped in front of the very closet he was hiding in.

"I trust you'll have an enjoyable trip, Master."

It must be one of The Circle with their apprentice!

"To be honest, my son, I look forward to it being over. It has been a trying week, and I feel this will be a trying weekend. But by this time next year it will be forgotten, and all those who currently pose a problem will be no more."

"Speaking of, Master, what do you want done with the prisoners?"

There was a pause as Acton felt a rustling to his right, a hand reaching in the closet. He heard a coat lifted off the rack, the thick wooden hanger returned a moment later.

"Make sure the bodies are never found," came the reply as a jacket was donned.

"Very well, Master, I shall take care of it personally."

Acton wanted to jump from the closet, tear the two of them into pieces and stomp on their twitching carcasses. He didn't care if he died, he just wanted to make sure that the "master" died a horrible, terrifying death like his beloved Laura. His foot inched forward, he could feel the adrenaline fueled courage pumping through his veins as he reached to push the jackets aside and fling himself at those responsible.

The sound of a door opening to the outside cut his offensive short as he caught a glimpse of the two men stepping out, the door closing behind them. He fell back against the wall, his heart still slamming, tears of anger and frustration and sadness welling at the opportunity lost.

An opportunity that would most likely have had him killed without anything beyond a few good blows being landed.

He was armed with chair spindles, in a house with an unknown number of hostiles, most likely with real weapons.

Hostiles who would soon discover he was missing once the apprentice went to fulfill his orders.

I need to get out of here!

Hotel Lido, Geneva, Switzerland

Reading sat on the edge of his bed and lifted a foot, massaging life back into it then doing the same with the other as Dawson poured himself a glass of water from what would probably be a five quid bottle of water from the minibar.

"Want one?" asked Dawson, holding up the bottle.

Reading shook his head.

"I'm on a budget."

Dawson looked at the bottle then the glass.

"Umm, how much do you think this is?"

Reading shook his head.

"No bloody idea, but I'm sure it would be cheaper if it were airdropped in."

Dawson looked at the rate card perched on top of the minibar and his eyebrows shot up.

"How much?" asked Reading.

"Enough for politicians to be fired by an ignorant public."

Reading chuckled.

"Sixteen dollar orange juice?"

Dawson nodded. Reading was surprised the Sergeant Major was aware of the political scandal that had begun in London. *Nobody outside of England realizes a glass of orange juice at a fine London hotel is actually ten quid.*

Dawson held up his glass.

"Well, I might as well enjoy it." He took a sip and made an exaggerated sound of enjoyment.

"Good?"

He smiled.

"Best damned water I've ever had," said Dawson, rolling his eyes. He sat down in one of the two chairs in the room. "Now down to business. Did you make the transfer?"

Reading nodded, taking his suit jacket off and flinging it into the other chair.

"I assume it's some sort of tracking device?"

Dawson nodded.

"We'll be able to track him for about thirty-six hours, then we're tracking his sewage."

"Pleasant. What's your plan?"

"Go in, get them out, hopefully clean with no casualties on either side."

"Unlike Scotland Yard."

Dawson pursed his lips.

"I think even you know we went to great lengths to not hurt anyone."

Reading waved his hand, cutting off the conversation.

"What about Jim and Laura?"

"We assume they've been taken by the Rosicrucians. We snatched a load of intel last night that's being reviewed now. No luck so far, just routine World Bank business, but we're trying to find a pattern."

"To hell with the Rosicrucians. I don't give a damn about them. I want to get my friends back, then go home to my other friend who's still in a coma, fighting for his life."

"I understand that, but you're wrong to ignore the Rosicrucians. If you pursue your friends, they just may take notice of you."

"What's that supposed to mean?"

"Many have died in the past few days at their hands, including friends of *mine.*"

Reading sighed, dropping his head and massaging his temples.

"Do we have any idea where they were taken?"

"We're assuming San Marino. That's where this Martin Lacroix guy lives. If they're not there, then somebody there might know where they've been taken."

Reading stood up and grabbed the phone off the nightstand.

"I guess I'm going to San Marino."

Dawson rose, draining his water.

"Do you need anything?"

Reading tossed his phone to Dawson.

"Put your contact info in there in case I need to reach you. You have mine already?"

Dawson nodded as his fingers flew over the keyboard. Finished, he tossed the phone back. Reading caught it one handed and stuffed it in his pocket.

"Anything else?" asked Dawson.

"I'd ask for a weapon but I'd never get it on the plane."

Unknown Location

Acton remained hidden in the closet, it too close to the front door and potential freedom to abandon to the vast unknown of the house. He heard doors opening and closing outside as an automobile was loaded with luggage and its passenger, then the sound of an engine as it pulled away. Moments later the door opened then closed, the apprentice walking by Acton's position, the footsteps fading away.

Acton listened, but didn't hear a door open. He was quite certain he would have heard the basement door being unlocked and opened from here, which meant he had some time before they would discover he was gone. He pushed the coats aside and peered out to find nobody. Taking a tentative step, he leaned forward, his head poking out into the open, and still he could see no one.

He extricated himself from the closet as quietly as possible, evening out the hangers to disguise his having been there, then stepped toward the door.

Footsteps echoed from somewhere.

He grabbed the door knob and twisted, pulling open the door and stepping outside, gently closing it behind him. He ducked to the side, away from the windows framing the large carved wooden door and pressed himself against the wall. Surveying his surroundings, he found himself looking upon a large front yard with a circular gravel driveway leading to a road several hundred yards distant. A statue of a robed figure sat in the center of the driveway near the house, surrounded by rose bushes, the bright red flowers in full bloom. He couldn't make out the details as it faced away from him, but he had little doubt it represented Rosenkreuz himself.

Footsteps on the gravel had him jumping over the railing and hitting the ground, ducking. He shuffled away from the steps and hid behind several large bushes. A figure, robed in dark brown, his head hidden from sight, walked by, then climbed the steps and entered the house. Slowing his breathing, he looked out at the yard. It was immaculately maintained, a brilliant green stretching uninterrupted to the road below, the rolling hills dotted with farms, vineyards and large homes.

The style of homes reminded him more of Italy than Switzerland. It was definitely a possibility. He had no idea how long they had been unconscious, and Italy wasn't that far a drive from Geneva, definitely less than ten hours if he remembered correctly. The sun was high in the sky, suggesting early afternoon.

A lone car drove by on the road below.

If he did escape, he'd have a hell of a time making any distance, especially since he had no clue where he was or which direction to head.

All he did know was that if he tried to cover that lawn, the likelihood of him not being seen was slim to none.

He skirted along the edge of the house, ducking past each window until he reached the corner. Peering around the corner he found it clear, as was the lawn, stretching to a nearby vineyard with rows of grapevines less than a hundred yards away. Reachable if no one were looking, and if he were spotted, he could at least hide for some time.

But would probably still be caught.

He needed a phone, or a guaranteed clear way out of here, but he knew time was at a premium. They would discover he was missing any minute now.

He looked at the house. There were no video cameras on this side. He had to admit he hadn't thought to check the front. There were four windows on the ground floor, and four matching above. Lattice work covered most of the side, vines spreading out from the ground to the roof, a look Acton encountered often in his work, but never really liked. To him it looked unkempt, especially during the winter, giving a home a bleak, desolate look of abandonment.

He crawled to the first window and took a peek inside. It was a dining room, empty, with no phone or weapon in evidence. He moved to the next window and found the kitchen. Knives stored in a large wood block were prominently displayed on the counter, a phone on the wall, and a chef with his back to the window preparing lunch.

Acton dropped.

The third window revealed an informal dining area, probably for the help. It too was empty but he assumed not for long. If he were lucky, they would have lunch before killing him.

He was rarely lucky.

His heart raced, his chest tightening as he thought of the luckiest thing to happen to him.

Then he heard a woman's cry above him.

And he'd recognize it anywhere.

There was a window open on the second floor, only several inches, and as he cocked an ear he heard nothing else.

Was I imagining it?

He continued to the fourth window and peered inside but found thick curtains blocking his view. Around the corner was a large patio, swimming pool and all the luxuries he would expect in a house of this size, clearly owned by one of The Circle, most likely Lacroix, richer than rich.

There was a shed about thirty feet away, on the same side of the house as the vineyard was. If he could make it there without being seen, he could use it to hide his escape.

He glanced back at the partially open window on the second floor, pausing for a moment, then shook his head.

You imagined it. She's dead.

He sprinted for the shed.

Unknown Location

Professor Laura Palmer lay flat on the bed, her muscles aching from her ordeal. She still sobbed at the thought of her beloved James thinking she was dead. Her chair had been kicked over and a cloth with something pungent on it shoved over her mouth. She had been out cold within seconds, barely hearing the shot that had been fired. Since she hadn't been wounded, she assumed it was a blank, or fired into the floor near her.

When she had awoken she was lying in this room, still gagged, still bound. But alone.

After a few minutes of self-pity, she realized her only hope was to escape and find James or find help. She had climbed out of bed and made quick work of the zip ties behind her back, her retired SAS man Lt. Colonel Cameron Leather having explained that most zip ties were rated to 180 pounds of force if not much lower, an amount easily generated by pulling the wrists apart and shoving your bum out while smacking the outstretched hands against the buttocks.

With her hands free, she had loosened the gag, leaving it around her neck, then used the broken zip tie to shim the one around her ankles. It had taken moments, but now she had to not only escape the room, but whatever building she was in, and then find help.

She peered out the window and saw a lawn that abutted a vineyard. There were vines with lattice work that she could easily climb down. She unlocked the window then began to push it open when she heard a key at the door. She darted for the bed, shoving the gag back in her mouth and bouncing onto the mattress. The door began to open as she crossed her ankles and shoved her hands behind her back.

A robed figure entered sending her heart into her throat. Her eyes darted to the open window, then quickly returned to the man now approaching. He tossed his hood back, a smile she could only reveal as wicked smeared across his face, the lust in his eyes obvious.

"My master says I am to kill you and make sure the body is never found. He is gone for three days and never told me when to do it, or what I could do in between."

He licked his lips causing her to almost gag in disgust as he drew a knife out from under his robes. He straddled her hips, leaning in with the knife, playing it over her forehead, then down her nose to the gag. He slid the knife under the cloth then jerked back, slicing it apart.

She yelped.

"Shhh," he whispered. "You don't want more of the household joining us, now do you?" he grinned as his tongue flicked at her now exposed mouth. "Or maybe you do?" He pressed his lips against hers as she squeezed her mouth shut, closing her eyes, refusing to let the humiliation overwhelm her. She knew she had to keep her wits about her if she were going to survive.

He placed his full weight on her, his arousal obvious, his hands beginning to explore her body. She kept twisting her head away from his, her eye on the knife as often as possible, until finally his overwhelming lust got the better of him.

He put the knife on the nightstand so he could begin to undress her with both hands.

She flipped her hands palm upward and moved them to her sides. He began to reposition himself, his lewd grin angering her even more. Her hands darted out from the sides, swinging up, the man's startled expression bringing her the first bit of pleasure since the experience started. She boxed his ears hard, causing him to yelp, then with her left hand grabbed the knife while he was disoriented, burying it in his neck up to the hilt, cutting off any chance of his calling for help.

She twisted.

His eyes bulged, his hands flailing for the knife as she used it to push him off of her and onto the other side of the bed. A pool of crimson quickly stained the white sheets, spreading rapidly as his life fluid drained from him. She yanked the knife from his throat then jumped out of the bed. Wiping the blood off the blade and onto the sheets, she placed the knife on the nightstand, grabbed the pillow and tried to wipe all sense of his saliva off of her, then straightened her clothes so she could feel human again.

She was tired of being the victim.

Grabbing the knife, she searched him and found a single key on his person, a key she had to assume was a master key that opened everything. And a cellphone. Her heart skipped a beat as she gripped it in her hand. It was an iPhone 5S, so new it probably hadn't even made it out of its first week. She pressed the button and the screen demanded a thumbprint.

She looked at the now dead man she had taken it off of, wondering if a dead thumb print would work.

He's still warm.

She grabbed his thumb and pressed it against the sensor.

The phone unlocked and her mind flipped through everybody she could think of that she could call, and realized she knew almost no one's phone number, almost all of her calls being done from her contacts list in her own phone.

Suddenly a number popped in her head only because it had an easy to remember sequence, and it had been recently mentioned by James.

Footsteps walked by the door and she froze, cursing herself for not locking it. They faded away and she tiptoed to the door, locking it with the key she had found, then turned her attention back to the phone.

And it too was now locked.

She pressed her assailant's thumb against the sensor again then sent a quick text message so she wouldn't be heard. She sent several more with as many details as she could provide, then found the setting to disable the thumb scanning. She slipped the phone into her pocket then went to the window to see if it was clear.

And the only person she saw was her beloved James, racing toward the vineyards.

Outside Gendarmerie Bourg-de-Four, Geneva, Switzerland

Dawson resisted the urge to look at his watch. He hated waiting. He was a man of action, or movement at least. Sitting in the driver's seat of an SUV waiting made him antsy. He was used to it, somewhat, a major part of his job spent just waiting, but it didn't mean he had to like it.

And it usually ended with him getting to blow something up or shoot at someone.

Today they hoped none of that would be necessary.

He looked at his watch.

"They're late."

"Certainly not operating like a fine Swiss watch," agreed Niner, who Dawson was sure was equally on edge, his partner Jimmy one of the two of his team locked up.

Dawson activated his comm.

"Bravo Seven, report."

Atlas' voice boomed over the earpiece.

"Our hacked transfer order has been accepted and actioned," he said as Spock climbed in the back of the SUV giving a thumbs up. "It looks like they've got some sort of mechanical failure on one of the vehicles that's delaying things, over."

"Gee, I wonder how that could've happened," asked Niner as he eyeballed Spock.

Spock's eyebrow climbed his forehead.

"Why look at me? It's not my fault I only got through the first two pages of Oil Changes for Dummies."

"BD, looks like they're going to proceed with only two vehicles," said Atlas, tapped into the security camera feeds from the other side of the Atlantic. "You should see them exiting the rear now."

Dawson looked in his rearview mirror and saw the gates open and two paddy wagons pull out and turn toward their position, the gates slowly closing behind them.

"Which one has our guys?" he asked.

"Locater has them in the lead vehicle. A review of the footage confirms two inside with them plus a driver and shotgun. Rear vehicle has six in the back, two in the front."

"Roger that," replied Dawson as he pulled out into traffic, several vehicles behind the mini-convoy. "Bravo Two, report, over?"

Red's voice came through on the comm loud and clear.

"We're in position, over."

Dawson glanced in the rearview mirror at his team, relaying his message to all listening.

"Remember, we want to keep casualties to a minimum." He paused as they made a turn, the convoy still following the expected route. "Bravo Two, proceed when ready, over."

"Roger that, out."

Dawson was still several vehicles back of the convoy, Red's not yet in sight.

"Coming up on your left," came Red's voice over the comm. Dawson looked and saw the silver BMW 335is convertible with Red and Mickey swing into view, top down, gunning it in the left lane then cutting in front of them. Dawson honked his horn and shook his fist. Mickey flipped him the bird as did Red who then looked at each other and laughed, darting back out in the left lane and jumping ahead of the two police vehicles. They suddenly braked, cutting in front, causing them all to jerk to a halt.

Dawson pulled up directly behind the second paddy wagon and threw open his door, marching past the two blocked vehicles toward the silver BMW and its two belligerent occupants.

"What's the bloody idea!" he yelled with his near perfect Aussie accent. "Where'd you learn to drive, mate?"

"Oh piss off you limey bastard! Don't you have a new baby or something to coo over?"

Somebody yelled something in French and they all turned to see the driver of the lead vehicle standing on the running board, half out of the vehicle, yelling at them to get out of the way.

Dawson dropped his head, raising his hands, apologizing as he made his way back to his SUV, the BMW's tires lighting up behind him as Red peeled away. As Dawson passed the rear of the second vehicle he took a glance at the rear doors and smiled. Spock had had enough time to do his job, which was to exit from the passenger side of the vehicle at the same time Dawson did, but while all eyes were on the altercation at the front, he instead sprayed the seams of the rear doors of the second vehicle with an incredibly strong adhesive that would bind the two doors together long enough that the six armed officers in the back would be useless.

Now they were only dealing with six instead of twelve.

Unknown Location

James Acton's feet shoved against the grass, his arms pumping at his sides as he sprinted as hard as his sore body could manage toward the vineyard and possible freedom. As he approached he spotted an opening in the thick vines and made for it, bursting through to the other side. He dodged to the right then hit the ground, peering through the intertwined branches and at the house he had just left.

As he caught his breath he waited to see if anyone had spotted him. He could see no activity from the house and began to relax slightly, continuing to watch. Still nothing. He looked down the row of grapevines and saw another opening just a few feet down. He scrambled over and pushed through, again pausing. He couldn't see the house through the two rows of vines so he assumed they wouldn't be able to see him. Climbing to his feet, still crouching, he peered over the top of the row he was in and nearly choked.

Somebody was climbing out of the side window that had been opened. The slight frame suggested a woman, but the clothes had him crying out for joy, slapping his palms over his mouth as he did so.

Laura!

There was no doubt. He would recognize her across an ocean. He rushed back to the first row of grapevines and hit the dirt, crawling forward so his head was sticking out just enough to see her progress. She had made it to the ground and ducked behind some bushes, obscuring her from sight, but her bright white blouse still stood out, noticeable even from here.

And definitely noticeable to the two robed figures approaching the back corner of the house.

Milton Residence, St. Paul, Maryland

Gregory Milton dragged one foot forward, almost dropping it on the treadmill, then the other, repeating this tortuous routine over and over as the machine droned on at an impossibly slow pace. His recovery would be long and painful, but the doctors were shocked at his progress. When he had been shot in the back they had said he'd most likely never walk again, but they had been wrong.

He was supposed to have died that day, but he had survived, fate placing a doctor at the same gas station at the time of the shooting. Then the spinal surgeons had said he'd probably regain some feeling, but not mobility. Now they were all changing their stories and the possibility was now dangling out there that he might stage a full recovery.

He'd never forget the day those Delta Force men had arrived at his house to collect his best friend, James Acton. He had stood up in a rage, stunning everyone in the room, including himself.

His progress had been rapid since, his young daughter telling everyone her daddy was walking all the time now and was better.

And she was the reason he was putting himself through all this torture.

Her naïve observations were way off the mark, but that optimism and blind faith in her father the superhero gave him the strength to forge ahead. He didn't know how long it would take, but he figured he had at least fifteen years before his daughter might marry, and he was determined to dance at her wedding.

He just hoped it didn't take fifteen years.

The renewed optimism was what kept him going, what kept them all going. Plans to retrofit the house for a permanently disabled person were cancelled. They already had the ramp out front and the master bedroom had been moved to the main floor, the bathroom downstairs retrofitted to his needs, the second floor a distant memory. But the rest of the plans to make the entire house accessible had been cancelled after he had stood up.

Now there was hope, and despite the pain, the frustration, the aggravation, he did his physical therapy every day, without fail, no matter how rotten he felt.

And every day, there was a hint of progress.

He was a numbers man, so he recorded everything, and he could tell from week to week he was improving, even if it sometimes didn't necessarily feel like it. His sense of feeling in his legs and feet continued to improve dramatically, he could go longer and farther every week on the treadmill, and he was starting to lose the gut that had started and regain the muscle mass in his legs, already a full three inches on each thigh.

He no longer cried when he saw himself naked in the mirror, his tiny legs getting skinnier with each month of inactivity, his stomach gaining an inch a month as he slowly gave up, silently suffering on his own, his family only seeing the brave face he put on when others were in the room.

But now there was a future in front of him, and he was fighting to reach that light at the end of the tunnel sooner rather than later.

And nothing would stop him from accomplishing his goal.

Milton looked up as his wife entered the room, holding up his cellphone. He frowned, not liking anyone to see him like this.

"You need to see this," she said, holding up the phone.

"Not now," he gasped as he kept plodding forward to nowhere.

She stepped forward and hit the big red *Stop* button in the center of the treadmill's console.

"No, you need to see this, now."

He gave her his "I'm not happy with you" glare then looked at the phone, a text message displayed on its screen. His eyebrows shot up as his jaw dropped.

"Help me to my chair," he said, and Sarah came to his side. He draped his arm over her shoulder, she holding his back and he stepped off the treadmill and dropped unceremoniously into his wheelchair. He took the phone and quickly began to read.

Greg help us. James and I have been kidnapped. Trace this message.

"Jesus Christ," he muttered as he rolled himself to the kitchen. "Get me the phone," he said and Sarah immediately grabbed it, placing it on the table in front of him. She also found a pad and pen for him before he had a chance to ask. He smiled at her gratefully.

"Have you read all these?" he asked.

"No, just the first one," she said, sitting down.

"Here's the second one," he said, reading, "We went to Geneva to help Bravo Team then James and I were kidnapped. He thinks I'm dead so isn't looking for me. If I don't make it out of here, tell him I love him and was thinking of him."

Tears rolled down Sarah's cheeks as he fought his own. Jim was his best friend since college, and though he was Dean and Jim's boss, they had remained incredibly close. This closeness meant they had also become very close with Laura as well. They were family and they were in trouble.

"There were three?" prompted his wife.

He nodded. "I just killed my captor. This is his phone. They are the Rosicrucians and are very dangerous. They killed Stucco and his family plus some people here including children. The main man seems to be Martin Lacroix from the World Bank. Don't risk yourself just get in touch with Delta. They will know what to do. Love you guys."

Sarah wiped her tears away with the back of her hand, then reached across the table and grabbed a tissue, blowing her nose.

"What are you going to do?"

"Make the same damned phone call I did last time this happened."

"That took a long time if I remember."

"Yes, but this time I know who to ask for by name."

Mike "Red" Belme's Residence, West Luzon Drive, Fort Bragg, North Carolina

Atlas grabbed the ringing phone off the table in front of him. At the moment it was just him and Donald "Sweets" Peters, Marco's replacement after he had been killed during the Triarii business, manning their temporary Ops Center, Casey getting some rack time so they could be manned 24/7. Since the arrest of Jimmy and Jagger things had been tense as they tried to gather intel. Several of their "go to" guys had hacked the Swiss police system and as far as they could tell there had been an anonymous tip phoned in on men with weapons, and somehow the two professors had been "lost". There was no record of them arriving at the police station, or being booked. And camera footage confirmed this. Internal reports had no explanation, but Atlas had no doubt they were taken by the Rosicrucians.

The question was why.

The professors had nothing to do with the incident in Geneva, and their abduction suggested anyone getting involved was now forfeit, there was some other reason the Rosicrucians wanted them specifically, or the Rosicrucians didn't know who they had.

"Speak," his voice boomed.

"Hello, umm, this is Dean Gregory Milton. I was put through to this number so I'm not sure if I have the right person."

Atlas' eyebrows narrowed. He knew the name from somewhere, and it didn't take a rocket surgeon to figure out it had to do with one of the two professors since this man had identified himself as a Dean.

"Let's assume they got it right," said Atlas. "What can I do for you?"

"I'm hesitant to speak over the phone, however I just received several emergency texts from the fiancée of one of my professors—"

"Professor Palmer?"

"Yes! Good, so I am talking to the right person, thank God! It sounds like they've been kidnapped."

"They have. Do you have any information for me?"

"I have the phone number from where the texts were sent. With it maybe you'll be able to trace where they were sent from?"

Atlas put the phone on speaker so Sweets could hear.

"You're on speaker, sir. Please relay the information to my colleague."

Milton quickly provided the phone number, along with the time of the texts then the actual contents. There was nothing really earthshattering, the intel merely confirming their hypothesis. But the phone number could prove invaluable in rescuing the professors, and finding where Lacroix might be at this moment.

"Got it," said Sweets between chews of a trademark chocolate bar, his sweet tooth already legendary in The Unit. "The phone was in San Marino and as far as I can tell, is still pinging off the same tower."

"Relay the coordinates to BD," ordered Atlas. "Sir, thank you for the information. We'll take it from here and have the professors contact you when we have them."

"Thank you very much."

Atlas ended the call and listened while Sweets passed the intel on to BD, their rescue op still underway.

"Good work," came Dawson's voice through the comm. "Relay the intel to Special Agent Reading. He's on his way there now."

"Will do, BD. Oh, and word just came down from above on Stucco."

"The usual?"

"Yup."

"How's Casey taking it?"

"As good as can be expected. He's getting some rack time now. They're calling it a natural gas explosion—"

"Of course they are."

"—so the families will never know what really happened. I think that has Casey pissed."

"He's not alone."

"Definitely not."

"We'll be back for the memorial service, but first we need to do a little house cleaning here."

Red's voice suddenly cut in.

"Bravo Two here, ready to proceed with phase two, over."

Sweets looked at Atlas with a smile on his face.

"Good hunting, Sergeant Major."

On route to Federico Fellini International Airport, Rimini, Italy

Martin Lacroix sat back in the plush leather of his Maybach 62. He pressed the button to recline as his chilled scotch on the rocks clinked in the crystal glass, prepared by his chauffeur just before he climbed in.

This is the life.

Sometimes he forgot how fortunate he was. He had come from nothing, an orphan, and had clawed his way through school despite the best efforts of those around him who would have him give up and join their lives of pathetic existence. He worked part time jobs, saved and scrimped where he could, secretly saving for his future, all the while studying every waking free moment so he could do well in school, knowing it was the key to a future better than he faced.

And all the hard work had paid off. Scholarships and accolades followed his hard work, and he went to university, then medical school, and became a doctor, soon heading into the research field.

Which was where his late master had found him.

Many conversations over many years had led his master to invite him into The Order, and once inside, he realized how little he truly knew, and how much he wanted to learn it all, to take advantage of it all.

And the only sacrifice was love.

He never understood why. Perhaps it was pillow talk The Order wanted to minimize, perhaps it was to honor the Founder, who had been a bachelor his entire life. Whatever the reason was, it didn't bother him, he preferred the life of a bachelor.

It brought him some of his greatest pleasures, and most of his problems.

He regretted most of his transgressions. In fact, if he had to admit it, he regretted them all, especially when his victims had to die. There was no reason for Maria Esposito to have to die. If he hadn't been arrested, he would have called his man and money would have been offered that very morning. Instead he had rotted for so long before he even got his phone call, that the girl had already been interviewed by the police and met with prosecutors. At that point she had to die, and die quickly, to prevent the charges from moving forward.

Such a pretty girl.

From what his alcohol impaired mind could remember.

As to the others, there was nothing he could do about that. He had known from the moment that first man had burst through the door that people were going to die, and die violently. The Order demanded it. Their secrets were absolute, the anonymity of The Order never to be risked. He had bought into it initially, his embarrassment and anger over what had happened to him all-consuming, but his decision to have markers left behind so those dying or discovering their loved ones dead would know it was *he* who was responsible, was foolhardy at best.

He was heading for the quarterly meeting of The Circle, and he had a sneaking suspicion it might be his last. He had been an embarrassment, a problem, and now he had allowed one of The Circle to be identified by others, if they were smart enough to put two and two together. The only thing that could save him would be finding the Catalyst, and right now he had every single resource available to him scouring the world to find out what happened to this one forgotten item of a massive collection, auctioned off piece by piece to the highest bidder.

They had never been closer, and through his sins, they might actually find that which had been lost centuries earlier over the love of a woman.

Perhaps that's why?

243

It was as good an explanation as any for why The Circle was so adamant that they all be bachelors, and all be men. Traditions were hard to break, and attempts in the past to let women in had proven unsuccessful, but he had no doubt they eventually would be. There were simply too many female researchers doing cutting edge work now. A few decades ago it was easy to ignore women since they were rarely given the chance, but now things were different. The one way The Order did recognize this was through funding. The Order didn't care what sex was doing the research if it might be of interest to them. It just meant that if the research were being performed by a woman, it was more likely her male assistant would be offered membership than she.

Women in The Order!

He shuddered at the thought. There was enough sexual tension in the world. The last thing he needed was to have the temptation of women at the quarterly meeting.

Women in The Circle!

That he could never see.

Then again, he never thought he'd see the Catalyst.

He pulled out his phone and dialed his apprentice, eager for news.

Unknown Location

Laura Palmer hid behind several bushes as she regained her bearings. She had seen James head into the vineyard, seeming to use a shed in the backyard as a blind.

And it had worked.

Which meant using the same plan again seemed reasonable. She drew the knife she had taken off her would be rapist and began to rise when she heard footsteps. She dropped back down on her haunches, but knew if they were at all observant, she would be seen. She needed a plan and fast.

The footsteps were coming from the backyard, and there were voices, which suggested at least two. If there were more, she probably didn't stand a chance, but two, along with surprise, she just might.

She jumped to her feet and covered the distance between her hiding place and the corner of the house just as the first person, covered head to toe in the same dark brown robe she had seen on her attacker, rounded the corner. A second followed immediately behind him.

She lunged forward, burying her knife in the first man's stomach, withdrawing as quickly as she could, not concerned with killing him, merely with taking him out of the fight. She plunged forward again, but the second man was ready for her, stepping aside and striking down with the edge of his opened hand on her forearm.

She yelped, dropping the knife as his other fist swung at her head. She ducked and thrust an uppercut at his chin, connecting, but not with the force she had hoped, still exhausted from her ordeal. She saw something move from the corner of her eye, but she ignored it, realizing if it was another attacker, she needed to disable this one before he arrived.

A punch landed on her left breast, leaving her wincing as she took several steps back. The man pulled a dagger from his robes and she gulped, realizing this could be the end. She made a stand, digging her right foot into the ground behind her, her fists raised. The man lunged forward and she blocked with her left hand, swinging it outward and catching the man's right arm, flinging it into the wall.

The knife scraped on the brick, momentarily getting entangled in the vines winding their way skyward.

She pressed the momentary advantage, snap kicking at his groin, instead catching his upper thigh as the man twisted to protect himself. Her leg still in the air, she leaned back and kicked again, this time at his head.

She connected.

His chin was tossed back with a grunt. She reached forward with her right hand, grabbing him by the wrist and digging her mid-length nails into the soft underbelly of his inner wrist.

He cried out and dropped the knife, she raising her knee and connecting with the family jewels. The man doubled over and she was about to drop an elbow on his head when the figure from earlier suddenly rushed forward. She spun to face him then she ducked, tears filling her eyes as the man whom she loved like no other swung a shovel, catching her assailant square in the face.

He crumpled to the ground.

"James!" she cried, careful to keep her voice low.

He dropped the shovel and grabbed her, pulling her into his arms as he showered her with kisses.

"Oh God, you're alive, thank God you're alive! I thought you were dead, I was sure you were dead! If I ever thought there was a chance, I never would have left. I'm so sorry!"

She hugged him back, hard, as if she hadn't seen him in months. It was a reunion she thought would never happen. It was obvious the intent of these people was to have them killed, but it was their own rules that had set her free. Bachelors only, no relationships, only carnal one-night stands permitted.

Meaning a horny young man was sent to kill a woman who could never complain or report to the authorities that he had raped her.

Send a sexually fulfilled man, perhaps she'd have been dead the moment he walked through the door.

The phone in her pocket vibrated and she jumped, breaking the embrace. She pulled it out and showed it to James.

"Where'd you get that?"

"From the man who tried to kill me in the bedroom upstairs."

"Oh my God, that was you!" James looked crestfallen. "I thought I imagined hearing you. I'm so ashamed!" he cried, his voice cracking.

She squeezed his cheek as she swiped the screen to access what appeared to be a text message.

She smiled, showing it to James.

If you two are done, I will be in the front yard with a car in thirty seconds. Hugh.

"How does he know we're here?" asked James.

"I sent Greg some texts."

"But—"

She put a finger over his lips.

"Why don't we ask him?" she said with a smile and a wink. She turned and ran toward the front of the house, James following her. As she rounded the corner she saw a blue Renault driving up the laneway at a casual pace. It rounded the circle, stopping in front of them as they stepped out from the bushes. James jumped in the front seat, Laura in the back, as Reading hit the gas, pulling away just as the front door burst open, half a dozen dark robed figures rushing into the driveway, blocking their escape.

"Blast!" yelled Reading, putting the car in reverse and flooring it. The car whined backward as the men rushed after them. Reading hit the brakes, shifted to first and surged toward them, cranking the wheel at the last second, sending the back end sliding toward their pursuers, the satisfying thumps of bodies discovering the futile physics of human versus automobile heard several times. Reading pulled away, around the sculpture in the center of the driveway, skirting it in the opposite direction of which he had come, then turned onto the laneway.

Within moments they were roaring down the road, nobody in pursuit.

James stuck a hand between the front seats and grabbed Laura's hand, squeezing it tight, then turned to their friend as he expertly executed their escape.

"What the hell are you doing here?" asked Acton.

"I could ask the same bloody thing!"

"We were kidnapped, thank you very much."

"And I was called in by the Bravo Team to help two of their men escape arrest by the Swiss police, and then find out you two have been kidnapped by forces unknown!" He shook his head as he made a turn. "I'm liable to lose my blasted post for this!"

"Border's coming up!" announced Laura, sighing in relief as she realized their ordeal was essentially over. Then a thought popped in her mind. "Where are we? Do we need passports?"

"No, you're in San Marino. It's an open border," replied Reading as he slowed down, driving through the ancient city gates that marked the border, and into Italy.

"Where to now?" asked James.

"Back to your universities if you know what's good for you," growled Reading.

James shook his head. "These people need to be stopped."

"Bloody hell," muttered Reading. "You two don't know *when* to stop!" He glanced in the rearview mirror at Laura. "Surely you aren't going along with this as well."

"Absolutely. These people are dangerous. Billions of lives could be at stake if they were to succeed."

"Bloody hell!" cried Reading, hammering on the brakes and bringing the car to a stop at the side of the road. "Why don't you two tell me what the blazes is going on?"

And for the next ten minutes they explained everything they knew, Reading interrupting from time to time with his own questions or curses.

"Bottom line is we don't know what their plan is or what they're capable of, but if they're willing to kill over people just seeing a file folder with a symbol on it, it must be bad," summed up James. "So are you in?"

Reading scowled at James then put the car back in gear, spinning the tires on the gravel shoulder and bursting back onto the pavement.

"If I'm not, you two will get yourselves killed, or worse, in a damned coma like Martin."

"How's he doing?" asked Laura, reaching forward and squeezing her friend's shoulder.

"No change." Reading's eyes glassed over. "I'm not optimistic."

The phone vibrated in Laura's pocket and she jumped, pulling it out. The call display simply said, 'M'. She held it up for the others to see.

"M as in Martin Lacroix?" suggested Reading.

James shook his head.

"No, M as in Master."

Route des Acacias, Geneva, Switzerland

"Equipment check," ordered Dawson as he tapped his body armor and checked his weapon, traffic at a standstill, the two police vehicles still directly in front of him. The light turned green and the first vehicle began to move forward, advancing into the intersection. The brake lights on the second vehicle went out as it moved too.

Suddenly the squeal of tires erupted ahead and Dawson watched as Red's BMW rental whipped through the intersection and impaled itself at almost forty miles per hour into the driver's side door.

"Let's go!" yelled Dawson as three doors of the SUV flew open and his team advanced. Dawson ran up the driver's side of the rear paddy wagon. The door opened and Dawson reached in, placing the Taser directly against the man's neck, stunning him as Spock did the same on the other side. Zip ties to the wrists, through the steering wheel, and his man was out of commission. Pounding could be heard from the rear of the vehicle as the occupants worked the glued door.

The driver of the lead vehicle had made the mistake of opening his door, giving Niner clear access to nail him with the Taser then train his weapon on the passenger. Dawson loaded a probe on his Taser as he ran up to the door, juicing him. Niner began to zip tie the two men as Dawson reached into the BMW, the engine steaming and Red still sitting behind the steering wheel, pushing the airbags back.

"You okay?" asked Dawson, undoing the seatbelt.

"Yeah. Safety systems are a bit better than on most things I get to crash."

Red climbed up onto the seat then stepped over to the passenger side and out onto the pavement. He waved off Dawson, who immediately returned to the rear of the first vehicle. He pounded twice.

"Anybody in there?" he asked, winking at Spock whose MP5K was trained on the door, along with Mickey who had been let out nearby to avoid risking him in the accident.

"Just two shaken and stirred men who enjoy long walks and cuddling by the firelight," came Jimmy's voice through the metal doors.

"And your company?"

"Visions of sugar plums dancing through their heads."

"Stand back, we're blowing the doors."

Spock placed the charge then prepped the trigger as they all stood to either side of the vehicle.

"Fire in the hole!" yelled Spock, who then pressed the detonator.

There was a small explosion and the doors flew open, the sound Dawson was certain deafening on the inside of the tin can. Spock and Mickey jumped inside, pulling the slightly disoriented pair out as sirens could be heard fast approaching in the distance.

"Let's go!" yelled Dawson, "we're about to have company!"

He rushed back to their SUV, jumping in the driver's seat and putting the vehicle in gear as the rest of the team climbed in. With the last door shut, he pulled around the three vehicles just as the rear doors flew open, one of the trapped officers inside sailing out feet first, almost as if he had been used as a human battering ram by the others inside.

Must have been the rookie.

Dawson rounded the smoking BMW and turned right, flooring it, dodging back and forth through the traffic as he put distance between them and the attack.

"Anybody hurt?" he asked, glancing in the rearview mirror.

Heads shook in response.

"My ears are ringing," said Red, "and I'll be stiff in the morning, but I'll live."

"And our friendly Swiss hosts? Did any get killed?"

A round of "Negatives" had him breathing easy. The operation had gone exactly according to plan, everyone was intact on both sides, and now they just had to make their getaway clean.

"Wings, report."

Wings' voice squawked over the comm.

"You've got half a dozen squad cars behind you, about three klicks back, plus four more headed right for you on the other side. You need to reach the next intersection before them or you'll be blocked, over."

"Roger that," said Dawson, flooring it. He could see the intersection in the distance, and beyond that, the flashing lights of the police. "Atlas, find us an alternate rendezvous, over."

"Take a right at this intersection," said Atlas over the comm. "Straight for two miles then there's a large parking lot at a stadium that has nothing going on there today. Should be lots of space for Wings to land, over."

"Wings, scout ahead and make sure."

"No need, I can see it from here, lots of space, but you're not going to be first, over."

"Shit!" yelled Dawson. "Buckle up boys, this is going to be rough."

He heard seatbelts clicking and Jesus handles being grabbed as he went full throttle toward the intersection. Suddenly overhead he heard the thumping of rotors and dust begin to fill the air around them, brake lights blazing on as he dodged between the last few cars, the flashing of police cars already turning into the intersection to block him filling his field of vision.

The SUV shook as Dawson cut it hard to the right, his side sliding into a squad car with a terrific crunch of metal. He kept the accelerator floored and pulled away from the crash and down the road Atlas had indicated.

Dawson looked behind and all he saw was a cloud of dust with brilliant red brake lights and flashing police lights lost in the confusion. To the right he could see the stadium approaching, the parking lot nearly empty, the gates down. He cranked the wheel to the right, blasted through the flimsy wood barrier and out into the sea of pavement where he raced toward a completely open area to the left.

"Let's go, Wings!" yelled Dawson as he screeched to a halt, the team exiting the vehicle and grabbing their gear. The thunder of Wings' helicopter overhead ended any further conversation as dust and litter was whipped about. Moments later the skids bounced down and the team loaded into the back as the confusion at the intersection cleared, the police cars resuming the chase toward the stadium.

Dawson climbed aboard last, sliding the door shut as Wings lifted off, angling the chopper directly toward the lead vehicle causing the driver to slam on his brakes as Wings blasted overhead, leaving the Swiss police in disarray, unable to pursue them. Wings kept low over the roof tops, his transponder disabled to keep him off standard civilian scopes and within minutes they were landing outside the city in a field where they had pre-positioned another SUV.

Dawson let Spock drive after all eight of them were in the new vehicle, Dawson acting as navigator as they headed for their new digs found earlier in the day, confident this time they hadn't been tracked.

Jimmy looked at Niner.

"So, what took you so damned long?"

Niner slugged him in the shoulder. Hard.

On route to Federico Fellini International Airport, Rimini, Italy

Martin Lacroix frowned as he heard the call go to voicemail. His apprentice had never missed a call in all the years he had known him, or if he had, there was a near immediate callback. It was almost a matter of pride with the man who had been with him for almost fifteen years, the last five as his finally selected apprentice. He knew the other candidates had been profoundly disappointed, and he had given them all the option to leave his employ and pursue other opportunities within The Order, but there had been no takers, for they knew the advantages of working directly for one of The Circle, apprentice or not.

He continued to stare at the phone, waiting for the callback, but it never came.

Perhaps something went wrong with the executions?

Ordering the deaths of the two professors hadn't fazed him at all. With the staged death of the fiancée gathering nothing beyond a vague reference to the cataloging of an estate, he knew there was nothing further to gain from Professor Acton, and since she hadn't been in his life at the time, the beautiful Professor Palmer had been of no use beyond the pawn she had already played.

She was *beautiful.*

He felt a twinge as he thought of her.

She would have been fun to wrestle with.

But she was dead by now, unless his apprentice had decided to have a little fun of his own. He felt a flash of jealousy that an underling should have some fun when he couldn't, but it passed. His last taste of fun had led to the current situation.

The phone still hadn't rung.

He dialed another number and it was immediately answered.

"Yes, Master, how may I help you?" asked the breathless voice.

"What's wrong? I can't reach my apprentice."

"The two professors have escaped. They had help from the outside. Your apprentice, Master, I'm sorry, but—" There was a pause, as if the man were terrified to say the words Lacroix already knew.

"He's dead."

"Yes, Master. One other is dead, several more are injured. They had help from the outside. A car with a single occupant. We got the license plate and are trying to track it now. All we do know is they definitely have left San Marino already."

Lacroix's jaw was clenched tight, his blood pressure building as the rage within seethed, it not yet finding an outlet. His fist flew into the passenger seat rest in front of him, startling his driver who didn't risk even glancing in the rearview mirror.

"They must be found," growled Lacroix.

"Yes, my master, we are doing everything we can."

"Very well."

"Master, wait! I have news!"

The excitement in the man's voice conveyed the subject matter to Lacroix better than any words could.

"You've found it."

"Yes, sir, well sort of. We found the estate that had the auction, and one of our operatives paid the auction house a visit."

"And?"

"And we found the buyer. It was part of a lot, so it wasn't purchased specifically. We've got two operatives heading there now."

"Where?"

"Barcelona."

"Tell them to exercise utmost caution. This could be the most important mission of their lives."

"I already have, my master, but I will remind them again immediately."

"Very well. Keep me informed. The Circle will want regular updates on your progress."

"Absolutely, Master."

Lacroix killed the call, tossing the phone on the plush leather beside him. If his people could find the long lost Catalyst, he would go down in history as one of the greatest members of The Order ever, and it might even put him in contention for Number One's position should he die. Though Number One had his own apprentice, upon the death, a vote was held amongst the surviving members of The Circle to determine who should be the new Number One, then they were all renumbered according to number of ballots received.

As the latest member to join The Circle, he was automatically Number Eight, a position he was certain he would maintain should a vote have been held two days ago. But now with the Catalyst almost within their grasp, he had a funny feeling he'd place much higher in the balloting.

And if he played his cards right, he just might become the most powerful man in The Order.

Then no one would be able to criticize him ever again.

Or delay his plans.

The Founder had taught it was imperative to keep the world's population at a safe level. That level had been exceeded in Europe and the result was the Dark Ages, not ended until the Black Death leveled things back out. But with advances in science and medicine, the world population had grown at an alarming rate during the twentieth century, with no diseases able to gain a foothold and bring the population down to acceptable levels.

Yes, those levels changed with time, the five hundred million number in his mind too low. His interpretation of the teachings was that the world population should be at a level sustainable for the planet. With modern farming techniques, that meant the ability of the planet to feed the population had grown. The problem was no longer food, it was other types of resources. The planet was being stripped of its resources to build massive cities and structures that could never be maintained indefinitely without outside replacements. Already companies were looking to the moon, Mars and the asteroid belt. They knew there was no way to sustain this rate of growth.

And once the resources ran out, the entire population, whether it was seven billion or twenty billion, would suffer, and potentially wipe each other out in a battle for what remained.

But if the population could be brought under control before the crisis occurred, there would be thousands of years' worth of resources for that smaller, sustainable population. He personally felt one billion was a reasonable number. It was large enough to maintain cultural and genetic diversity, to populate the entire planet in reasonable pockets, and to sustain an economy of global proportions where capitalism could still thrive.

The question for The Order had always been how to achieve that. Disease had always been believed to be the only way, but he had come up with a different method that he was certain would work, and could be implemented within a generation without the public even knowing. In fact, it was already being implemented, with those on the left and right cheering it on, totally unaware of how this great advance could be twisted and turned into the greatest population die off in the history of humanity.

And if he were to lead The Order, he could implement it within less than five years, leaving the planet with his one billion target, living in the richest nations of the world, leaving the remainder of the planet to sustain and improve the lifestyles of those that survived and would flourish in the new reality, with The Order carefully guiding things in the background.

Rue de la Tour de I'lle, Geneva, Switzerland

"What have you got for us?" asked Dawson, the secure phone on speaker with Atlas.

"When the professors escaped they managed to steal the apprentice's phone. I've traced the number they think might belong to Lacroix and I'm showing his last location at an airport in Rimini, Italy."

"So he's flown the coop," said Jimmy. "Where to?"

"We've got a private flight leaving there not even an hour ago. It's due to land in Colmar, France in less than an hour."

Dawson's head bobbed. "Good. Niner and Mickey should already be in the air thanks to Professor Palmer letting us borrow her jet again. Relay the new info to them; they might be able to get there first."

"Casey's doing that now, already confirmed that they should get there about ten minutes before," replied Atlas. "Professor Palmer's plane should then be refueled and back in Geneva within a little over an hour to pick you up."

"Equipment?"

"Our French connection is already on his way with everything we asked for. Should rendezvous with the advance team about an hour after they arrive."

Dawson smiled as there was a knock on the door.

"Excellent work," he said. "Hold on for a second, we've got someone at the door."

Jimmy and Jagger covered the door as they waited for the second coded knock.

It came and Jimmy opened the door, Jagger still with his weapon trained on the entrance until the new arrival was recognized and confirmed clear. Dawson saw Jagger's shoulders relax as Wings and Red entered, closing the door behind them.

"Good news?" asked Dawson.

Red smiled, looking between Jimmy and Jagger.

"I think they're going to love them."

Dawson grinned as Jimmy and Jagger frowned.

"Do we *really* need to go that far?" asked Jimmy. "I'm willing to hike it out if necessary."

"Hey, you're the ones who were stupid enough to let yourselves get caught," said Mickey with a grin, flopping down on a nearby cot. "Besides, it's not like we're crossing the Atlantic. You'll survive."

Dawson turned back to the comm unit sitting on the table.

"What's the status on their files?"

"We hacked the system and removed all electronic records of those two bozos ever having been there along with their prints and mug shots."

"Paper records?"

"Swiss policy is electronic records only. Some green initiative."

"Thank God for the eco-movement," said Jimmy. "I'd really like to come back to this country sometime."

"Looks like we got lucky," said Dawson. He pointed to a pile of supplies sitting on a table, then the bathroom. "Now why don't you two ex-cons get yourselves ready?"

"But if there's no records, do we really need to do this?" protested Jimmy. "Come on, BD, live dangerously!"

Spock's eyebrow shot up as Dawson's head dropped, giving Jimmy the eye.

"Red, get your knife. I want their heads shaved as closely as yours."

Red stood, pulling his Bowie knife from its sheath.

"Fine! Fine!" said Jimmy, waving Red off and grabbing the bag from the table. "I think you guys just want to see me in lipstick again."

"Again?" asked Jagger as he followed Jimmy into the bathroom. "Do I need to be worried stuck in here with you?"

There was a smack of a hand hitting an ass.

"You're not my type," said Jimmy as the door closed, Jagger's reply cut off.

"Touch my ass again and I'll—"

Milton Residence, St. Paul, Maryland

Gregory Milton had sat at the kitchen table since the moment he had made the call to Fort Bragg. It had been hours, and his newly found sense of feeling in his legs and particularly his ass were starting to really bother him. His wife sat at the table with him, silently surfing on her iPad to keep him company, she quickly having discovered he was in no mood to chat.

His best friend—scratch that, his best *friends*—were in trouble and he had no idea what was going on.

"We'll have the professors contact you when we have them."

That was the last he had heard.

Surely they would have rescued them by now?

Then again, they were in a different country, there was travel time, maybe they had their own priorities?

There were dozens of perfectly plausible reasons for not having heard yet, and every time he reached for the phone to make a call, Sarah would reach out and place her hand gently over his.

"Give them time," she would say. "You calling won't speed things along."

He shifted in his chair, his right ass cheek finally demanding relief.

"Can I get you anything?" the ever attentive Sarah asked.

He shook his head, then stopped as his stomach rumbled.

"Tea biscuits and a glass of milk?"

She winked at him, knowing exactly what he was doing. Occupying her time. She stood up and poked her head out into the hallway leading to the stairs.

"Niskha, do you want to help Mommy bake tea biscuits for Daddy?"

The reply was the pounding of tiny feet on the floor overhead, then the much less confident footsteps on the stairs.

He'd never tire of hearing those little feet and his chest tightened a bit as he realized that in a few years, those feet wouldn't be so little anymore.

The phone rang and they all jumped as he grabbed it. He didn't recognize the call display.

"Hello?"

"Greg, it's me, Jim!"

He felt a sense of relief wash over him as every muscle in his body relaxed, including some he didn't remember being able to feel anymore.

"Thank God! And Laura?"

"She's right here beside me."

"Hi Greg!" he heard her call.

"We're here with Hugh, still in Italy. We managed to escape and I think we're safe now. But we need your help."

"Name it," said Milton, grabbing the pen and pad of paper.

"I need you to find an old photograph."

"A photograph? What the hell for?"

"Daddy swore!" whispered Niskha to her mother's leg.

And when it was explained to Milton, he realized the danger his friends had been in was far from over.

Colmar-Houssen Airport, Colmar, France

Niner stepped onto the tarmac first and shivered. It was damned cold, and in the too near distance the mountains made it clear why, their snowcapped peaks lost in the covering of snow stretching down the entire height into the nearby valley. Mickey stopped beside him, admiring the view.

"Man I love mountains," he muttered, then stepped toward the small terminal. Once inside it didn't feel that much warmer to Niner, which was something he found quite often in these types of locations, central heating seeming to be a North American necessity, everywhere else a luxury. A fire roared in a nearby hearth, and they both walked over to warm themselves as they waited for their baggage to be brought inside.

The door opened letting in a rush of cold air as a lone staff member relegated to the outdoor duties pulled their two bags in on a trolley. One was a bright purple, the other lime green, Red's idea of a joke.

"Your covers are two gay lovers on a nice romantic getaway to the mountains for some skiing, hot chocolate and rubdowns in front of the fireplace," he had said. "Who knows where the evening could lead?"

Niner had jumped up and down, quickly clapping his hands together while Mickey had groaned.

"You had to partner me with him on this, didn't you? You know he'll take it too far."

Red grinned.

"I'm counting on it."

The man who had brought their luggage in had looked old enough to be Niner's grandfather, causing Niner to feel a twinge of guilt until he witnessed the old man slinging them around like they were filled with feathers. Instead of offering to help, Niner took a moment to get into character.

He decided to have fun, channeling Eddie Murphy from Beverly Hills Cop—hands on the hips, shoulders shoved forward, elbows back, head cocked to the side with his lips puckered. He turned to Mickey who Niner was sure had to clench his sphincter to avoid shitting his pants in laughter.

Mickey decided to play the alpha and stepped toward the lone counter, a woman who might have been the luggage guy's wife manning it.

"Bonjour, parlez vous Anglais?" he asked.

"But of course, monsieur."

Mickey pushed his fake passport forward. "You have a vehicle for us, under Green?"

"Of course, monsieur. It is outside, fully gassed and ready to go." The woman held out a pair of keys which Mickey took, handing them to Niner.

"Thanks, sweetie," whispered Niner, putting his head on Mickey's shoulder.

The woman smiled at him.

Niner flashed her one in return.

"Would you like Heinrich to put your luggage in your vehicle?" she asked, pointing to the old man.

Mickey shook his head.

"No, I think we can manage. Thank you very much."

Niner walked over to the two bags and stood beside them. Mickey picked up his own bag while Niner stared at his, hands on his hips. Mickey shook his head and picked up the second bag as Niner skipped behind him, wiggling his fingers at the lady behind the counter in a fabulous goodbye.

Moments later they were in the SUV, the engine running, a feeble heat pushing through the vents as the cooled engine slowly warmed up. Niner pointed at a set of landing lights in the distance.

265

"That must be Lacroix."

Mickey nodded toward a convoy of three black sedans that had just arrived.

"I'm guessing those are for him."

Niner nodded.

"It's good to be the king."

On route to Barcelona, Spain

One of the many things Acton loved about Europe was the size. From Barcelona to San Marino, the Alsace in France to Switzerland, it all fit in the size of Texas, with heavy populations throughout, which meant plenty of fast, regular flights.

As soon as his good friend Greg had found the photo, he was able to use it to track down where and when the auction had been held, then the Delta guys had been able to find the purchaser located in Barcelona.

After a brief debate, Reading the only dissenting opinion, they were on a flight for Barcelona, hopefully ahead of their opponents, but most likely not. The Order would have operatives scattered throughout the world. Most likely they had already dispatched a team, and perhaps even had the item in their possession. And if they did, any hope of stopping the Rosicrucians might be lost.

Acton wasn't one to believe in magic or special powers, but he was one to believe in science and the fact some knowledge was lost over time. A prime example being Damascus steel. An advanced form of sword making employed for centuries, now lost, no one knowing how the swords were made, or what made them of such strength, the gun having replaced the need.

How much other knowledge had been lost to history? How many claims had been made over the years of rediscovered technology, rediscovered methods or medicines? As an archeologist he could think of dozens off the top of his head. But a magic cube? That he doubted just as he doubted the power the Triarii claimed the crystal skulls possessed.

To him the Catalyst, as The Order called it, provided a golden opportunity. To him it was bait, pure and simple. If they could possess it, then use it against The Order, they just might be able to stop them from whatever it was they were trying to accomplish.

They just had to get there first.

The seatbelt indicator chimed and a flight attendant who spoke an impressive number of languages began to announce their descent into Barcelona. Acton prepared himself as Laura and Reading continued to sleep. How either of them could was beyond him.

He decided to let them rest for an extra few minutes, now wishing he had been able to relax enough to do the same.

Looking at Laura, her head lolled to the side, facing him, he felt an overwhelming rush of emotions as he recalled how he felt when her death had been faked, at how close she had come to being raped repeatedly then murdered, and how he had left her behind, convinced she *was* dead, despite his hearing her cry out.

He still felt ashamed.

He fished a handkerchief from his pocket and dabbed his eyes dry. As he stuffed it back in his pocket he felt a hand on his arm. He turned to look at Laura who had a concerned expression on her face.

"Are you okay?"

He nodded.

"Sorry, just remembering."

She sat up and took his arm in both hands, squeezing as she leaned over and gave him a comforting kiss.

"It's over. Forget about it."

He nodded, placing his forehead against hers.

"It would be over if it weren't for you two," muttered Reading, apparently not as asleep as Acton had presumed. "If it weren't for you two,

I'd be in London, relaxing in front of the telly, watching Foyle's War or some other fine example of British television, while I devoured a bag of crisps. But no! Here I am on some foolhardy journey to Spain, chasing down a magic box, so you two don't get yourselves killed."

Laura reached over and squeezed their friend's arm.

"And we appreciate it very much, don't we James."

"Absolutely!" he said, grinning. "We'd appreciate it even more if he stopped bitching about it!"

Reading glared at him and Acton laughed, reaching over Laura and giving the man a gentle punch in the shoulder as their plane touched down.

"Into the thick of it again," muttered Reading as the plane turned onto the taxiway.

Acton kept the smile on his face as he peered out the window, but deep down, he couldn't help but wonder if Reading were right, and that they shouldn't be here. They had escaped the Rosicrucians once almost through blind luck. With their precious Catalyst retrieved, they might very well have forgotten about them, relegating them to history as they looked to the future.

But if they interfered?

They'll kill us for sure.

Sarrià, Barcelona, Spain

Carlos Mendoza eyeballed the house from the passenger seat, double-checking the brass numbers on the gate against the address they had been sent. It matched. His heart jumped in excitement. The honor he and his partner Juan Delgado had been bestowed was incredible. It would cement their names in the annals of The Order for eternity, and might even allow them to move up within the organization, perhaps enough to be noticed by a Master looking for an apprentice.

Becoming an apprentice was all he had ever thought of when he had found out the true organizational structure of The Order. He was a medical doctor with a thriving practice, as was Delgado. They had cofounded their clinic six years ago almost immediately after medical school, their aim to help the poor. The recession had hit Spain particularly hard, the country's foolish dalliance with green energy causing businesses to flee the high energy prices, taking their precious jobs with them.

It had nearly bankrupted the country, and now with youth unemployment approaching fifty percent, doctors willing to devote some of their time for free to those without medical care were in high demand. They profited while those around them suffered.

It was a conversation between them and a former medical school friend that led them into The Order after several years of vetting, vetting they hadn't even known was occurring, their opinions being tested, their beliefs challenged.

But eventually The Order's existence had been revealed, and when he heard about what they could offer, he jumped at it. It wasn't until recently he had caught wind of their secret agenda, and even that didn't really bother him as he saw the misery day in and day out at his clinic.

Population reduction executed quickly and in a controlled manner.

Leaving the planet to return to the paradise it once was.

It was a fantastic idea, if you were on the right side of the equation, and being a member of The Order guaranteed that.

Especially after today.

Delgado pressed the buzzer at the front gate. A moment later it was answered.

"Yes? Can I help you?"

"Police, we need to ask the homeowner some questions."

"Come right up," said the voice, a buzzer sounding as the gates slowly opened.

Delgado pulled through and up the winding, treed drive to the massive house. Mendoza looked up at it in awe.

"I really hope we don't have to search it."

They had been sent a picture of what they were looking for. When they had been fully initiated into The Order, they had been taught the history, and featured prominently was the Catalyst. Legend had it that the Founder, Rosenkreuz himself, had stolen it from heathens in the Middle East, but was never able to unlock its powers, despite having seen them demonstrated. It was on his journey back to get the writings on the cube translated that it had been lost to the Rhine River in Germany, half a millennia ago. The Order had hunted centuries for it, and the hunt continued to this day, unabated, but with little hope that it could be found.

And now today, out of the blue, Mendoza received the call, the excited call, that it had been found, and the search, with no leads in over five hundred years, was now only ten years behind, and perhaps today, if they were fortunate, they would possess what was lost to them due to revenge by an apprentice over his master's killing of a girl.

Mendoza had to admit the bachelor rule was trying at times. It meant dating, not relationships, and if he liked someone, he'd have to cut it off before true feelings developed. Sometimes he wondered if it was worth it, but after going out with someone, someone he could see spending time with, and the doubts began to creep in, he'd review the latest research on The Order's secure website, and realize it all *was* worth it.

Especially after the plan was executed.

And if he and Delgado retrieved the fabled Catalyst today, they stood good chances of being leaders in the new world order that would prevail. But they had to retrieve the item, with their instructions followed to the letter. The Catalyst had been bought as part of a lot at an auction in France almost a decade ago, its importance unknown to the purchaser. To Mendoza it looked like an ornate cube, and if it weren't for knowing it was the Catalyst, he too would probably have paid it no more mind than any other box. He might have even tossed it in the trash.

He shuddered at the thought.

What if they did do just that? Then it could very well be lost forever.

Then again, knowing The Order, they'd probably track the garbage truck to the dump, purchase the dump, then mine it until they found what they were looking for.

For The Order would stop at nothing to retrieve the Catalyst, and no one, including the current owners, were exempt, their death warrants already issued, regardless of whether or not they still possessed the item.

It was strange how the idea of letting billions die affected him less than the thought of killing a handful of innocent people he was about to meet.

Treat them like patients. Don't form any attachments. It's just a job.

Delgado stopped in front of the large front doors where a woman was standing, a young boy, perhaps eight, beside her, his head cocked to the side as he took in the sight of the new arrivals.

"May I help you?" asked the woman, her expression curious but in no way fearful.

Mendoza smiled, holding up his fake Cuerpo Nacional de Policía ID.

"CNP, Ma'am. Are you Señora Ortega?"

She nodded.

"What is this about?"

Her expression had definitely changed, more concerned now but still no fear. For what had she to fear from them? They were the police, so he was certain she was perfectly content helping them. Any concern might be that they were here about a loved one being hurt.

Mendoza held out the photograph, cropped, of the item they had been instructed to retrieve.

"We're looking for this item," he said. "It was purchased by your husband almost ten years ago at an estate auction in France."

"He bought this?"

Mendoza nodded, already fearing they might be wasting their time.

"You haven't seen it?"

She shook her head.

"No."

"It was part of a lot. There would have been perhaps another dozen pieces with it."

She shrugged.

"Antiques were my husband's interest, not mine. After he died this household's interest died with him."

"So you don't recognize the item."

"I'm sorry, no."

The boy tugged on her shirt and she bent down. He whispered in his mother's ear, then she stood upright with a smile on her face.

"Lalo says he has seen what you are looking for," she said, tousling the boy's hair as he buried his shy face in her leg. "Follow me, I'll show you where."

Mendoza looked at Delgado and could sense the struggle Delgado was undergoing. It was the same one he was battling. The battle to hide their elation. Could they about to be the first in The Order to see the Catalyst after all these years? Could their names about to be remembered forever in the history of The Order? Could the Catalyst have the rumored powers, be the source of the Lazarus myths, eternal life through some ancient science forgotten to man?

His control cracked as he followed the woman and her son inside, a smile breaking out. The boy looked over his shoulder at Mendoza and his eyebrows narrowed. Mendoza immediately wiped the smile off his face, instead turning his head away to look around the beautiful home filled with antiques and artifacts from around the world, an eclectic collection whose very diversity seemed to result in each piece fitting in with every other piece.

It was breathtaking.

They descended a set of stairs into the basement, the air a welcoming cool, the boy now eager to get to their destination, running ahead to a door at the end of a short hall. He opened the door and went inside, holding it open for them. Mendoza followed the mother inside, Delgado behind him, as the boy rounded a large, dusty desk, jumping in the high back leather chair that sat behind it, a grin on his face.

"This was his father's office," said the mother. "I haven't been in here since he died. I apologize for the mess."

"No need to apologize, ma'am," said Mendoza. "So, little man, where is it?"

The boy pointed behind them and as Mendoza turned a smile spread across his face. On top of a book shelf filled with tomes perhaps as ancient as the relic they sought sat the Catalyst, one of five pieces spread across the top, the dust thick, cobwebs stretching from it to the items around it.

Mendoza looked at Delgado whose smile was even bigger than his. Mendoza turned to the mother as he reached behind his back.

"Thank you so much, Señora Ortega, you have no idea how important a day this is, and how your names shall be remembered throughout history for the small part you played, and the sacrifice you made."

"Sacrifice?"

His hand whipped from behind his back, his Beretta gripped tightly, the safety flicked off. Her eyes bulged as she froze momentarily then dove toward her son, screaming in horror as she realized what was about to happen. Mendoza emptied his clip at the diving form, Delgado doing the same.

It was over in seconds.

Her bloody, twitching body landed on the desk, her blood mixing with the dust as the boy jumped on the body, trying to cover her, trying to protect his mother from a resumption of the assault he had just witnessed. Mendoza stepped over to the boy, looking him in the eye as he raised his gun to the youngster's forehead.

"I truly am sorry for this."

Entering the Vosges Mountains, Alsace Region, France

"These roads are starting to get bad," commented Mickey as he pushed forward through the snow, the convoy they were following mere taillights in the distance. According to the GPS there were no roads for their targets to take, so Mickey wasn't worried about losing them, but he did press a little harder on the accelerator each time they rounded a bend in the winding pass through the mountains.

It was becoming quite evident this meeting Lacroix was attending was somewhere very exclusive, very secluded. The towns ahead were few and far between according to their GPS, and with the roads getting worse, Mickey was beginning to wonder if the rest of the team would be able to make it through.

The taillights rounded another bend ahead and disappeared. Mickey gave their SUV a little more gas, but not much as the traction control kicked in, warning him his attempts to overcome physics weren't appreciated.

Niner was uncharacteristically quiet as they proceeded, even he apparently sensing the need for Mickey to concentrate. He was jacked into the comms as was Mickey in case any new info was to be broadcast. The last bit was the successful departure of Professor Palmer's plane. Assuming the rest could get out of Geneva successfully, then they should be here in three, maybe four hours.

By then hopefully they'd have some intel of their own to share.

He was a little worried for the professors and that Interpol agent. He understood why they were doing what they were doing, but they weren't trained for this, although he did have to admit they were a hell of a lot better trained than pretty much any civilian he had encountered. He just felt this mission they had taken upon themselves should wait until these Rosicrucians were taken care of.

"A penny for your thoughts."

"Huh?" Mickey glanced over at Niner who still had his eyes on the road ahead. "Sorry, just thinking of the professors. I think they should be waiting. They don't know what they could be getting themselves into."

Niner nodded. "True, but after what they've been through, I think a little leeway might be in order."

"Leeway usually gets people hurt, or worse."

"True, but retrieving that artifact could be critical, and we aren't exactly swimming in resources here. Three extra sets of hands shouldn't go to waste."

Mickey frowned at Niner's comment as he regained sight of the convoy.

"Agreed. I just hope they're not walking into something big."

Niner shifted in his seat.

"Do you really think it would still be there after all these years?"

"It doesn't matter if it's there. What matters is if the Rosicrucians think it's there. They have the photograph, so they know it's out there. There's no way in hell they aren't tracking it down and sending a team."

Niner nodded, biting his lip.

"True." He pointed ahead as brake lights and signal lights flashed through the rapidly encroaching darkness. "Something's up."

"Anything on the GPS?"

"No roads indicated. Maybe that's their destination?"

Mickey continued forward and soon they passed a large gate, fresh tire tracks slicing through the several inches of snow, the taillights visible farther up a long laneway, at the top of which stood what appeared to be a large castle, older than anything back home probably by hundreds of years.

Its façade, bathed in electric lighting, indicated modern renovations. Mickey kept on moving, barely slowing down as Niner held his phone up, holding the button to take a rapid series of pictures at high resolution.

Soon they were around another bend, the castle lost in the snow.

"There's a village coming up in about half a mile," said Niner, eying the GPS as he transmitted the coordinates of the castle to the rest of the team. "Let's see if we can find somewhere to stay there."

Mickey nodded, continuing to grip the wheel tightly as the road wound along the mountainside, finally opening into a small valley, a picturesque slice of history being revealed, a village that if it weren't for the electric lighting, would fit perfectly into another century. It was the very picture of the perfect romantic getaway, and here he was, sharing it with Niner, who was to his dismay already transitioning into his character.

As they drove deeper into the village, they encountered a smattering of locals, all seeming to stop and stare at their vehicle as they drove by.

"You'd think they'd never seen tourists before," commented Mickey.

"Maybe they're just stunned we were stupid enough to drive up here in this weather, at this time of the day."

"Perhaps." But as he watched in the rearview mirror, he saw people going inside their businesses and homes, lights being turned off, shutters closed, and the general appearance of a village from the Old West closing up as if a gunfight at high noon was about to begin. "Something's not right."

"There's a hotel," Niner said, his intonation already changed, Mickey shaking his head as he pulled in front of the building, it too seemingly dark.

Mickey climbed out, pulling the collar up on his jacket and shoving his hands in his pockets as he followed Niner up the few steps and toward the double front doors. The wood steps creaked under their feet and the shutters smacked against the timber framed sides of the three story building.

Niner pulled on the doorknob and to Mickey's surprise it actually opened. They stepped inside to find a welcoming fire roaring to their left and what appeared to be a landlady standing behind a counter, her expression of surprise mild to say the least.

In German, rather than French, she asked, "May I help you?"

Mickey, fluent, responded.

"Do you have any rooms? Just for tonight, we're passing through and want to ride out the storm."

"Storm? Bah, this is nothing," replied the woman, batting her hand at the wind outside. "Tomorrow is the real storm. You should turn around and go back before you get stuck here."

Mickey smiled, thankful Niner was playing his part quietly right now, not sure how tolerant these people might be despite the pleasant demeanor.

"All the same, I think we'd rather take our chances. Do you have a room? Two if possible?"

The woman shook her head.

"Sorry, but we are sold out."

Mickey's eyebrows shot up his forehead.

"Sold out? But there are no cars outside? How can you be sold out?"

"This is the annual fest, people come from all over the valley, mostly hiking or skiing in. You won't find a room anywhere."

Mickey frowned, looking at Niner. If this village was having some annual festival, there certainly was no evidence of it. The streets had seemed fairly quiet, and there were no decorations or banners suggesting any type of gathering.

They were being lied to.

If it weren't for the reaction of the villagers who had seen them arrive, he might have thought it was discrimination, but Niner had played it quiet, beyond his loud colors there was no other evidence of the part he was playing.

"Ya vol!" he heard a voice say, muffled through a doorway, then the distinct sound of a receiver being slammed on an old style phone. A door behind the desk suddenly opened and an older man, perhaps early sixties, walked through with a distinctive limp. He whispered to the woman, something Mickey couldn't pick up, then she nodded as the man disappeared back through the door.

"You are fortunate. We have a last minute cancellation. We can give you a chalet if you don't mind driving up the mountain a short way."

"A chalet sounds perfect," said Mickey, signing the guest book as it was spun around. As he put his alias down, he noted the date of the last arrival was two days ago, and they were signed out the next day.

Full?

Geneva Cointrin Airport, Geneva, Switzerland

Dawson, dressed in a black suit and tie, stood beside the coffin, his head bowed in remembrance. Behind him Red did the same, his hand resting on the coffin of his friend, the somber look of Dawson mirrored. The rest of the team were already aboard the private plane, but moving dead bodies from Switzerland to an international destination still involved some paperwork, even if not flying commercial.

Paperwork that was taking longer than Dawson liked.

Two airport security personnel were talking in whispers behind the special luggage counter, a lineup of at least a dozen waiting to check their own special items from pets to corpses.

Finally one of them stepped out with a sheaf of papers in their hands.

"I apologize for the delay, Mr. White. Per procedure, I will need to see each of the deceased so I can compare it to the photo ID."

Dawson nodded, knowing this was coming, but dreading it nonetheless.

"Of course."

He undid the screws holding the top half of the coffin, then lifted the lid as Red did the same behind him. He looked down at the light grey face of Jimmy, the makeup Jagger had applied garish, overdone to the extreme as if he were a gag corpse at a Halloween party rather than the real thing. The man held the passport up to the face then nodded, moving on to the next casket. Dawson closed the lid and suddenly there was a stifled sneeze from inside.

The security guard spun around as Dawson rubbed his nose.

"Sorry, must be the dry air," he said, sniffing.

The guard's eyes remained narrowed, but Dawson stifled a second forced sneeze, praying Jimmy would keep it together, this idea no longer seeming like such a good one.

Thankfully Jagger had no involuntary spasms or twitches, and they were on their way to the tarmac with their two caskets. Minutes later the caskets were loaded into the underbelly of their plane, then they themselves joined the rest of the team.

Dawson didn't breathe easily until the plane's landing gear had cleared the runway.

"Okay, get them out of there," he said as the team jumped to their feet, removing floor panels and gaining access to the storage compartments. Spock and Red climbed down into the small compartment, these private jets never designed to move a lot of cargo, and quickly unscrewed the lids.

Jimmy was the first to push himself up and out of the casket, hands pulling him into the passenger compartment, his makeup smeared under his nose where he had wiped it earlier.

"My God, remind me to update my paperwork so I'm cremated if I die. There's no way in hell I want to spend eternity in one of those!"

Jagger joined him in his displeasure.

"That had to have been the most unpleasant experience I've ever had, and I had to bunk with Niner and his fart jokes for two weeks in Baghdad."

"Well, in about twenty minutes you're over the border, hopefully thinking about how next time you won't become wanted men in a friendly country where we can't go in guns-a-blazin' to rescue you," said Red.

"Yeah, yeah. It wasn't all chocolate bars and yodeling in there, you know. There was some really disturbing food served. They eat sauerkraut with everything! My delicate stomach still hasn't recovered."

"Next McDonald's we see, we'll stop so you can soothe your sophisticated palate," said Spock.

"Thank you very much," replied Jimmy with an exaggerated bow. "Now, if you'll excuse me, I have to take my makeup off." He made a show of flicking non-existent hair off his shoulder, then super-modeled it toward the bathroom, Jagger aping him all the way.

As the team roared in laughter, Wings cut through the frivolity with a toss of a comm unit to Dawson.

"It's Atlas, he has an update."

Dawson fitted the earpiece in place.

"This is Bravo One, go ahead, over."

"Bravo Seven here. I've got some updates for you. Niner and Mickey are situated and have relayed their coordinates, along with our target's. Apparently the gathering is at some sort of castle. I've sent satellite imagery to your accounts. Unfortunately there are no birds scheduled to pass over that area until tomorrow so I won't be able to give you numbers. I've passed the advance team's location on to our supplier. He says he can be there before you arrive. Also, the professors and Special Agent Reading have landed in Barcelona. ETA at their target ten minutes, over."

"Okay, if we're hitting a damned castle, make sure our supplier has a lot of C4. The walls tend to be thick on those things."

"Already done."

"Any luck on that intel we gathered?"

"Not really. It's like trying to put a puzzle together where you haven't got a clue what the end product looks like. So far everything is World Bank related, but they've got their fingers into so much, there's no way to know if it's something we should be paying attention to. We're trying to flag anything that might deal with population control, but I'm not confident at this point."

"Okay, keep at it. It might just be that these guys are fanatics with a pipe dream, but I'm not willing to risk it. Out."

Dawson looked up as Jimmy exited the bathroom, his old self again.

"Looks like we're hitting a castle, gentlemen."

"Oh, goody," said Jimmy as he took a seat, sounding anything but thrilled at the prospect.

Sarrià, Barcelona, Spain

"That's odd," said Reading as they arrived at their destination. "The gates are open."

Acton shrugged. "Maybe they're just welcoming people?"

"This isn't Maryland," said Laura. "This is Spain. With the economy the way it is, there's no way they'd leave their door basically open."

Reading pulled up to the intercom rather than just drive in, his manners demanding it. He pressed the button to buzz those inside and waited. And waited. He pressed again.

Nothing.

"Either no one is home, or we're already too late," he said.

Nobody said anything, all probably thinking the same thing. Acton was already picturing a bloodbath, the only question in his mind how large of one. As Reading navigated the winding drive to the front entrance, Acton began to feel even more uneasy than he already had since the airport.

"I'm not sure this is a good idea," he said as they pulled to a stop.

"Now you finally come to my side," said Reading, throwing his hands up in the air. "Don't you think it's a little late for that now?"

Acton nodded. "Oh, it's too late all right," he said, pointing at the doorway.

Blood covered the porch, drag marks where a body had been pulled inside ending at the closed door.

"Bloody hell," muttered Reading as he stepped out of the car. "We have to check it out, there may be injured."

"Agreed," said Acton as he joined Reading, Laura right behind them. "Just remember we don't have any weapons." Reading grunted in acknowledgement, then pushed the front door open, tentatively poking his head inside.

"We've got a body," he said quietly, opening the door all the way, then stopping to listen. "I don't hear anything."

He stepped inside, Acton and Laura following, tip toeing through the front hall and past the body of what appeared to be a maid.

"Do you think they're still here?" whispered Laura.

Reading shook his head.

"No, the only cars outside were in the garage. These guys wouldn't park there, they'd be out front."

"Maybe they didn't take the car through the gates?"

"Then why were they opened? There's a side gate for pedestrians."

Laura flashed a look at Acton.

"I guess that's why he's the detective and we're not."

Acton flashed her a grin, catching something in a reflection. He turned into a room and found another body, this time a man.

"Looks like a gardener," he said.

"This is going to take too long," said Reading. "We can safely assume that they have been here, are probably gone, and they got what they were looking for. We're just looking to see if anyone is alive that needs help. I'll start upstairs, you two finish this floor then check to see if there might be someone in the basement."

Acton and Laura spread out, taking a room at a time as Reading trotted up the stairs to the upper level. No more bodies were found, and as they were about to head to the basement, Reading returned.

"Anything?" asked Acton.

"Nil."

"Where's the family?" asked Laura. "We've only found staff."

"Maybe they're out?"

"Could be, but there are two vehicles in the garage and no more spaces," replied Laura.

"Look who's the detective now," smiled Reading as they descended into the basement. They didn't find anything until they reached a door at the end of the hall. Reading entered first and gasped, holding out his hand, blocking the others. "You don't want to see this."

Acton shook his head.

"We've come too far to stop now."

He stepped inside and nearly cried out at the horror. What looked like a mother was lying across a desk, her body riddled with bullets, and a small boy, no more than ten, was draped over her, as if to protect his mother, he too shot.

By a single bullet to the forehead.

He spun to stop Laura from entering the room but it was too late. She cried out and turned her body away from the sight, covering her eyes with her hand in a useless effort to block what she had already seen. Acton turned away, wrapping his arms around his fiancée as he looked about the room, avoiding the bodies.

"It must have been here," he said. "This is the family. The family must have taken them to where the Catalyst was, then they killed them."

Laura pointed to a bookshelf opposite the desk.

"It looks like something is missing on top."

Acton looked and saw four artifacts across the top, a gap between the third and fourth that looked like it might have held something. He grabbed a chair and stepped up so he could see the dust covered top of the bookshelf. There was a clear square shape in the fourth spot, the perfectly clean area leaving little doubt the Catalyst had been here.

He stepped down and nodded to the others.

"They definitely have it."

"What now?" asked Laura.

"Well, if I had just found a long lost relic that my Master and my Order had been looking hundreds of years for…"

"I'd make a phone call," finished Laura.

Reading speed dialed their mini ops center, putting the phone on speaker as Atlas immediately answered.

"This is Reading. We're here and everyone's dead. We've confirmed they found and have the artifact. Is there a way for you to tell if a phone call was made from here?"

"I can do better than that," said Atlas. "We just tracked it down now and I was waiting for your call. The *Master's* phone was just called from Barcelona. We have the number and are tracking them now."

Reading motioned for Acton and Laura to follow him as he stepped out of the office, rushing down the hallway and up the basement stairs as Atlas continued to talk, much of it lost to Acton as Reading held the phone out in front of him. It wasn't until they climbed into the car and Reading handed the phone over that he was privy to the rest of the conversation.

"I'll need you to contact the local authorities and tell them there've been multiple murders here."

"Will do."

Reading pointed at the GPS in the dash.

"Okay, feed me those coordinates," he said as Acton selected the appropriate menu and typed in the relayed coordinates. The GPS programmed a route and displayed the result.

"Looks like they're only ten minutes ahead of us," said Acton.

"It appears they've been stopped there for over thirty minutes," replied Atlas. "Probably either to eat or to admire their prize."

"Okay, we're on our way to those coordinates. We'll call you to get new ones in case they've left."

"Roger that, out."

The call ended as Reading pulled through the gates, leaving the horror scene behind. Acton looked back at Laura who gazed out the window, her eyes glassed over.

"Are you okay?" he asked.

Her head turned slowly, nodding.

"Just thinking of the mother and her boy."

A single tear rolled down her cheek and Acton reached back, taking her hand and squeezing. He didn't bother saying anything, he knew words of comfort weren't possible. There was nothing positive to take from the situation. Instead they drove in silence as they all paid homage to the massacre victims they had left behind.

The silence was finally broken by Reading.

"We're almost there," he said. "Call Atlas and see if he's got an update for us."

Acton nodded and dialed, Atlas answering right away.

"We're almost there, any updates?"

"They left not even two minutes ago. I've got your position on my screen. Turn left at the next intersection," he said.

Acton put the phone on speaker.

"Turn left at the next intersection," he repeated.

Reading turned, just making the light, and accelerated.

"They've just left the city. They don't seem to be in any hurry on the highway, so you should be able to catch up to them no problem."

"And what do we do if we catch up to them?" asked Acton to no one in particular. "We have no weapons."

Atlas' voice came through the speaker.

"Just catch up to them in case they smarten up and turn their phone off. I've got a Spec Ops Command buddy of ours heading your way."

"Spanish Special Forces?" asked Reading.

"Yup. He's got a few gifts for you. He's coming from the north so you'll intercept each other in about twenty minutes. Stand by to receive instructions."

The line went dead and Acton looked at Laura then Reading.

"Is the fact that we'll be armed better?"

Laura frowned, but said nothing.

Reading however had no problem expressing his opinion.

"Of course not. It means we're obligated to fight if it becomes necessary to do so."

"So *not* better."

Schloss Rosen, Riquewihrweiler, France

It was a lavish if not exciting gathering. The finest of wine, spirits and champagne flowed, the hors d'oeuvres were to die for, and Lacroix knew the dinner that awaited would be exquisite, The Order sparing no expense at these quarterly gatherings of The Circle. The gathering was small, intimate, with just seven of the eight members in attendance, Numbers Two through Eight each being absent once every seven meetings so the eight were never together in the same place at once. The missing member would always be on another continent, far away from any natural disaster that might befall the others.

It was a security protocol implemented centuries before when the entire Circle had almost been captured by a local prince hell bent on their demise. It had resulted in The Circle moving its base to this very castle, now named Schloss Rosen, or the Rose Castle, where they had continued for centuries until modern travel and communications allowed them to move farther apart.

He had been to dozens of these gatherings. To call them enjoyable would be to insult parties that actually were enjoyable. Informative might be a better word. It was one thing to deliver news over the Internet, quite another to do it in person, which meant sometimes a member might hold back some tidbit that he knew would fascinate the others and make him the center of attention at least until the next tidbit was revealed.

But tonight all mouths were wagging over the Catalyst. Nothing would be able to top the news he had brought them, and with the phone call he had just received, he was about to cement his name in the history of The Order.

Lacroix rounded the corner and entered the room, having left only moments before to take the call. The entire room, including servants, all members of The Order, turned to face him. It was customary to leave the hoods of the robes up, but tonight he meant to make a statement, wanting everyone to recognize his face as the words were spoken.

He flipped his hood down to his shoulders as a smile spread across his face and he opened his arms wide.

"Brothers, I have news."

He left the words to dance their way through the room, the small group seeming to move closer to him without their feet moving, their bodies leaning forward in anticipation.

"I am proud to announce that we have the Catalyst!"

Cheers erupted as they surged toward him, all his past transgressions immediately forgotten and forgiven as hugs and pats on the back were exchanged, even the wait staff hugging each other, then some rushing off to return moments later with a tray of champagne flutes filled to celebrate.

Number One took Lacroix by both shoulders, looking him in the face for the first time. The man looked even younger than the last time he had a glance.

"You shall go down in history, Number Eight."

Lacroix almost found himself choking up. For the first time since joining The Circle he actually felt a part of it, the gathering suddenly making sense. This was a brotherhood, these men were supposed to be his extended family, his brothers, their vow of bachelorhood preventing any other type of family.

Finally, after decades, he found he had a family, one that was now embracing him, welcoming him back into the fold after years of embarrassment, his penance complete, his contribution strengthening the brotherhood beyond anything it had known since its origins.

A staff member entered the room and approached Number One, who let go of Lacroix and turned to the man.

"What is it?"

"A message from the village, Master. We have a problem."

Niner and Mickey's Chalet, Riquewihrweiler, France

Niner sat perched on a chair, a pair of binoculars glued to his eyes as he surveyed the castle below, their chalet offering them a perfect view of the magnificently restored structure. Even from here he could see there was a party of sorts going on, a grand ballroom at the back well lit, floor to ceiling glass extending from one end to the other, rising two full stories above the ground, definitely a new feature, any castle designed for defense never leaving an opening like that.

Not to mention the lack of glass when it was probably built.

He lowered the binoculars to rest his eyes for a few moments. Mickey had a fire going in the fireplace which was already taking the edge off the frozen solid room. He was bundled up with everything he had brought, it still ice cold by the window, his breath prominently displayed every time he exhaled.

"Looks lightly guarded at the back, mostly forward defenses," said Niner, raising the glasses again. "When the guys get here it should be pretty easy to take the rear and use those windows to get our targets."

"Foolish set up if you ask me."

Niner nodded.

"Clearly they're not expecting uninvited guests."

"Arrogance once again."

"Well, it is France after all, not the Middle East."

"True." Mickey threw another log on the now roaring fire then stood up, stretching. "Speaking of, did you notice how there's an awful lot of Germans around here?"

Niner shrugged.

"Sure, they like to visit every few decades or so. Helps the French practice waving those big white flags."

Mickey chuckled.

"No, I'm serious. At the airport, the guy's name was Heinrich. The woman spoke with a German accent. At the hotel, it was a Gasthaus, which is clearly German. The guy on the phone was speaking German, and they both had German accents."

"We're close to Germany. Probably just ancestral."

Mickey nodded as he walked toward the front door.

"Could be, just a little odd that the French haven't made their presence known a little more and let this tiny enclave of Deutschland continue. If I were..." Mickey's voice trailed off and Niner looked over his shoulder. "What the hell is that?"

Niner stood up and joined Mickey at the door.

"What?"

"Take a look."

Niner looked through the small frosted window in the door. Outside he could see the snow continuing to fall, albeit much gentler than before, their SUV parked out front, and walking up the road from the village below, dozens upon dozens of people armed with shotguns and rifles, their flashlights leading the way.

"We've gotta get out of here," said Niner as he searched the room for any type of weapon, cursing their supplier for not being here on time.

"It's too late," said Mickey, backing away from the door. Niner rushed to the tiny window and saw the crowd spreading out. A glance at the window he had just been using to recon the castle showed half a dozen people marching by.

"Suggestions?" asked Mickey, grabbing a discarded ski pole, tossing a cane to Niner.

"We take advantage of the situation," said Niner, putting the cane aside and opening a pouch in his suitcase. He retrieved a small bottle of pills, removing the lid. "It's obvious these people work for the Rosicrucians. If we play our cards right, they might take us down to the castle rather than kill us."

"No resistance?"

"No resistance." Niner swallowed a pill then tossed the bottle to Mickey who took one as well. The door was kicked open, a shotgun barrel advancing, followed by its owner. Niner raised his hands and looked at Mickey who tossed his ski pole to the floor, raising his hands. Mickey shrugged.

"I guess we're the inside team now."

Highway C-16, Spain

Mendoza leaned forward and frowned. He had been watching their backs like a hawk, convinced they were being followed, but every time he saw nothing. No evidence of anything except cars travelling in the same direction, some passing them, some turning off, others continuing at their speed, occasionally long enough for him to have Delgado pull over or slow down so he could be certain.

And all along there had been nothing.

Until now.

A blue sedan had been racing down a straight stretch then suddenly slowed, pulling from the left lane into the slower right, and had kept itself several cars back since then, even making a point to slow down from time to time if they got too close.

This time he was convinced he was right.

"We've got a tail."

"Not again."

"Blue sedan, four cars back. He's been with us for almost ten minutes."

"Do you want me to slow down?"

"Next exit pull off, we'll take the local roads through the Pyrenees."

Mendoza knew it would be slower, but the local roads through the mountains were in his mind safer if they were being followed. They were only one lane in each direction, almost impossible to pass, and if they were lucky to get a truck or two between them and their tail, it would be almost impossible for them to catch up.

"Fine," muttered Delgado as he signaled, turning off the highway as the GPS adjusted their route. He ignored her chattering as he knew the way like the back of his hand.

"See, they followed us."

Delgado glanced in the rearview mirror and pursed his lips.

"Perhaps you're right."

He pulled onto the secondary highway and floored it, racing toward the winding road through the Pyrenees Mountains. The blue sedan fell behind a bit, but seemed to keep pace, only a little farther back than before.

"I told you!"

Mendoza grabbed his gun and made sure it was loaded.

"Let them catch up, I'll take care of them."

Delgado eased off the accelerator.

"Are you sure that's wise?"

"Better than having them follow us until they can get reinforcements."

"Never thought of that," said Delgado as he slowed down even more. They rounded a bend, losing sight of the sedan, then suddenly it whipped around the corner as Mendoza leaned out the passenger side window, opening fire at the hood of the car.

Tires squealed and the vehicle swerved toward the guardrail on the left then corrected itself as the driver regained control after dropping more than half his speed. Suddenly Mendoza could see muzzle flashes as they returned fire. Delgado floored it as Mendoza ducked back in.

"I knew it!" yelled Mendoza as he reloaded. Bullets continued to ping off the car. Suddenly they jerked to the left, Delgado battling with the steering wheel.

"They got a tire!" he cried as he cranked the wheel back to the right, trying to keep them on the narrow road. They bounced off the guardrail and back toward their side. Delgado spun the wheel to the left, having overcompensated, and Mendoza screamed as they rounded a bend to find themselves careening directly at a large truck heading in the opposite direction.

The truck jerked to the left, the driver apparently figuring it was better for him to hit the rock carved out of the side of the mountain than the guardrail he'd most likely slice through. Smoke billowed from its brakes as the truck slid down the road, blocking both lanes.

Delgado was spinning the wheel back to the right but it was too late. The car's right front bumper nailed the front tire of the truck. The car felt like it was just tossed aside as an inconsequential chunk of metal by the massive vehicle, and they suddenly found themselves heading for the guardrail. There was a crunch and the car leapt over the thin strip of metal and wood designed to somehow keep two thousand pound vehicles from certain death.

Mendoza raised his hands, covering his face as did Delgado. It was an odd feeling as the car leapt into nothingness, like he was on a roller coaster, the strange weightless sensation giving him the impression they were at the top of the rise, about to plunge to the exciting conclusion.

The front tipped forward, removing all doubt this was a ride to the death, the river carved out in the valley below over millions of years rapidly approaching, both men now holding their hands out as if they might stop their fall if they pushed hard enough against the ground they were about to hit.

Mendoza dropped his gun, struggling to reach between his legs for the Catalyst. His fingers kept touching it, refusing to gain a grip, when suddenly he grabbed a corner, yanking it to his lap. As his head rose once again above the dash, he gasped, the front of the car suddenly smashing into the ground, the hood crumpling rapidly toward them, then airbags bursting into their faces and their sides as the car stood on its end, then slowly fell forward and onto its roof.

The car seemed to swivel, then bounce, a curious sound and sensation enveloping them as Mendoza pushed the airbags away, the compressed gas quickly dissipating, leaving him to realize they were in the river, the car floating on top as the roof filled with water.

Mendoza looked over at Delgado, but his neck was twisted, clearly broken. Mendoza released his seatbelt, falling onto the roof. He screamed in agony as he realized his legs were crushed under the foot-well, now stuck above him, his body pulling at them, gravity a cruel torturer. He pushed at the door, but it was useless. The car spun as it hit something, then suddenly the window smashed in as it smacked against a rock, spraying Mendoza with glass and water. As he gasped for breath, he tried to pull his legs free but it was no use, the agony causing him to almost black out.

He gripped the Catalyst tight with both hands as the progress of the car seemed to slow, the top now filled with water, weighing it down, the buoyancy almost neutralized. The car hit something and he felt the rear get forced high into the air, all the water in the car rushing to the front, his head almost submerged. He extended one arm, pushing on the roof, desperate to keep his head above the water, the other arm gripping the Catalyst like it was his first born child.

He could feel the car begin to spin slowly around whatever obstacle they were hung up on, then suddenly it smacked back down, jarring the Catalyst from his hands. He cried out, reaching, but it simply floated out the window, his ice cold fingers unable to grip the priceless artifact.

He lunged for it, his fingers squeezing around the corner, its escape halted, and he pulled it toward him, reaching out with his other hand to secure a tighter grip. He felt the cube smack against something, the jarring impact wrenching it from his grip as he cried out in horror, the water now to his nose, his eyes dipping above and below the water as his breathing turned to gasps when air momentarily became available.

But it didn't matter anymore. He could see the Catalyst floating on the water above, just outside the window, travelling with the car, hopelessly out of reach, then suddenly slipping past and out of sight, lost to The Order, and to history, its secrets once again locked away.

Schloss Rosen, Riquewihrweiler, France

Dinner was served, and they all sat at the table, Number One at the head, the others, three down each side. With him being Number Eight, Lacroix would normally be relegated to the far end, across from Number Six or Seven, depending on who was missing at any particular gathering, but regardless, as far from Number One, and those of the most influence, as was possible.

But tonight Number One, the Master of all, had requested Lacroix be seated beside him. There were no grumblings this day, even from Number Three, his most outspoken detractor, who had wisely ceded his seat to the master's left, he now relegated to the end of the table.

Which suited Lacroix just fine. He realized it was most likely a one-time honor, but he didn't care. His feelings of euphoria continued, the camaraderie, the fellowship, still overwhelming. Hoods were down all around, the excitement too much to bear as the night continued and the alcohol flowed. Someone told the story of how the Catalyst had been lost in the first place, a story well known to all, but listened to with rapt attention by everyone. He told the story of how he himself had found the photo while researching the archaeologists—an embellishment to say the least— then interrogated the prisoners himself, faking the female professor's death, proving Professor Acton had no idea where the Catalyst was hidden. He left out the part where they had escaped, killing his apprentice. Today was a day for joyous stories, success stories, where the triviality of facts would not get in the way of the legend now being woven, with his name featured prominently at its center.

It was everything he could dream of, everything he had ever hoped for, and with each passing moment he was certain his future included the coveted head of this table.

As he finished his story, a servant bent down and whispered in the master's ear, pointing to a doorway. Lacroix looked and saw what was obviously a resident of the local village standing in the shadows, his head bowed, his cap literally in hand.

The village of Riquewihrweiler belonged to The Order. It had for centuries. They weren't members of course, The Order having no need for ordinary commoners. They did recruit muscle from the village when they absolutely needed it, but that was it. Almost all members were doctors or scientists. But the villagers were a valuable asset. Over the centuries they had helped repel those who would harm The Order, and each new generation was raised to revere the residents of the castle, to render it service whenever demanded, and to lay down their lives should it be necessary.

The village was isolated, forgotten, the armies of Germany even ignoring it, several doctors prominent in Hitler's Third Reich, along with the long line of rulers before him, members of The Order. Which was why security was always so light at these events. No one knew where they were, and the villagers, all armed, were mere minutes away.

But things were different tonight. Somebody *did* know where they were, the proof the two Delta Force members locked away in their dungeon, a remnant of yesteryear.

Lacroix could see the rage overcome his master, a sight that was both terrifying, and wondrous.

"What?" he roared, dropping his fork on the table with a clatter. "Again?" He turned to the table. "We have *more* company." He looked at the servant. "I've had enough of their interference. Kill them all! Now!"

Approaching Riquewihrweiler, France

"That must be where the party is," said Red as all heads turned to see the well-lit structure towering at the top of a long drive. Guards were evident patrolling the front, two at the gate eyeballing their vehicle as they drove by, Dawson thankful they had blacked-out windows courtesy of their supplier. They were all armed now with Glocks thanks to a care package left in a storage compartment in the back, but they didn't have enough for a sustained battle, merely an inglorious retreat they might survive.

If all went to plan, their supplier would have delivered their requested gear to the chalet.

But things didn't appear to be going to plan.

They had been unable to reach Niner and Mickey, which could be explained as easily as bad reception due to the storm, or something equally as simple—they were captured or worse.

"Anybody notice anything odd?" asked Jimmy from the third row of seats in the back as they entered the village.

Dawson looked around from behind the wheel, noticing nothing but a quiet village in the middle of a mild snowstorm.

"What?"

"Everything's in German, no French flags, and every time we drive by somebody, they stare at us then go inside."

Dawson frowned, realizing Jimmy was right. He knew enough from history to know this area had traded hands too many times to count between the French and Germans, so perhaps it was as simple as that. But that didn't explain the behavior.

"Maybe they just don't like tourists," he said.

They turned up the road leading to the chalet, Niner having sent instructions to Atlas when they first arrived. As they reached the top they saw two vehicles, one with its engine running.

"That's odd," said Red. "Henri maybe?"

Dawson nodded at the suggestion of their supplier.

"Has to be. No one else knows we're here."

Dawson pulled up and turned the vehicle around should they need to make a quick getaway down the hill, then parked. Everyone climbed out as the driver's door opened on the idling SUV.

"It's about time you arrived. I was about to give up," said Henri in a thick French accent.

"Sorry *we're* late, there was an accident at the bottom of the pass, held us up for over an hour." Dawson pointed at the chalet. "Aren't they in there?"

"There's no answer if they are," said Henri, who then pointed at the ground. "But look."

Dawson looked at the snow, noticing it was covered in pockmarks, hundreds of them.

"Footprints?"

"Oui. They were much more obvious when I arrived *two* hours ago. They come from down there"—he pointed toward the village at the bottom of the road—"then go all around the cabin." Henri paused, looking at Dawson. "I have a bad feeling."

Dawson motioned for everyone to spread out as he and Red approached the door. Red tried the knob and shook his head.

Locked.

He knocked several times, but there was no answer.

Dawson nodded and Red kicked in the door, stepping back as Dawson rushed in with Jimmy. They quickly cleared the one room structure. Jimmy pointed at the fireplace.

"Fire's still burning, but not much left of it. Judging by the amount of ash, and assuming it was relatively clean when they got here, I'd say they've been gone a few hours."

Dawson agreed, stepping outside.

"They're not here," he said to his men. "Help Henri unload our gear, then let's get ready. I have a funny feeling we're being watched." He looked at Henri. "And if I were you, I'd get my ass out of town as quickly as possible."

"You don't have to tell me twice, monsieur. I feel like a fool for having stayed as long as I did."

"It's appreciated," said Dawson, shaking the man's hand. "Did you receive our payment?"

Henri waved his hand, dismissing Dawson's statement.

"You saved my ass in Algeria. How about we say I no longer owe you one?"

Dawson smiled, grabbing Henri's shoulder.

"Despite everything I know about you, and what everybody says about you, you're a good man."

"Maybe my English isn't very good, but I think I have just been insulted," grinned Henri.

Dawson laughed, slapping Henri's other shoulder.

"You're English is perfect, my friend."

Henri laughed and climbed in his vehicle, shutting the door. His window rolled down and he stuck his head out.

"You be careful. There's something strange happening here."

Dawson nodded.

"Don't worry, we'll be out of here before they know what hit them."

Henri didn't look convinced, the smile he gave half-hearted as he pulled away. Dawson watched him turn the corner at the bottom of the hill, noticing several villagers eyeballing the vehicle as it disappeared. Dawson pointed at Spock and Jimmy.

"You two take first watch."

Everyone else entered the chalet and huddled around what remained of the fire, the stone at least still radiating a noticeable amount of heat.

"Get the fire going. They know we're here, that's for sure. We want them to think we're planning on staying awhile. I want everyone geared up and ready to go in five minutes." He turned to Red. "Comms?"

Red tossed him a unit.

"Finally got through to Atlas."

Dawson fitted the unit on.

"Bravo Seven, Bravo One, how do you read, over?"

"Five by five, Bravo One. Before we get cut off, I have important intel for you, over."

"Go ahead, over."

"Two beacons have been activated and are located in the one-four corner of the structure, together. That must be our boys. It looks like they've been in the same location for hours, over."

Dawson felt a chill run down his spine.

"No movement? So we don't know if they're alive?"

"Negative, no way to tell. Also, the professors and our Interpol guy just landed. They'll be heading your way shortly, over."

Shit! He had hoped to be done and out of here before they had a chance to arrive. While he understood their desire to see the job through, and commended them for it, he didn't want to have to worry about three civilians, despite whatever experience they might have. But three extra sets of experienced hands might prove useful.

"Understood. If you can communicate with them, warn them we think the village might be compromised."

"I'll try, but cellphone reception is extremely poor."

"Okay, we're going in any minute now. Keep this line open, out."

He turned to Red who was already geared up and at the window with a set of binoculars.

"Report."

"I can't see the front from here, but if what Niner relayed when he arrived is correct, we've got at least a dozen there. The rear has only four guards, all seem to be huddled around two heating ducts. They don't seem to be too worried about an attack from the back. The rear number three wall is almost all glass with a small gathering going on inside. I'm guessing our Circle members and then some servants."

"Good," said Dawson as he finished putting his gear on. "Everyone ready?"

Everyone stepped forward, fully prepped. He pointed at Wings and Jagger.

"Switch off with Spock and Jimmy so they can get geared up."

The two men nodded and stepped outside, their two comrades entering moments later.

"Gear up. We leave as soon as you're ready."

Jimmy nodded.

"Good, that crowd at the bottom of the hill is getting bigger."

"How many?"

"About a dozen now, nothing we can't handle."

Dawson frowned. "Seems clear that coming back here after the attack isn't an option." He turned to Red. "Any sign of vehicles there that we can commandeer?"

Red nodded. "Yup. There's a bunch of SUV's and cars parked along the four side."

Dawson pointed at Spock as he pulled on the last of his gear.

"You and Wings secure one of those SUVs for us when we get down there. Did Henri bring us the kit for that?"

Spock nodded, patting one of his pockets.

"One car decoder, check. Should have a vehicle hot and ready for us within two minutes."

"Good, once it's ready, defend that side against anybody coming from the front."

"Will do."

Wings suddenly burst through the door.

"Crowd is getting big. If we're getting out of here, I suggest we do it now."

"Okay, get Jagger in here, barricade the door and windows; we're going out the back."

The men sprang into action, locking everything down, closing the curtains on all the windows and stacking the minimal furniture against the door and the one window large enough to enter by. At best it bought a few minutes.

"Rig the door, something gentle that will scare the shit out of them for a bit."

Jimmy smiled and quickly set up a mercury switch trigger that would detonate a small block of C4, enough to make a large noise, but not kill anyone.

The back door was already open, the rest of the team outside when Dawson and Jimmy finally exited, closing the door. The men were snapped into their short stunt skis provided by Henri at Niner's suggestion, poles in hands and goggles down. Dawson stepped into his, as did Jimmy, and within moments they were skiing down the hill toward the castle, the only light from the stars and a half moon.

Dawson took a glance over his shoulder and saw a large group, well lit by their lanterns and flashlights, begin to surround the chalet. Moments later Jimmy's surprise activated, cries of fear but not pain echoing down the slope as they continued their silent approach.

"Report if you see the rear guard, over," he said over the comm.

"I've got two left side in my sights," replied Spock.

"I've got eyes on two on the right," said Wings.

"Take them out when you both have the shot," ordered Dawson.

Spock replied first. "Ready to engage."

"Ready on the right," replied Wings.

"Engaging."

Two pops, followed by two more, sounded and Dawson, who had just got eyes on the targets on the left, saw both crumple. He couldn't see those on the right.

"Two down on the left," said Spock over the comm.

"And two down on the right," added Wings.

"Okay, Spock, Wings, secure us a ride. Red and Jimmy take the right. Jagger you're with me on the left."

Spock and Wings blasted past the rear left of the castle and out of sight as Dawson came to a stop with Jagger to the left of the large well-lit window, the other side of which hosted the quarterly gathering.

"Begin setting charges, report when done," he ordered.

Dawson began placing C4 charges with detonators along the rear wall from the three-four corner on his left toward the center of the rear number three wall, meeting up with Red who was doing the same from the other side. Within minutes three of the four sides were wired with enough explosives to bring down any good sized structure.

How a centuries old castle might react, Dawson had no idea. All he cared was that the explosion was big enough to delay anybody from following them.

Jimmy and Jagger reported successfully completing the laying of their charges, then joined Dawson and Red who were kneeling just below the bottom of the windows, the snow behind them lit a brilliant yellowish white.

Spock's voice burst from the comm.

"Vehicle secured, second SUV closest to the rear number three wall. Taking up position to cover the four wall at the one-four corner now."

"Roger that," said Dawson as he peered over the lip and through the window with a small mirror. "I'm seeing seven guys in robes sitting at a table, several waiters moving about, no guards."

"Confident," said Red.

Dawson disagreed.

"Arrogant." He frowned. "But where's the eighth?" He looked across the entire room again, but couldn't see any other robed figures. "Anybody have eyes on the eighth?"

"Negative," said Red, "but the table is only set for seven."

"Shit!" Dawson shook his head. "I was hoping we'd get them all."

"Seven should stop them shouldn't it?"

Dawson was about to reply when he shifted slightly, something catching his eye. He could see someone is street clothes running into the room, all eyes shifting to the man who appeared terrified to be there.

Suddenly several people at the table jumped up, looking out the large window and up toward the chalet.

"They know we're here," announced Dawson. "Shoot everything in sight that doesn't look like Niner or Mickey in three...two...one... execute!"

Dawson jumped to his feet, raising his MP5K and emptying a magazine into the window and at the table as the others did the same around him. As the massive glass panes collapsed, it obscured the view, but he didn't care. He kept firing, ejecting the first spent clip and loading the second in record time as his thoughts were consumed by images of Stucco and his family, of his own sister and niece, of Inspector Laviolette and his family, and the one little innocent girl who had started it all off by fighting back.

Maria Esposito.

Reading was behind the wheel, Acton in the passenger seat and Laura in the back. They had intentionally sped past the castle, not wanting to attract any attention.

"If anything is happening there tonight, it hasn't started," commented Reading as they entered the village. "Now where did they say the chalet was?"

"Through the village square then take a left. There's a road that leads up to it," said Acton, pointing toward a large open area with a fountain in the center. "This must be it."

Reading slowed, the snow still coming down fairly heavy and their SUV already providing a little fun on some of the roads when trying to accelerate.

"There's the—" began Acton, pointing to the left, when he stopped. "What the hell?"

Reading saw what his friend was talking about and hit the brakes, the SUV skidding to a halt.

"Bloody hell," he muttered, then yelled, "make sure your doors are locked!" He slammed his elbow down on the lock beside him to make sure, then turned to Laura. "Break out those weapons!"

Laura flipped open one of the storage bins in the back and pulled out three Glocks, handing them out along with several clips each. Reading refused his as he put the vehicle in reverse, a crowd of at least fifty people approaching them at a run, shotguns and rifles at the ready. "Load mine, Jim." He hit the gas as Acton loaded their weapons then stuffed the gun under Reading's right leg.

"Loaded, safety is on, three clips sitting in the cup holder in the console."

"Roger that," said Reading as the vehicle reversed itself. He cursed again as his rearview mirror filled with more villagers, all armed. "We're cut off!"

Suddenly gunfire erupted, their vehicle taking multiple hits. Reading put the vehicle in drive and hammered on the gas, deciding a moving target might be harder to hit. He raced toward the approaching crowd then cut to the left, rounding the fountain when he suddenly cried out, a sharp pain in his shoulder overwhelming him. His right hand darted to his left shoulder, the pain shooting through him like repeated jabs of a spear as he desperately tried to hang on to the wheel, his left hand losing its strength.

He lifted his foot off the gas and tried to press the brake, his entire body becoming weak as he heard his friends yelling, neither yet realizing what was happening.

Suddenly they slammed into the side of a building, jarring them all as Acton shoved the gearshift into park, finally realizing something was wrong. Reading could feel hands on him now, shouts of concern, but everything was dim and distant, nothing even seeming real anymore as the white hot pain in his shoulder overwhelmed him, thoughts of his former partner flashing before his eyes as he prayed for God to take him rather than leave him comatose in some lonely hospital, a chunk of meat to be mourned, waiting for it to die, rather than a corpse to be mourned and buried, the pain slowly forgotten, the happy memories remaining to be enjoyed forever.

Niner looked at Mickey, shifting uncomfortably, his ass numb from the cold stone floor they were both sitting on.

"I really wish I hadn't of worn these pants," he muttered. "I can barely feel my ass anymore."

Mickey looked over at him then the pants.

"Me too, those damned things are so tight I can see the pulse in your nuts."

"It was part of the character."

"Which once again you overplayed."

"What are you saying, that it's over? After all I've done for you?" cried Niner. "I've kept in shape, I take care of your every whim, and this is how you treat me?" He glared at Mickey. "It's another man isn't it? Who is it? Spock? I know you get turned on by his eyebrow. Or is it BD? I know you love taking orders from him!"

Mickey moved away slightly.

"Seek help."

Gunfire erupted from somewhere in the structure and Niner pushed himself to his feet, as did Mickey.

"You hear that?"

"I think Atlas heard that."

"About time those guys showed up. I was getting a little tired of our accommodations," said Niner as he smacked his hands against his ass, popping the zip ties, Mickey doing the same.

"Now what?" asked Mickey as he looked out the ancient bars of their prison cell, nobody in sight.

"I don't know, I was thinking of taking off my pants."

Mickey mocked horror.

"Do you have any C4 in those?"

Niner's eyebrows narrowed as he looked at Mickey.

"I barely have a pulse in these pants. Where the hell would I hide a brick of C4?"

Mickey shrugged, eyeing the pants again.

"Are you staring at my ass?"

"It looks good in those jeans."

Footsteps pounding down the hall ended their jibes as they both ducked to either side of the bars and out of sight. Niner pressed himself into the corner, Mickey doing the same as the footsteps skidded to a halt, gunfire erupting as their cell was sprayed, bullets and shards of stone ricocheting indiscriminately, Niner dropping to the floor in pain as he took a hit in the thigh.

The barrel of the gun extended into the cell and twisted toward him, their attacker finally realizing where they must be hiding.

Niner lunged forward but faltered, his thigh wound worse than he thought, the trigger squeezing as he fell to the ground.

His eyes rose to meet Mickey's to say a silent goodbye to his friend but Mickey had already leapt, his arms extending out in front of him. The weapon began to fire as he grabbed it, pushing the barrel up then his momentum twisting it out of the man's hands. He hit the ground, rolled, the gun now his and spun, firing at their attacker before he knew what was happening.

Niner pushed himself to his feet, jumping forward on one leg and reached out, grabbing the now dead man before he could fall backward and out of reach. He pulled him toward the bars as Mickey slung the weapon over his shoulder. Niner quickly found a set of keys, tossing them to Mickey, plus several clips.

He let the body slide to the ground as Mickey unlocked the cell door.

"Let's get the hell out of here before more come," he said, draping Niner's arm over his shoulders and helping him over the body and out into the hall.

Niner winced with each step.

"Good thing I wore these tight pants. There's no way I can lose any damned blood since there's none left down there."

Mickey chuckled.

"I think the four horsemen of the apocalypse could charge by and you'd have something funny to say about it."

Spock popped back up, took aim and removed another target from the census database. He was hidden behind the front tire of a large SUV near the front of the line of vehicles, Wings doing the same at the lead vehicle but from the rear, giving him a nearly full view of those guarding the front of the castle. As soon as the gunfire had begun in the back they had started taking out targets. At his count he had eliminated six before they even began returning fire in any method other than blindly. Wings had counted out seven kills.

There appeared to only be three remaining, all behind a large fountain, now frozen, in the front of the castle. Three guards didn't bother him necessarily; he was certain more were inside. What concerned him was the fact that their escape route was right past these three men. They had expected those they didn't kill to retreat into the castle, or around the other side, but these three had either decided through bravery to stay outside and fight, or through cowardice to remain behind cover.

"We need a tank!" yelled Wings, firing a few rounds to keep their enemies' heads down.

"One tank, coming up!" promised Spock as he eyed the SUV behind him. He pulled his scanner out and hit the button for it to start probing the frequencies, the vehicle quickly chirping as it unlocked. "Cover me!" he yelled, and Wings fired off several more rounds as Spock pulled open the door and crawled inside, keeping himself below the windshield. He hit the start button in the dash and the vehicle roared to life. "You navigate!" he yelled, using the comm as he put the vehicle in gear and let the automatic pull him forward, one hand ready to push a pedal, the other up grabbing the steering wheel. The vehicle moved forward, quickly gaining speed as he heard Wings' voice.

"Hard left now!"

Spock spun the wheel one handed.

"Straighten out in three…two…one…now."

He let go of the wheel and it spun above him, the vehicle straightening out with a jerk.

"I'm behind you, using you as cover, turn right until I tell you to stop."

Spock turned the wheel, a little more gently this time as bullets pinged off the hood, the windshield taking several hits, the safety glass splintering into thousands of pieces still held together by the laminate.

"Straighten out!"

He let go of the wheel and felt the SUV slowly align itself.

"Little to the left."

He adjusted with a tweak.

"Perfect. Floor it!"

The gunfire the SUV was taking was now steady, and due to their enemies' restricted angle, either they didn't have a clear shot at the tires, or were just poor marksmen. Spock pushed himself up into the seat so he could take advantage of the airbags, keeping his torso low, then pulled his right leg into position, flooring it.

The vehicle surged forward, causing him to roll back into the seat, the console painfully jabbing his ribcage, but he continued to press on the accelerator. He felt the gears shift and he estimated he had to be at thirty by now.

"Hold on!" he heard Wings' yell and he braced himself as best he could.

The crash was tremendous, far more jarring than he had expected. The front of the vehicle almost came to a complete halt for a moment, then the rear wheels, still with traction, pushed it up and over the fountain, the gunfire stopping. Airbags popped, the engine cut off and he found himself momentarily dazed as several bursts of gunfire erupted outside his window, then suddenly the door was pulled open.

His foot drew back and he was about to nail whoever was stupid enough to poke their head in when he heard Wings.

"Take it easy, it's me."

Spock breathed a sigh of relief as he felt hands pulling him out. His feet hit the ground and it took him a moment to regain his bearings. The SUV's front wheels were propped up on top of one of the tiers of the fountain, and three freshly bloodied corpses lay on the other side.

"Let's get out of here before somebody decides to check how the front is holding."

Spock nodded and Wings helped him back to their original position, Spock finally able to run on his own as they arrived.

The gunfire inside continued.

Acton popped Reading's seatbelt and pulled him toward the center console then handed him back as Laura pulled. Together they got him in the rear seat just as the crowd enveloped the vehicle, fists pounding on every surface as Acton climbed into the driver's seat. The vehicle was still running and he put it into reverse, flooring it, the sound of the rear smacking against bodies, the tires bouncing as they drove over the villagers, disconcerting to say the least.

He had no plan, he had no idea what to do, and at the moment didn't even know where to go. He spotted the chalet in his rearview mirror and decided it might make a good destination, its position elevated. He spun the wheel and shoved the stick into drive, hammering on the gas as the four wheel drive pulled them through the snow and up the slippery lane to the chalet, leaving the villagers behind.

Arriving at the drive in front of the chalet, he saw two SUVs parked for a quick getaway, but judging by the chalet's smashed in windows and blown apart front door, there was no way the Delta team was there. He spun the vehicle around, angling the front to point down the hill as he watched the villagers racing toward them, slipping on the snow and ice.

He turned to the backseat.

"How's he doing?"

Laura had already ripped off Reading's shirt and tied a tourniquet.

"He's losing blood. We need to get him to a doctor."

"That's not happening soon," said Acton, turning back to see the villagers were now halfway up the hill. "Do what you can, and buckle up. This is going to get rough."

He gunned the engine and braced his arms against the steering wheel.

Here goes nothing.

Lacroix, being at the head of the table with Number One, had been amongst those to hear the news first. But rather than stand and stare out the window like most did, he had spun out of his chair, and at a crouch ran toward the nearest exit. Gunfire had torn into the massive windows that looked out upon the mountains and he had hit the floor, covering his head as the shattered shards scattered in every direction including his.

His robes had proven useful in protecting him from the glass, the hood having flipped up and covered his head as he hit the ground, his hands tucked into his long sleeves. The gunfire was far more terrifying than the glass. He looked back as he crawled toward the door and already saw several of The Circle on the floor, or still in their chairs, dead. Guards poured into the room from the side areas, adding to the deadly crossfire he found himself under.

"Help!" he yelled, and three of the guards advanced toward him, their weapons belching lead toward the window, their attackers still unseen. He felt hands grab his shoulders and then his body being pulled toward the line of guards slowly advancing, determined to reach whoever might still be alive, their own lives inconsequential to that of The Circle.

He felt one hand let go, the sound of a body dropping to his left, then the grip on his other arm lost as the other guard was felled. He looked up and saw two more rushing forward, both gunned down within inches. He pushed against the marble floor with his sandaled feet, using his bare hands to try and create some traction, pulling himself along, the tiny shards of glass ripping at his hands. Within moments he was in agonizing pain, a bloody trail slowly being left in front of him as his robes then mopped up the mess. The guards had advanced past him now, rushing toward the table where dinner had just finished minutes before, aperitifs being enjoyed as they all spoke of what they might learn from the Catalyst when it arrived.

A servant darted from a nearby alcove and grabbed his arm, pulling him the final few feet to safety.

"Thank you, my son," said Lacroix as he was helped to his feet. "We must get out of here, quickly."

The young man nodded, pointing at a door on the other side of the area they were tucked away in. A door that lay out in the open.

Lacroix cursed, poking his head out to see what was happening. The line of guards had reached the table, two of his brothers being pulled back to safety, but there were less than a dozen men left, and they were dropping like flies as they tried to save The Circle.

"Let's go!" ordered Lacroix, grabbing the boy and positioning him between himself and the attack. They made it half way before the boy took a hit, crying out. Lacroix grabbed him, holding him up as a human shield as he continued for the door. He tossed the body aside as he burst through to safety.

Dawson popped up from below the window, firing another spray of gunfire at floor level, taking out a retreating guard and the now bloody corpse he had been dragging. They hadn't expected this many guards on the inside, so their plan to charge in and eliminate the soft resistance had been halted, and instead they remained outside using the castle wall itself as cover while those inside willing to die for their masters did just that. If their opponent had been smart about it, they would have sent most of their team outside and around the castle to engage the enemy.

Instead, they were clearly either poorly trained, or poorly motivated. If you don't value your own life, and instead believe another's is more important, you don't take the necessary precautions to protect yourself so that you can actually fulfill the mission to save the other.

As a soldier Dawson was willing to die to protect another, but that didn't mean he ignored the value of his own life. If he did, he would have died years ago *trying* to save someone, rather than surviving, and actually *succeeding*.

The gunfire quickly dwindled, then stopped.

"Clear!" yelled each of his team.

"Spock, report."

Spock's voice came over the comm.

"Front is clear for the moment, over."

"We're heading inside now, out."

Dawson flipped up onto the floor as did the others. Glass crunched under their feet, blood soaked the marble.

"Check the honored guests. See how many we've got, and if any are alive. They might know where the eighth guy is."

They quickly cleared the room, six brown robes, all dead, along with several dozen dead guards. It seemed nobody who had entered the room had survived, except for one man.

"Are any of them Lacroix?" he asked.

The round of negatives and shaking heads had him cursing.

"Of all the ones to escape!"

He pointed toward the rear of the room.

"Let's get our men, then find Lacroix."

Dawson gritted his teeth, advancing with his team, fuming.

There's no way in hell Lacroix escapes tonight.

Niner hobbled forward, Mickey carrying much of his weight, when the gunfire above stopped. They paused to rest and listen, both looking up the stairwell they had begun to climb.

"Who won?" winced Niner.

"Those were MP5's firing at the end, not the Uzi's these guys are packing," replied Mickey. Niner had to admit the pain in his thigh was preventing him from being as aware as he should be in their surroundings.

Footsteps rapidly descending the stairs had them both scrambling back. Mickey pushed Niner into a dark corner, covering him with his body as a robed figure burst past them.

"Hands up!" ordered Mickey, stepping from the shadows.

The man came to an abrupt halt, his hands shooting up over his head.

"Turn around."

The man slowly turned and Niner smiled when he saw who it was.

"Dr. Lacroix! You have no idea how happy we are to see you."

His pain momentarily forgotten, he hobbled out into the dim light as Mickey advanced, weapon raised.

"There's a lot of people who are looking very forward to meeting you," said Mickey as he quickly patted down the man, relieving him only of a cellphone.

More footsteps could be heard from above and Mickey kicked Lacroix in the nuggets, putting him on the floor as Niner took up position on one side of the stairs, Mickey the other, his weapon raised.

Niner couldn't see who was coming, but Mickey tensed up as the steps suddenly seemed on top of them, the winding stone stairs hiding everything to the last second.

"Flash!" yelled Mickey, stepping back.

"Thunder!" came the reply and Niner grinned as Mickey lowered his weapon. Four of their comrades burst into the hallway, relief clearly written on their faces at the recovery of their friends. Within seconds Jagger had Niner on the ground, taking care of his thigh wound.

"I see you found somebody in your travels," said Dawson, standing over Lacroix, his weapon trained on the man's chest. Dawson placed a boot on the man's right hand and pressed down, the man crying out in pain.

"Ready to talk?"

Lacroix shook his head vehemently.

"Never."

Bodies bounced off the large bumper and the crowd slowly parted as the momentum the SUV had built up racing down the hill proved to be too much. What Acton couldn't understand was the motivation of these people. How deep did the blind devotion to The Order have to extend for ordinary people to be willing to sacrifice themselves to capture or kill strangers? If he didn't know better, he'd think they were drugged, but he *did* know better, their reaction times too swift. What it seemed to him was that these people were willing to sacrifice themselves perhaps not to serve The Order, but rather to escape it.

The crowd suddenly parted at the bottom of the hill and Acton's eyebrows shot open as the well at the center of the square was suddenly revealed in front of them. He hammered on the brakes, the entire vehicle shuddering as the ABS kicked in and he cranked the wheel to the right. The left wheels skidded into the base of the fountain and the vehicle tipped slightly to the left, then stabilized.

Instantly they were surrounded, hammers, axes, clubs, swinging at the vehicle, the windows smashed out within moments as hands reached inside, grabbing at them, tearing at their clothes and hair. Several shots fired from the backseat caused a momentary pause and Acton tore himself away, pushing again on the gas, grabbing his weapon as he fired blind out his window when suddenly a large hay cart was pushed in front of them.

He hammered on the brakes, but it was too late. They hit the side of the cart, pushing it between the very buildings lining the street they needed to clear.

They were immediately surrounded by villagers, this time with guns pointing directly at all three of them.

Acton raised his hands, as did Laura. He looked at her through the rearview mirror.

"I'm sorry."

Lacroix stood against the stone wall, doubled over in pain as yet another blow buried itself into his stomach. He had refused to answer any questions so far, and had no intention of changing that position, no matter what these men did to him. Even if they killed him, he didn't care. His position in history was clear. *He* had found the Catalyst. *His* team had retrieved it, and even if he were dead, his name would go down in history.

He would never be forgotten.

"Where's the eighth member?" asked the man he recognized as Command Sergeant Major Dawson, leader of this group.

"I will never tell. I *can* never tell. No one knows where the eighth member goes when we are at our retreat. If we knew, it would defeat the purpose of them not being here."

Another blow landed and he doubled over again, the taste of blood now in his mouth.

"Do what you want with me, it doesn't matter. There is no way you can stop us, we have the Catalyst now. No matter what you do now, we are unstoppable."

Dawson grabbed him by the chin, holding him up so he could look him in the eye.

"I have some bad news for you."

Lacroix looked at him, the smile on his opponent's face a little too satisfied for his liking. *What possible news could have this man so happy, so self-satisfied?*

"There is nothing you could tell me that could possibly matter to me. I know I am to die, and I have accepted my fate. My name will go down in history as one of the greatest masters to ever serve The Order. The Order has always been, The Order *will* always be. It is your destiny, should you survive, to praise us and our brilliance when we release our knowledge to the world. It is the betterment of mankind that drives us, and there is nothing you or your pathetic team can do to stop us."

"You don't have the Catalyst."

Lacroix froze, a surge of fear and doubt propping him up.

"What? I don't believe you."

"Your two operatives were intercepted outside of Barcelona. We killed them. Your precious Catalyst is gone. You will never see it. Your Order will never see it. It is once again lost to history, never to be found by your kind."

The words were spat out, each sentence jabbing at him as his confidence waned, as his future faded, and as his name, moments ago to be engraved into the permanent history of The Order and the world, now turning to mere dust, blown away by the sands of time.

He was to be forgotten to history, his name a whisper of embarrassment, his example used as a screening criteria to make sure others like him never joined The Circle.

Tears welled in his eyes, then the sense of satisfaction he could see in his opponent's backstopped his will, a rage slowly building.

"We survived half a millennia without it, we will continue on," he sneered. "There is nothing you can do to stop us."

"What are your plans? What is it you are trying to accomplish?"

"I will never tell. I don't care what you do to me. You can't stop it, it's too late." Lacroix stood as erect as his sore body would allow him. He squared his shoulders and looked at the faces surrounding him, finally settling on his nemesis, Dawson. "You might as well kill me."

Dawson looked directly in his eyes then raised his weapon, pushing it against Lacroix's forehead.

"Very well."

Lacroix never heard the shot.

"Ready the vehicle, we're on our way out, one wounded, over."

Dawson's status caused the hair on Spock's arms to stand up as he exchanged glances with Wings, both concerned over the casualty report. He fired up the vehicle and pulled around to the front of the castle as the doors burst open and the rest of the team rushed out and down the steps, Mickey and Jimmy carrying Niner by the shoulders. Wings jumped into the back, pushing open doors as everyone piled into the rows of seats.

Gunfire rattled in the darkness and Dawson, now in the passenger seat, motioned for Spock to move.

"Let's get the hell out of here before they discover our surprise!"

Spock floored it and spun around the crushed fountain and down the winding drive toward the gates at the bottom as more gunfire erupted from behind them, Spock watching in the rearview mirror as more guards poured out the entrance.

"Everyone get on the passenger side!" he yelled as he hammered on the brakes, the slippery drive providing little traction as they slid through the metal gates, the ABS vibrating to no avail as the team jumped to the right, grabbing onto anything they could to redistribute the weight. The two sets of wrought iron gates burst apart in the center, the mass of metal flung to the sides as Spock fishtailed through and out onto the road at far too high a speed. He was already cranking the wheel to the right before he even hit the gates, jamming the brakes into the floor as he forced the vehicle into a sideway skid toward the precipice on the other side.

The SUV was now perpendicular, aimed up the road toward the village, still sliding toward the guardrail as it suddenly regained traction and began to climb, gravity killing much of its speed as his tires spun up the hill, the wheel still cranked to the right as he continued to try and turn the skid so the rear end would hit the guardrail as gently as possible.

"This isn't going to work!"

The rear quarter smacked the guardrail, too hard. There was a jerk from the rear end then the truck slipped, and a series of "whoahs!" erupted from the back as everyone realized what was happening. "Everyone out!" yelled

Spock as he continued to apply gas, the vehicle no longer moving forward, it instead starting to slip backward, its rear driver side tire over the edge.

Dawson jumped out the passenger side as the rear doors opened, the men climbing out as quickly as they could, Niner still needing to be helped. A crunching sound had them all spinning as the guardrail gave way. Spock felt his other front tire slip over the edge, the vehicle beginning to tip. He turned to Dawson, their eyes meeting, and for the first time that he could remember, he was certain he was going to die.

"Tell my family—"

Dawson leapt forward, his left hand extended, and Spock reached for it on instinct alone, not even registering what was happening. He felt the iron grip of his friend wrap around his wrist as the SUV tipped some more, dragging Dawson farther into the vehicle, his feet now off the ground. Spock could feel Dawson tugging on his arm and Spock reached over with his left hand and grabbed hold of the dash, twisting himself so his feet were on his door, now at a 45 degree angle. He could hear shouting from the other side, then Dawson suddenly jerking as someone pulled on his legs.

The SUV slipped some more, then tipped over the edge, Spock staring at Dawson.

"Let me go or we both die!" he yelled, not wanting to be responsible for his friend's death. He let go of Dawson's wrist. "Please BD!"

Dawson's face was red, veins popping, as he reached forward with his other hand and grabbed hold of Spock's free hand.

"No more die!" he grunted, and Spock knew there was no reasoning with him. He wrapped his fingers around Dawson's wrist again as the SUV slipped away. The passenger side door dragged along their bodies, tearing at Spock's left arm and breaking the grip he had. He felt his body continue to fall, Dawson right with him, then suddenly jerk to a halt. He looked up, dangling by one hand to see Dawson holding onto him, Wings hanging onto Dawson's belt, completely over the cliff edge, and two pairs of hands holding his legs, their saviors out of sight.

"Grab my hand!" yelled Dawson.

Spock flung his left side up, Dawson catching the hand, and they both crawled their fingers to each other's wrists and grabbed on.

"Let's go!" yelled Jagger from out of sight. "Pull together now!" There was a tug, and they all moved up several inches. Another tug, another few inches. Spock could feel his grip loosening.

"I don't know how much longer I can hold on!" he yelled, his arm sore from where the truck door had hit it.

"I've got Wings' belt!" yelled Jagger. "Spock, can you climb?"

"I think so." He looked at Dawson. "Swing me up."

Dawson nodded and they swung to Spock's right, then to the left, and back. As the momentum picked up Spock let go of Dawson with his right hand on the upswing, reaching up and grabbing a fist full of ass, his hand then slipping down and hooking onto the belt, his fingers bent inward like claws.

"Got it!" he grunted. He immediately reached up and grabbed onto Wings' left arm with his free hand, Dawson letting go then clasping both hands under Spock's foot.

Spock straightened his leg, pushing against Dawson's hands and shot up half a body length, grabbing onto Wings' belt, letting go of Dawson. His left arm screamed in protest, but there was no way he was quitting now. If he did all three of them were liable to go over the edge, and like Dawson had said, Stucco was enough.

No more die!

Spock looked to the left and right, then spotted a small foothold in the rock. He shifted his body weight to the right, extending his boot, and planting it on the several square inches of rock, relieving much of his body weight from the human chain.

"Can anyone reach my hand?" he yelled. "I'm to your left!"

A hand suddenly appeared directly above him, then the face of Niner, the only man not involved in the rescue. Spock let go of Wings' belt in a leap of faith, his hand darting up toward Niner's outstretched arm. He missed the catch, but Niner's reflexes proved true and he felt a strong grip wrap around his wrist. He let go of Wings and reached up, holding onto Niner's arm as he winced, his leg still probably in agony.

"Okay, let's pull!" yelled Wings as the lighter load was quickly yanked up the side of the cliff. Another set of hands quickly appeared and Spock grabbed on with his left hand, and moments later he too was over the lip, lying beside a gasping Niner, the rest of the team prone or sitting on the ice cold pavement.

Gunfire up the road toward the village had them all turning toward the sound.

"Now what?"

"It must be the professors," said Dawson jumping to his feet, grabbing Spock by the hand and helping him to his feet. Spock grabbed Dawson by both shoulders.

"Thanks, BD."

"Anytime. Next time I drive," he said with a wink. Shots rang out from the drive leading to the castle as several guards slid and stumbled their way toward them. Spock grabbed his weapon and fired off several rounds as did Dawson and Red. Their targets dropped. "Let's blow this thing and help the professors," ordered Dawson.

Red pulled the detonator from a pouch and flipped the guard up to reveal the switch.

"Fire in the hole!" he yelled, then flicked the switch.

There was a rumble as a series of explosions ripped around three sides of the massive structure. Flames blasted out the sides, dust and debris showering the mountainside in every direction, little of it reaching their position due to the front not having been rigged.

"That was kind of anticlimactic," said Niner, now on his feet. "I was expecting something bigger."

Red shrugged his shoulders.

"They don't build 'em like they used to."

"Look!" yelled Jagger, pointing toward the castle as the right side number four wall, barely visible from this angle, suddenly collapsed down several feet, then fell outward, pancaking the vehicles parked along the side. The rear wall followed, collapsing inward, triggering secondary explosions, the rest of the structure teetering on the brink, then finally giving in, the remaining walls collapsing inward, more explosions erupting as the fuel that powered and heated the castle erupted along with what appeared to be several weapons caches. The blast lit the night sky, a ball of fire and black smoke lighting the side of the mountain for several seconds, then collapsing back down as the remains continued to glow and pop as rounds of ammunition succumbed to the heat.

"Is that better?" asked Red looking at Niner.

"Much. I'm a dying man, you know, if I'm going out, I want it to be with a bang like that, not that whimper you initially delivered."

"Dying eh?" muttered Red as he grabbed Niner by the arm and draped it over his shoulder, Jimmy doing the same on the other side. "We should be so lucky."

"When my leg is back to a hundred percent, I'm kicking your ass," he said as they all began to climb the hill toward the village ahead.

"I'll pencil you in for around Valentine's Day, but only if you wear those pants."

"I said *kick* your ass, not *kiss* your ass."

"Ohhh, that makes more sense."

Dawson turned.

"Let's pick up the pace. You two stick with Niner, we'll go on ahead."

Spock and the others began a tactical run up the hill, prepping their gear as Niner's wisecracks faded into the distance.

Hands grabbed at them, tore at their clothes, their hair, anything they could grab. The guns seemed to have been forgotten, their intention either now to tear them apart, or capture them for interrogation. Acton punched at the one closest to him, catching the man on the nose, then pushed himself between the seats into the back, draping himself over Laura and Reading as she struggled with her own set of attackers.

Suddenly a terrific explosion ripped through the night causing everyone to pause, even their attackers. Acton looked through the window to see all eyes looking down the blocked road toward the castle. The night sky flickered and flashed, then a massive fireball shot up into the air, their attackers now completely withdrawn from the vehicle.

The explosion collapsed, the night sky dark once again, but silence reigned. Then a voice sliced through the shock and awe of their attackers, something yelled in German that Acton took a moment to translate.

They're all dead!

And with those few words, the crowd slowly receded into the darkness, the carts blocking the roads removed, the wounded carried away, leaving an eerie silence almost as terrifying as the rage of the attack, the only sounds the slamming of doors and shutters as a village, sustained by The Order for centuries, mourned its passing, wondering what an uncertain future would bring.

Pioneer Cemetery, Boise, Idaho
Three Days Later

The ceremony for Stucco and his family was moving, the gathering large, the pomp and circumstance impressive. It was a worthy funeral, even if the cause of death was a lie. Acton had shook his head in disbelief when he had heard about the cover up. Even he was angry, and he barely knew Stucco. But they were soldiers, their missions top secret, and this heinous, barbaric act would remain a secret to all but those involved.

As they walked toward the cars, the Bravo Team along with Acton and Laura congregated along the car lined street, Niner in crutches, many of the others showing some wear and tear from their ordeal. But the unit was back together, back on duty, and ready to serve. The sight of Niner had him thinking of their friend Reading who had survived and was recovering quite quickly. Acton had spoken to him this morning and he seemed in good spirits.

"Do you think it's over?" asked Acton to the group in general.

Dawson shrugged.

"We know one of The Circle survived. Let's hope that's enough to stop them, or at least delay them."

Acton frowned, not very confident.

"Stop, I doubt. Delay, possibly. But delay for how long, and delay what? We still don't know what their plan is."

"And perhaps we never will."

"Until it's too late," muttered Laura.

"Let's hope you're wrong, Professor, otherwise all of this was for nothing."

Unknown Location

Exactly one week after the Schloss Rosen attack

The last beep sounded, indicating the final member had connected to the meeting. It was a somber event, but also an event of renewal, and Number One, the new Number One, welcomed those logged in.

"Welcome apprentices," he said, deepening his younger voice, those gathered having no idea who he was, or how he normally sounded. He needed to command the respect of the others, especially with so many deaths. They would learn to respect him in time, as he himself earned their respect, but for now, an iron grip must be maintained.

"I am now Number One. The Circle is complete, The Order continues, undeterred. Those who would try to take us down, have failed, as have all others in the past, for The Order is eternal, and The Circle is unbreakable. Rejoice now, apprentices, for today you are masters, masters in the greatest organization to have ever existed."

He sucked in a breath as he looked at the agenda in front of him.

"Now to business." He looked at each of the robed faces on his screen. "Number Seven, please bring us up to date on the progress your late master was able to make in our plan."

A robed head lifted, revealing nothing but the chin of the new master.

"Much progress has been made, the plans well laid. Recent events will *not* impact rollout of the new strains to the Third World. We anticipate adoption throughout the developing world within less than ten years, at which point we can trigger the plan."

"Excellent," smiled Number One, content that it would be he that would be in power to oversee The Order's greatest triumph.

And he at the head of the new world order that would prevail.

Costa Brava, Spain

Sophia dug at the sand with her red plastic shovel, certain she had found some sort of buried pirate's treasure. The box didn't seem that big, but she could only see one corner. She continued to dig, then abandoned the shovel, scraping at the sand with just her fingers. Soon a second corner was revealed, then a third. Within minutes she had enough of the treasure chest showing to see, much to her disappointment, that it indeed was small.

But still big enough to hold plenty of gold that might help her family. She knew they were poor, her daddy having lost his job, her mommy as well, and all she ever wanted to do was help them.

This could be the key.

With a final effort she yanked it from the sand, then brushed it off. It was a perfect square with strange symbols written all over it, but no obvious way to gain access. She searched for an opening but couldn't find any.

Daddy will know how!

She jumped up and ran toward home, only a few minutes from the beach. She found her daddy in his study. He looked up.

"What have you got there?"

She shrugged.

"Treasure chest?"

Her father smiled, getting up from his chair and taking the curious box to the backyard, spraying it clean with the hose. He handed it back to her after trying to find a way to open it with no success.

"Perhaps you will have better luck," he said. "Now why don't you put that in your room, and perhaps someday you will solve the puzzle."

She hugged him then ran to her room, jumping onto her bed as she began to struggle with the box, pulling at it, pushing at it, and finally hitting it with everything she could think of.

And nothing happened.

After fifteen minutes of failure she lost interest and tossed the cube in her box of toys in the closet, running back to the beach to see if she could find some seashells to glue to her find.

THE END

ACKNOWLEDGEMENTS

The inspiration for this book came from a buddy of mine, the "real" Chris Leroux, who sent me a link to an article on the Georgia Guidestones. After reading about these, I became fascinated about who could be responsible and stumbled upon the Rosicrucians. I had heard of them before, but knew nothing of them. Researching them, then creating a history of their continued existence was a blast.

Thanks to Ian Kennedy for his invaluable assistance with regards to explosives and triggers. Thanks of course to my main researcher, my father, who once again has outdone himself.

And one final thing as a reminder to those who have not already done so. Please visit my website at www.jrobertkennedy.com then sign up for the Insiders Club. You'll get emails about new book releases, new collections, sales, etc. Only an email or two a month tops, I promise!

And to my wife, daughter, parents and friends, thank you once again for your support. And to you the readers, thank you! You've all made this possible.

ABOUT THE AUTHOR

 J. Robert Kennedy is the author of twelve international best sellers, including the smash hit James Acton Thrillers series, the first installment of which, The Protocol, has been on the best sellers list since its release, including a three month run at number one. In addition to the other novels from this series, Brass Monkey, Broken Dove, The Templar's Relic (also a number one best seller), Flags of Sin and The Arab Fall, he has written the international best sellers Rogue Operator, Depraved Difference, Tick Tock, The Redeemer and The Turned. Robert spends his time in Ontario, Canada with his family.

Visit Robert's website at www.jrobertkennedy.com for the latest news and contact information.

The Protocol

A James Acton Thriller, Book #1

For two thousand years the Triarii have protected us, influencing history from the crusades to the discovery of America. Descendent from the Roman Empire, they pervade every level of society, and are now in a race with our own government to retrieve an ancient artifact thought to have been lost forever.

Caught in the middle is archaeology professor James Acton, relentlessly hunted by the elite Delta Force, under orders to stop at nothing to possess what he has found, and the Triarii, equally determined to prevent the discovery from falling into the wrong hands.

With his students and friends dying around him, Acton flees to find the one person who might be able to help him, but little does he know he may actually be racing directly into the hands of an organization he knows nothing about...

Brass Monkey

A James Acton Thriller, Book #2

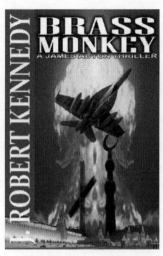

A nuclear missile, lost during the Cold War, is now in play--the most public spy swap in history, with a gorgeous agent the center of international attention, triggers the end-game of a corrupt Soviet Colonel's twenty five year plan. Pursued across the globe by the Russian authorities, including a brutal Spetsnaz unit, those involved will stop at nothing to deliver their weapon, and ensure their pay day, regardless of the terrifying consequences.

When Laura Palmer confronts a UNICEF group for trespassing on her Egyptian archaeological dig site, she unwittingly stumbles upon the ultimate weapons deal, and becomes entangled in an international conspiracy that sends her lover, archeology Professor James Acton, racing to Egypt with the most unlikely of allies, not only to rescue her, but to prevent the start of a holy war that could result in Islam and Christianity wiping each other out.

From the bestselling author of Depraved Difference and The Protocol comes Brass Monkey, a thriller international in scope, certain to offend some, and stimulate debate in others. Brass Monkey pulls no punches in confronting the conflict between two of the world's most powerful, and divergent, religions, and the terrifying possibilities the future may hold if left unchecked.

Broken Dove

A James Acton Thriller, Book #3

With the Triarii in control of the Roman Catholic Church, an organization founded by Saint Peter himself takes action, murdering one of the new Pope's operatives. Detective Chaney, called in by the Pope to investigate, disappears, and, to the horror of the Papal staff sent to inform His Holiness, they find him missing too, the only clue a secret chest, presented to each new pope on the eve of their election, since the beginning of the Church.

Interpol Agent Reading, determined to find his friend, calls Professors James Acton and Laura Palmer to Rome to examine the chest and its forbidden contents, but before they can arrive, they are intercepted by an organization older than the Church, demanding the professors retrieve an item stolen in ancient Judea in exchange for the lives of their friends.

All of your favorite characters from The Protocol return to solve the most infamous kidnapping in history, against the backdrop of a two thousand year old battle pitting ancient foes with diametrically opposed agendas.

From the internationally bestselling author of Depraved Difference and The Protocol comes Broken Dove, the third entry in the smash hit James Acton Thrillers series, where J. Robert Kennedy reveals a secret concealed by the Church for almost 1200 years, and a fascinating interpretation of what the real reason behind the denials might be.

The Templar's Relic

A James Acton Thriller, Book #4

The Church Helped Destroy the Templars. Will a twist of fate let them get their revenge 700 years later?

The Vault must be sealed, but a construction accident leads to a miraculous discovery--an ancient tomb containing four Templar Knights, long forgotten, on the grounds of the Vatican. Not knowing who they can trust, the Vatican requests Professors James Acton and Laura Palmer examine the find, but what they discover, a precious Islamic relic, lost during the Crusades, triggers a set of events that shake the entire world, pitting the two greatest religions against each other.

Join Professors James Acton and Laura Palmer, INTERPOL Agent Hugh Reading, Scotland Yard DI Martin Chaney, and the Delta Force Bravo Team as they race against time to defuse a worldwide crisis that could quickly devolve into all-out war.

At risk is nothing less than the Vatican itself, and the rock upon which it was built.

From J. Robert Kennedy, the author of six international bestsellers including Depraved Difference and The Protocol, comes The Templar's Relic, the fourth entry in the smash hit James Acton Thrillers series, where once again Kennedy takes history and twists it to his own ends, resulting in a heart pounding thrill ride filled with action, suspense, humor and heartbreak.

Flags of Sin

A James Acton Thriller, Book #5

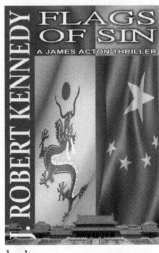

Archaeology Professor James Acton simply wants to get away from everything, and relax. A trip to China seems just the answer, and he and his fiancée, Professor Laura Palmer, are soon on a flight to Beijing.

But while boarding, they bump into an old friend, Delta Force Command Sergeant Major Burt Dawson, who surreptitiously delivers a message that they must meet the next day, for Dawson knows something they don't.

China is about to erupt into chaos.

Foreign tourists and diplomats are being targeted by unknown forces, and if they don't get out of China in time, they could be caught up in events no one had seen coming.

J. Robert Kennedy, the author of eight international best sellers, including the smash hit James Acton Thrillers, takes history once again and turns it on its head, sending his reluctant heroes James Acton and Laura Palmer into harm's way, to not only save themselves, but to try and save a country from a century old conspiracy it knew nothing about.

The Arab Fall

A James Acton Thriller, Book #6

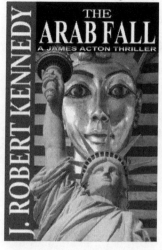

The greatest archeological discovery since King Tut's tomb is about to be destroyed! The Arab Spring has happened and Egypt has yet to calm down, but with the dig site on the edge of the Nubian Desert, a thousand miles from the excitement, Professor Laura Palmer and her fiancé Professor James Acton return with a group of students, and two friends: Interpol Special Agent Hugh Reading, and Scotland Yard DI Martin Chaney.

But an accidental find by Chaney may lead to the greatest archaeological discovery since the tomb of King Tutankhamen, perhaps even greater. And when news of it spreads, it reaches the ears of a group hell-bent on the destruction of all idols and icons, their mere existence considered blasphemous to Islam.

As chaos hits the major cities of the world in a coordinated attack, unbeknownst to the professors, students and friends, they are about to be faced with one of the most difficult decisions of their lives. Stay and protect the greatest archaeological find of our times, or save themselves and their students from harm, leaving the find to be destroyed by fanatics determined to wipe it from the history books.

From J. Robert Kennedy, the author of eleven international bestsellers including Rogue Operator and The Protocol, comes The Arab Fall, the sixth entry in the smash hit James Acton Thrillers series, where Kennedy once again takes events from history and today's headlines, and twists them into a heart pounding adventure filled with humor and heartbreak, as one of their own is left severely wounded, fighting for their life.

The Circle of Eight

A James Acton Thriller, Book #7

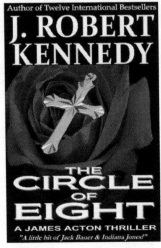

Abandoned by their government, Delta Team Bravo fights to not only save themselves and their families, but humanity as well.

The Bravo Team is targeted by a madman after one of their own intervenes in a rape. Little do they know this internationally well-respected banker is also a senior member of an organization long thought extinct, whose stated goals for a reshaped world are not only terrifying, but with today's globalization, totally achievable.

As the Bravo Team fights for its very survival, they are suspended, left adrift without their support network. To save themselves and their families, markers are called in, former members volunteer their services, favors are asked for past services, and the expertise of two professors, James Acton and his fiancée Laura Palmer, is requested.

It is a race around the globe to save what remains of the Bravo Team, abandoned by their government, alone in their mission, with only their friends to rely upon, as an organization over six centuries old works in the background to destroy them and all who help them, as it moves forward with plans that could see the world population decimated in an attempt to recreate Eden.

The Circle of Eight is the seventh installment in the internationally best selling James Acton Thrillers series. In The Circle of Eight J. Robert Kennedy, author of over a dozen international best sellers, is at his best, weaving a tale spanning centuries and delivering a taut thriller that will keep you on the edge of your seat from page one until the breathtaking conclusion.

The Turned

Zander Varga, Vampire Detective, Book #1

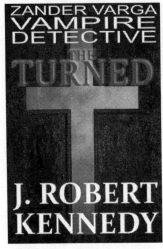

Zander has relived his wife's death at the hands of vampires every day for almost three hundred years, his perfect memory a curse of becoming one of The Turned—infecting him their final heinous act after her murder.

Nineteen year-old Sydney Winter knows Zander's secret, a secret preserved by the women in her family for four generations. But with her mother in a coma, she's thrust into the front lines, ahead of her time, to fight side-by-side with Zander.

And she wouldn't change a thing. She loves the excitement, she loves the danger. And she loves Zander.

But it's a love that will have to go unrequited, because Zander has only one thing on his mind. And it's been the same thing for over two hundred years.

Revenge.

But today, revenge will have to wait, because Zander Varga, Private Detective, has a new case. A woman's husband is missing. The police aren't interested. But Zander is. Something doesn't smell right, and he's determined to find out why.

From J. Robert Kennedy, the internationally bestselling author of The Protocol and Depraved Difference, comes his sixth novel, The Turned, a terrifying story that in true Kennedy fashion takes a completely new twist on the origin of vampires, tying it directly to a well-known moment in history. Told from the perspective of Zander Varga and his assistant,

Sydney Winter, The Turned is loaded with action, humor, terror and a centuries long love that must eventually be let go.

Depraved Difference

A Detective Shakespeare Mystery, Book #1

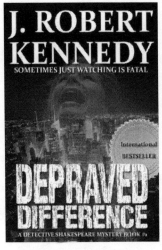

Would you help, would you run, or would you just watch?

When a young woman is brutally assaulted by two men on the subway, her cries for help fall on the deaf ears of onlookers too terrified to get involved, her misery ended with the crushing stomp of a steel-toed boot. A cellphone video of her vicious murder, callously released on the Internet, its popularity a testament to today's depraved society, serves as a trigger, pulled a year later, for a killer.

Emailed a video documenting the final moments of a woman's life, entertainment reporter Aynslee Kai, rather than ask why the killer chose her to tell the story, decides to capitalize on the opportunity to further her career. Assigned to the case is Hayden Eldridge, a detective left to learn the ropes by a disgraced partner, and as videos continue to follow victims, he discovers they were all witnesses to the vicious subway murder a year earlier, proving sometimes just watching is fatal.

From the author of The Protocol and Brass Monkey, Depraved Difference is a fast-paced murder suspense novel with enough laughs, heartbreak, terror and twists to keep you on the edge of your seat, then knock you flat on the floor with an ending so shocking, you'll read it again just to pick up the clues.

Tick Tock

A Detective Shakespeare Mystery, Book #2

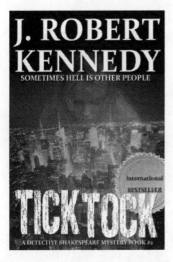

Crime Scene tech Frank Brata digs deep and finds the courage to ask his colleague, Sarah, out for coffee after work. Their good time turns into a nightmare when Frank wakes up the next morning covered in blood, with no recollection of what happened, and Sarah's body floating in the tub. Determined not to go to prison for a crime he's horrified he may have committed, he scrubs the crime scene clean, and, tormented by text messages from the real killer, begins a race against the clock to solve the murder before his own co-workers, his own friends, solve it first, and find him guilty.

Billionaire Richard Tate is the toast of the town, loved by everyone but his wife. His plans for a romantic weekend with his mistress ends in disaster, waking the next morning to find her murdered, floating in the tub. After fleeing in a panic, he returns to find the hotel room spotless, and no sign of the body. An envelope found at the scene contains not the expected blackmail note, but something far more sinister.

Two murders, with the same MO, targeting both the average working man, and the richest of society, sets a rejuvenated Detective Shakespeare, and his new reluctant partner, Amber Trace, after a murderer whose motivations are a mystery, and who appears to be aided by the very people they would least expect—their own.

Tick Tock, Book #2 in the internationally bestselling Detective Shakespeare Mysteries series, picks up right where Depraved Difference left off, and asks a simple question: What would you do? What would you do if you couldn't prove your innocence, but knew you weren't capable of murder? Would you hide the very evidence that might clear you, or would you turn yourself in and trust the system to work?

From the internationally bestselling author of The Protocol and Brass Monkey comes the highly anticipated sequel to the smash hit Depraved Difference, Tick Tock. Filled with heart pounding terror and suspense, along with a healthy dose of humor, Tick Tock's twists will keep you guessing right up to the terrifying end.

The Redeemer

A Detective Shakespeare Mystery, Book #3

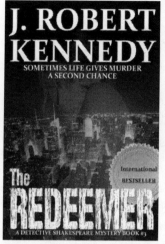

Sometimes Life Gives Murder a Second Chance

It was the case that destroyed Detective Justin Shakespeare's career, beginning a downward spiral of self-loathing and self-destruction lasting half a decade. And today things are only going to get worse. The Widow Rapist is free on a technicality, and it is up to Detective Shakespeare and his partner Amber Trace to find the evidence, five years cold, to put him back in prison before he strikes again.

But Shakespeare and Trace aren't alone in their desire for justice. The Seven are the survivors, avowed to not let the memories of their loved ones be forgotten. And with the release of the Widow Rapist, they are determined to take justice into their own hands, restoring balance to a flawed system.

At stake is a second chance, a chance at redemption, a chance to salvage a career destroyed, a reputation tarnished, and a life diminished.

A chance brought to Detective Shakespeare whether he wants it or not.

A chance brought to him by The Redeemer.

From J. Robert Kennedy, the author of seven international bestsellers including Depraved Difference and The Protocol, comes the third entry in the acclaimed Detective Shakespeare Mysteries series, The Redeemer, a dark tale exploring the psyches of the serial killer, the victim, and the police, as they all try to achieve the same goals.

Balance. And redemption.

Rogue Operator

A Special Agent Dylan Kane Thriller, Book #1

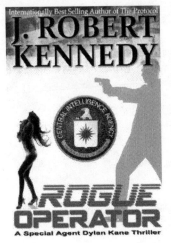

TO SAVE THE COUNTRY HE LOVES, SPECIAL AGENT DYLAN KANE MIGHT HAVE TO BETRAY IT.

Three top secret research scientists are presumed dead in a boating accident, but the kidnapping of their families the same day raises questions the FBI and local police can't answer, leaving them waiting for a ransom demand that will never come.

Central Intelligence Agency Analyst Chris Leroux stumbles upon the story, and finds a phone conversation that was never supposed to happen. When he reports it to his boss, the National Clandestine Services Chief, he is uncharacteristically reprimanded for conducting an unauthorized investigation and told to leave it to the FBI.

But he can't let it go.

For he knows something the FBI doesn't.

One of the scientists is alive.

Chris makes a call to his childhood friend, CIA Special Agent Dylan Kane, leading to a race across the globe to stop a conspiracy reaching the highest levels of political and corporate America, that if not stopped, could lead to war with an enemy armed with a weapon far worse than anything in the American arsenal, with the potential to not only destroy the world, but consume it.

J. Robert Kennedy, the author of nine international best sellers, including the smash hit James Acton Thrillers, introduces Rogue Operator, the first installment of his newest series, The Special Agent Dylan Kane Thrillers, promising to bring all of the action and intrigue of the James Acton Thrillers with a hero who lives below the radar, waiting for his country to call when it most desperately needs him.

Containment Failure

A Special Agent Dylan Kane Thriller, Book #2

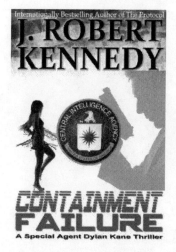

THE BLACK DEATH KILLED ALMOST HALF OF EUROPE'S POPULATION. THIS TIME IT WILL BE BILLIONS.

New Orleans has been quarantined, an unknown virus sweeping the city, killing one hundred percent of those infected. The Centers for Disease Control, desperate to find a cure, is approached by BioDyne Pharma who reveal a former employee has turned a cutting edge medical treatment capable of targeting specific genetic sequences into a weapon, and released it.

CIA Special Agent Dylan Kane has been given one guideline from his boss: consider yourself unleashed, leaving Kane and New Orleans Police Detective Isabelle Laprise battling to stay alive as an insidious disease and terrified mobs spread through the city while they desperately seek those behind the greatest crime ever perpetrated.

The stakes have never been higher as Kane battles to save not only his friends and the country he loves, but all of mankind.

In Containment Failure, eleven times internationally bestselling author J. Robert Kennedy delivers a terrifying tale of what could happen when science goes mad, with enough sorrow, heartbreak, laughs and passion to keep readers on the edge of their seats until the chilling conclusion.

Made in the USA
Middletown, DE
30 November 2023

44189659R00217